TFS INGENUITY

The Terran Fleet Command Saga – Book 1

*****

Tori L. Harris

ISBN: 978-0-9961796-2-1
TFS INGENUITY
THE TERRAN FLEET COMMAND SAGA – BOOK 1

Published by Tori L. Harris
AuthorToriHarris.com

Edited by Monique Happy
www.moniquehappy.com

Prologue

Sol System, Near the Jovian Orbital Path
(0609 UTC - 9.5x10^8 km from Earth)

The probe's brief appearance in normal space was intentionally discreet. The small ship, if it could even be called a ship at less than a meter in length, was designed to be all but undetectable to the technology available to any species it was expected to encounter during its mission. That certainly included the rather primitive species represented by the approaching squadron of nine warships and four support vessels.

Had any of the approaching ships been scanning the area roughly one hundred fifty thousand kilometers to port with their most powerful optical sensors, they might have detected a small flash of light, followed a few seconds later by another. Otherwise, they were provided no warning whatsoever of the devastating attack that was now imminent.

The probe's quick reconnaissance of the enemy squadron provided a wealth of data with which to plan an attack. Since the scan was completely passive in nature, there were no detectable sensor emissions. With optics, of course, there was no getting around Einsteinian physics. The probe's sensor suite received only a few seconds worth of "new light" during its encounter with the enemy ships, but this had been more than enough. The high resolution scan still covered a spherical volume of space with a diameter of over one million kilometers. Any targeting data beyond that distance was deemed less reliable, but could still be used in case things didn't go exactly as planned during the coming engagement.

Now at a safe distance and camouflaged by a particularly dense group of asteroids orbiting between the fourth and fifth planets in the Sol system, the probe rejoined its mothership. Even before the docking process was complete, all of its valuable reconnaissance data had been uploaded, causing the fifty-meter-long mothership to pause momentarily and consider its options.

The approaching enemy squadron was composed of well-known ship types with well-known capabilities – with one notable exception. Based on its emissions and power levels, that particular ship did appear to be significantly more advanced than the others, but it was of little consequence. The mothership calculated that it still enjoyed an overwhelming advantage in every category from power generation, to shielding, to speed and maneuverability, to weapons. The outcome of a confrontation with this enemy was all but certain. No, the real question was the best course of action in support of its mission directives, which was orders of magnitude more complex than destroying the inferior enemy squadron.

Over five hundred years earlier, the mothership had been given three directives that would govern its mission for centuries to come. In descending order of priority, they were:

1. *Neutralize any direct threat to the Pelaran alliance.*

2. *Cultivate the species inhabiting the third planet of the Sol system (Terra) as a Pelaran regional proxy.*
3. *Prevent damage to Pelaran property and economic interests, except when in conflict with the first two directives. This includes self-preservation of all Guardian Cultivation Systems (GCS).*

The Makers were many things, but micromanagers they were not. The Guardians they created had been given wide discretion to interpret both the intent of their mission directives as well as their practical application. Each mission could, after all, last a thousand years or more (based on the orbital period of Terra).

In the case of the approaching enemy ships, directives one and three were not a factor. These primitives clearly represented no direct threat to any member of the Pelaran Alliance … at least not yet. Based on the design of their ships, their technology was at least a millennia behind even the most backwater Alliance affiliate. Directive three actually did evaluate to a nonzero probability, largely due to the unknown capabilities of the previously unknown ship in the enemy formation. Realistically, however, the threat to the Guardian was deemed inconsequential.

No, as usual, the problem was directive two, how best to cultivate an adolescent race, in this case the Terrans, in such a way that they became the dominant regional power while also creating a sense of loyalty, indebtedness, and dependency upon the Pelaran Alliance. At the moment, directive two simply implied that the approaching ships could not be allowed to approach Terra, but where the Humans were concerned, nothing was ever as simple as it seemed. While they did share the common genetic heritage with the Makers as required of all cultivated species, the Terrans were proving to be a race of petulant, arrogant children that was nearly impossible to control.

Cultivation of proxy species had been considered a morally superior method of maintaining regional stability for thousands of years. The system had been codified in various treaties between ancient, immensely powerful civilizations and alliances, and was designed to prevent their ever coming into direct open conflict (the results of which would be unthinkable). It allowed less populated areas to develop along a reasonably natural technological and cultural timeline without the need for excessive intervention. Still, it was sometimes difficult for the GCS to understand why a simple purge of any species deemed a threat to regional stability was not also considered a morally viable option.

As the Humans illustrated on a daily basis, practical application of cultivation theory was an incredibly delicate and complicated undertaking. The general idea was to choose a species with genetic ties to an Alliance member (preferably a civilization developing along a similar cultural path). The selected species was then guided through the most unstable and dangerous portion of their maturing process. This was accomplished primarily through the rapid introduction of key technologies at a rate between ten and fifty times their projected developmental timeline.

Unfortunately, cultivation theory rarely followed a cookbook approach. Deployment of a Guardian Cultivation System depended on a myriad of factors including the mean intelligence of the species under cultivation, regional galactic population density, and literally thousands of other factors. It was also critical to ensure that the cultivated species did not experience an accidental first contact with another species or a premature discovery of non-native technological artifacts.

On average, a species received guardianship approximately three to five hundred years before its first, tentative steps into interstellar space. How long the GCS "loitered" in the region depended in large part on how quickly the cultivated species reached the required level of self-sufficiency and regional supremacy. In the case of the Humans, it had sometimes been difficult to imagine that they would ever fully realize this goal, but they *had* come a very long way in a relatively short period of time, hadn't they?

With its brief contemplation on the finer points of cultivation theory completed, the time for action in support of directive two had arrived. The question now was what action to take? The most conservative approach was to immediately intercept and destroy the approaching enemy squadron. There was absolutely no doubt that they were enemies of the Humans, or eventually would be (even though the Humans had only the vaguest notion that they even existed). They were the Wek, the most aggressive member species of an expansionist coalition known as the Sajeth Collective. Controlling species like the Wek and their potentially bothersome regional alliances was one of the primary objectives of the cultivation program.

Another option was to even the odds a bit and then allow the Humans to deal with the remaining threat themselves. In cases like this where the species under cultivation were still relatively weak militarily, this approach, while potentially messy, sometimes yielded dramatic results. Typically, the resulting loss of life and property spurred even the most passive of civilizations to the realization that their neighborhood of the galaxy was not nearly as safe as they had once imagined.

The final option was to do nothing and see how the Humans fared on their own. In this scenario, however, even this small squadron of enemy ships had more than enough firepower to render the Humans defenseless in a matter of minutes, and potentially extinct a few hours later. This scenario might require the GCS to intervene in close proximity to the planet, which would most likely render it visible, openly announcing its presence to the Humans. Although the Guardian sensed that the time for direct contact was rapidly approaching, it calculated that the optimum time had not yet arrived to do so.

So many things to consider, and so much potential for complete mission failure. Not for the first time in the past five centuries on station near Terra, the Guardian experienced an uncomfortable mix of what the Humans might call anxiety and boredom. Consciousness, it turns out, was overrated. This was certainly true when it included self-awareness of one's own personal responsibilities. The GCS indulged itself for several hundred femtoseconds by observing that when you happen to be a sentient spacecraft possessed of world-shaping intelligence and brimming with a godlike array of weapons, an overdeveloped sense of irony wasn't particularly helpful either.

Mere seconds after the Wek squadron emerged from months of hyperspace travel, the Guardian had completed a detailed reconnaissance, assessed the situation, and determined that they must be destroyed immediately in accordance with directive two.

In the extremely unlikely event that the Guardian itself was destroyed in combat, a communications drone detached and positioned itself inside a crater on a nearby asteroid. The drone would remain hidden in this location during the coming battle. If the GCS was lost, it was capable of returning to Pelara on its own with a complete mission log in its memory core. With its limited power generation capabilities, however, the trip would take several Terran years. Under those circumstances, it was unlikely that a follow-up mission would be undertaken in the near term. The hapless Terran civilization would be categorized as presumed destroyed, pending confirmation at a later date.

Fortunately for the unsuspecting Terrans, The Makers had been designing starships for a thousand years before any species in the Sajeth Collective had discovered the basic principles of atmospheric flight. They had designed the Guardian Cultivation System for a broad spectrum of missions, but it was particularly well-suited for this type of engagement.

When it came right down to it, the key to successful long-range space travel and space warfare was actually quite simple. The ship capable of generating the most power tended to travel farther and faster, and then dominate its enemies after arriving at its destination. With technology perfected and handed down across hundreds of generations of Makers, the GCS was capable of producing a vast supply of power. So vast, in fact, that compared with the ships in the approaching squadron, its power output was practically without limitation.

Although this was the first tactical encounter the Guardian had experienced in over fifty years, its combat-related systems treated the situation as merely routine – nothing more than a precisely calculated response to the current threat. With Terra less than one light hour from the approaching squadron, the time for action had come.

With another faint blue flash, the Guardian spacecraft engaged its hyperdrive and transitioned to a position well above, but as near as possible to the center of the Wek formation. So much of space combat strategy was dictated by the speed of light (in so-called "normal space" at least). It was the one rule that all participants were forced to, if not obey, then at least acknowledge as having a significant influence on tactics. To achieve initial surprise, the Guardian calculated that it had approximately one hundred milliseconds for Sol's light reflecting off its hull to cover the distance to the closest Wek ship. The first salvo from its array of pulsed antihydrogen beam weapons arrived a mere thirty milliseconds later.

The GCS was a small vessel with only sixteen beam emitters, but this was sufficient to assign every target in the Wek formation at least one impact. Each of the support vessels and smaller warships were targeted by only one emitter, leaving two for each of the largest three vessels, including the one with unknown capabilities. The beam weapons were designed to fire packetized pulses in rapid succession, which allowed each pulse to (very briefly) interact with the hull of the target before the next pulse arrived. Aiming points were predetermined based on the reconnaissance probe's positional data as well as each vessel's energy signature. The known, or most probable, location of an enemy ship's power systems was usually the target of choice for the opening salvo.

The Wek support ships were positioned slightly behind the warships. So it was that a five-hundred-meter-long supply vessel was the first to receive the Guardian's fire. Although the beam's coherence was reduced slightly as it interacted with the vessel's shields, the majority of the packetized antihydrogen particles reached the target's hull, striking at a velocity only slightly less than the speed of light. Atomic level annihilation occurred instantaneously at the point of impact, tearing into the ship's armor plating and releasing vast quantities of energy. As subsequent packets of energy arrived at the same location, the heavier alloys in the ship's hull were disrupted to a state exceeding their atomic binding energy. Runaway fission reactions occurred as the antimatter came into contact with the hull's more vulnerable inner layers. At this point, a jagged line beginning at the original point of impact and exiting on the opposite side of the ship erupted with a continuous series of nuclear detonations. The ship was instantly ripped in half, each section trailing multiple streams of gas and debris, including the bodies of her Wek crew, as they spun off into space.

Much the same occurred with the other ships in the enemy formation. The warships, with more powerful shields and heavier armor, withstood the Guardian's fire slightly longer than the support ships, albeit only milliseconds longer. From the point of view of the Wek squadron, they had reached the Terran system after months of hyperspace travel only to be destroyed within mere seconds of their arrival.

With the immediate threat neutralized, the Guardian ship ceased fire. A quick battle damage assessment confirmed the destruction of the entire Wek squadron with one exception – the warship of unknown capabilities. The ship had simply no longer been present in the enemy formation when the attack began. This was always a risk when conducting a Before Light Arrival, or BLA attack. Opening fire on an enemy before there was any possibility of their detecting your presence provided a tremendous tactical advantage, but there was always a chance that the disposition of the enemy's forces could have changed during the brief period between reconnaissance and battle. Generally, this was only a concern when fighting a much more advanced enemy. The fact that it had happened in this particular battle was troubling to the GCS.

The new enemy ship type, now designated SC Fader 1, had clearly reentered hyperspace within seconds of its initial arrival in system. Executing multiple hyperspace transitions within a short period of time was a surprisingly difficult technical challenge, even for civilizations that had possessed FTL technology for centuries. In fact, this was not a capability previously encountered in any of the spacefaring species within five hundred light years of the Sol system. The Wek, or one of their allies, had either achieved a lucky technological breakthrough, or, worse, unauthorized technological sharing was taking place within this region.

The Wek ship could be tracked, of course, but doing so would take time and require the use of other Pelaran resources. The most immediately pressing question was why the ship had chosen to depart the area immediately after its arrival. The possibilities included everything from a preplanned tactic designed to foil an expected BLA attack to the enemy actually detecting the Guardian's reconnaissance probe. None of the most likely explanations were good news for directive two.

As the implications of the Wek incursion unfolded in the Guardian's consciousness, one outcome now seemed all but inevitable: The time for direct first contact with the Humans was near at hand.

Chapter 1

TFS Ingenuity, Earth-Sun Lagrange Point 1
(0725 UTC – 1.5×10^6 km from Earth)

"Captain Prescott to the bridge," the ship's voice announced in the captain's ready room. He had just gotten comfortable and was nearly asleep on the long couch lining the wall opposite his desk after nearly twenty hours of nonstop activity on his newly commissioned ship. While slightly irritated at the interruption, he couldn't help but stifle a chuckle every time he heard the (female and vaguely suggestive, he thought) synthetic voice. *Not only do I have the coolest damn job in the history of mankind, but my ship's voice is <u>hot</u>,* he thought glibly. *What more could a man ask for?* He had been making observations like this to himself more and more frequently of late, often having a hard time believing that any of this was real. His ship, TFS *Ingenuity*, was, after all, the very first vessel in Earth's history that could actually be classified as a true starship.

Tom Prescott had every reason to feel that his life over the past couple of years had been guided inexorably to this point by a bizarre series of lucky breaks. He was a humble man by nature, with a fervent sense of gratitude, but he often wondered whether others in similar positions throughout history had felt the same way. Had Chuck Yeager or Neil Armstrong realized the enduring significance of what they were about to do? He doubted it, and figured he shouldn't waste any time doing so either. One thing was for sure, *Ingenuity* was as far removed from the Bell X1 or the Saturn V as they had been in their day from a dugout canoe. Both of them (as far as he knew) had been the products of strictly Human creativity and invention. His ship was something entirely different. Not only was she infinitely more complex, but she was also the result of the first collaborative effort, of sorts, with an extra-terrestrial species. As incredible and exciting as this still seemed to him, he couldn't help but feel a vague sense of disappointment that this miracle of engineering wasn't a solely Human achievement.

With a concerted effort to appear more professional and alert than he felt at the moment, Captain Prescott stood and walked the already familiar ten steps to his command chair on the bridge.

"Sorry to bother you, Captain," his executive officer, Commander Sally Reynolds said apologetically as he emerged from his ready room. "Fleet Control is telling us to prepare for an immediate departure."

"Departure? Why is that? Do they need another hyperdrive calibration run?"

Although she had been officially commissioned three days earlier, *Ingenuity* still had a lengthy "punch list" of items requiring his crew's attention. Most of these had been identified during her shakedown cruise over the past month. The list ranged from the simple – installing the cappuccino machine in the galley – to the incredibly complex – minute adjustments to the sensor network designed to monitor the ship's engines during a transition to hyperspace flight.

"I don't think so, sir. They are also requesting a secure video conference with the two of us in five minutes."

Not for the first time since his crew reported aboard, Prescott fought back the urge to make a snarky comment regarding "Fleet's" affinity for the dramatic. Even the newly minted title "Terran Fleet Command," or TFC, seemed a little over the top for an organization in command of precisely one starship – and an unarmed one at that. He had heard, but had not been able to confirm, that the name was at least partially due to requirements imposed by Earth's somewhat anonymous benefactor. The "ultimate gift horse" was the rather uncomfortable analogy that kept popping into his mind.

"Status, Mr. Lau?" Tom asked.

"Still holding position at L1, sir," the navigator reported promptly, turning to face his captain out of habit. "Engineering reports all systems in the green. Hyperspace transition available within fifteen minutes. Also, sir, the board is clear. No contacts."

"I would hope not, Mr. Lau, but please go right on reporting what's on the threat board anyway. Oh, and Korwin, you don't have to turn around and look at me when you have something to say. I appreciate the courtesy, but it's more important for you to keep your eyes on the road. Just be sure to speak up so we can hear you while you are looking in the other direction."

"Yes, sir, sorry about that," Lieutenant Lau replied rather sheepishly, but with a boyish grin on his face. Every member of *Ingenuity's* crew was hand-picked from a huge pool of volunteers representing the absolute best that each member nation of TFC had to offer. Like their captain, each of them was also amazed to some extent at their monumental good fortune in being selected.

"Commander, I guess we had better go have a chat for a minute before this call, huh?" Prescott rose without waiting for a reply and headed back in the direction of his ready room.

"Lieutenant Lau, you have the bridge," Commander Reynolds ordered automatically as she followed her captain. "Notify Engineering to expect a hyperspace transition within the hour." As she turned her back to the ship's small bridge, an already well-rehearsed choreography took place. Lieutenant Lau was relieved in his position at the Navigation console by one of the two other officers who immediately emerged from the "lounge" opposite the captain's ready room. Before the captain and XO had even left the room, each of *Ingenuity's* five required bridge positions was crewed and ready.

"Well, sir, one thing about a fleet that only has one ship," Reynolds said as they reached the privacy of the ready room, "if they weren't busy being a nuisance to us, what else would they have to do with their time?"

"True enough, and I guess we shouldn't have expected anything else under the circumstances, but the timing of this message seems a little odd to me." Like most experienced officers, Prescott was a bit of a stoic where the motivations of his military and political betters were concerned. "They know that everything we have been doing for three months has been regimented and scheduled almost to the minute. Now they throw an unscheduled hyperspace transition at us forty-eight hours before we are fully operational? It just seems a little odd, that's all."

"Maybe E.T. phoned home again," Reynolds quipped as she seated herself at the conference table opposite the large view screen that made up the outside wall of the ready room.

"God, I hope not," Prescott moaned, uncharacteristically rolling his eyes. "Well, let's stop speculating and find out what the latest crisis is, shall we?" Retrieving the tablet from his desk, he called up the secure video feed from Fleet's (also brand new) Near Earth Real-time Data network.

Of all the amazing toys his planet had been surreptitiously gifted over the past several years, the NRD network was one of his personal favorites. Predictably enough, it was lovingly referred to as "NERD net" by just about everyone who ever used it in a sentence. In spite of the rather inane acronym, however, the technology was truly incredible. Like most of the other advances the mysterious data streams from space had offered, Humans were probably at least a century away from creating anything approaching its capabilities without outside help. Prescott, in spite of his PhD in Aerospace Engineering and Master of Science in Applied Physics, had only a general idea of how it actually worked. His understanding was that the NRD comm array, mounted between the railgun turrets on *Ingenuity's* ventral surface, was used to access a network of communications beacons permanently deployed in hyperspace. The array, as well as the beacons themselves, utilized technology similar to his ship's hyperdrive engines to provide for the near instantaneous transmission of high bandwidth data streams to any location within one light year of Earth.

The implications of this were almost as colossal as faster-than-light, or FTL, travel itself. At the moment, it meant that his vidcon with Fleet could proceed without the usual annoying delays associated with the signal traveling at a glacial three hundred thousand kilometers per second back and forth to Earth. Even sitting in his planet's own backyard at Lagrange point 1, traditional, radio-based communications signals would normally be delayed by roughly five seconds each way, rendering conversations awkward but still possible. During calibration runs of *Ingenuity's* hyperdrive, however, she had traveled to the outer reaches of the solar system. While the ship ran "wind sprints" out to near the orbit of Pluto, video and telemetry feeds of the entire mission had been streamed back to Earth in real-time. At that distance, a one-way transmission to Earth that would have originally taken over five hours arrived as if the ship was sitting in low earth orbit. In terms of command and control, it was truly revolutionary technology.

One unfortunate limitation, however, rendered communications impossible while ships traveled at faster-than-light speeds. The design required individual comm beacon nodes to remain stationary at a precisely defined position in hyperspace. Since it was generally agreed that starships should remain mobile while communicating, their comm arrays were designed to simply forward data to the nearest network node. From a practical standpoint, this meant that a ship was required to transition back to normal space before it could reestablish communication with the network. Over time, it was hoped that increasing starship speeds and expansion of the network would lessen the impact of this limitation. There were already plans to begin deploying additional comm beacons as Fleet ships started the process of exploring nearby star systems.

Prescott's reflections were interrupted as Terran Fleet Command's official service seal appeared on the screen, followed a few seconds later by the careworn face of Admiral Kevin Patterson, Chief of Naval Operations.

"Good morning to you both," the CNO greeted. "This vidcon is classified Top Secret, code word MAGI. Your ready room has been automatically secured for this briefing."

"Understood, Admiral, and good morning to you as well," Prescott replied, sounding a bit more tired than he would have liked.

"MAGI" was the aptly applied code word designating any information related to Extra Terrestrial Signals Intelligence, or ETSI. Just about everyone on planet Earth was now aware that the existence of intelligent alien life had been confirmed beyond a shadow of a doubt, although there were many who stalwartly refused to believe that it was actually true. In fact, even those who embraced the idea of communicating with an alien race tended to be blissfully unaware of the sweeping implications for their world.

The signals had been arriving now for nearly fifty years and appeared to originate from hundreds of different star systems. Although the data streams were not encrypted per se, their content was of little use to the casual listener. In fact, detailed transcripts of the data were now available on hundreds of publicly accessible websites. For the most part, however, the information was of such an esoteric nature that open access was of little consequence. The true secrets associated with the ETSI data streams were known to only a select few.

"I'll come straight to the point, Tom," Patterson continued. "As you know, we have deployed thousands of surveillance drones to hopefully give us a heads up of any alien activity in our neighborhood. A little over an hour ago, we detected a number of very large explosions near Jupiter's orbit on the opposite side of the sun from our current position. The closest drone was about ten light minutes away from the activity, but the data was transmitted back to Earth via NRD net, so we had the opportunity to get some assets pointed in that direction in time to take a look. Here's what we saw." Admiral Patterson's image retreated to the top right corner as a starfield filled the majority of the large screen. The image distorted repeatedly as the surveillance satellite adjusted its optics in an effort to find whatever was in the area prior to the explosions. Suddenly, a single ship loomed large in the display before the image distorted again and zoomed out to reveal a formation of at least ten individual ships.

"What the hell?" Reynolds gasped, briefly losing her normally unflappable military bearing.

"What the hell indeed, Commander Reynolds," the CNO answered without skipping a beat. "Keep watching, you haven't seen anything yet." The satellite had been given instructions to capture as much detail as possible of whatever was in the area prior to the time of the explosions. The video was being played in slow motion, which provided nearly two minutes of footage as the camera focused and panned across each ship in the formation. There appeared to be a total of twelve. They weren't what you would call beautiful by any stretch, their hulls portraying a rather boxy, utilitarian look. They gave the impression of being huge, however, even though there was nothing to provide a sense of scale in the video feed.

"Are we assuming that all those things that look like guns on the big ones are indeed guns, Admiral?" Captain Prescott asked with more good humor than he felt at the moment.

"They sure look like guns to me, Tom," Admiral Patterson grumbled, "and I don't know why we would assume otherwise at this time. You'll see the good news on that subject shortly, if I can call it that."

Each of them returned their attention to the video feed, which had zoomed out to once again reveal the entire formation of ships. As if the appearance of this small fleet of ships within their own solar system wasn't surprising enough, they knew from the admiral's comment that something even more extraordinary was about to occur. Captain Prescott thought he saw a tiny flash of light appear just above the formation a fraction of a second before every single ship on the screen exploded simultaneously. "Dear God!" was the only thing he was able to say for several seconds while he struggled to process what he was seeing.

The video froze momentarily, then displayed a split screen with close-ups of two of the larger ships before beginning a playback loop of the incident. The effects of whatever weapon was being used was remarkably similar in both frames. Unlike most Sci-Fi movies Tom had ever seen, the ships didn't vaporize in a spectacular expanding ball of plasma. Instead, the explosions, while clearly huge, were more localized to specific locations on the ships. It was more like what you would expect to see if a giant cutting torch burned its way from one side of the hull to the other in a split second, literally slicing the ships in two and sending each half spinning off in different directions. Secondary explosions were clearly visible as the sections rotated toward the camera before exiting the field of view.

Prescott and Reynolds stared at the screen in stunned silence as the admiral continued. "I really don't even know where to begin, other than to tell you that analysis of all this data is underway, but it will take some time as you can imagine. We've been getting MAGI data now for fifty years, so all of us knew that something like this would probably start happening at some point, but there was obviously no way for anyone to know what to expect. The data we have been getting over the past several years has greatly improved our situational awareness, at least within the solar system, but we are clearly not yet prepared to defend the planet against any sort of alien attack."

"They don't want us to be able to defend ourselves?" Reynolds asked, surprised to be hearing MAGI data discussed in such a general way.

"Let me rephrase. Whoever is sending the data seems almost paternalistic towards us. It's almost like a father who wants to take his son hunting for the first time, but doesn't believe he's quite ready for the responsibility of carrying his own rifle, if that makes sense."

"I suppose it does, but did they come right out and say, 'Sorry, kids, no weapons for you?'"

"Not exactly, Commander," he laughed. "The data we receive often includes engineering specifications and blueprints that are crafted specifically for our benefit, or, if not ours, then some other humanoid species that just happens to be about our size, has our level of technological knowhow, and speaks English," Patterson said with a wry smile. "Those blueprints almost always include what I would describe as 'terms and conditions' documents that read a lot like legal contracts. One of the common threads we see over and over again are exhortations against the weaponization of any technology we borrow from the data."

Prescott's eyebrows went up. "Borrow, sir?"

"Oh yes, Captain. As I said, some of the documentation they provide looks like it comes straight out of our Judge Advocate General's office. They make it very clear that they are granting us limited use of their technology, not ownership of it. They also appear to be willing to enforce the terms of our implied contractual agreement, if necessary. As I'm sure you surmise, the merits and potential pitfalls of using this data has been debated now for decades. Given that whoever our patron is must be hundreds, if not thousands of years more advanced than we are, we have endeavored to be in strict compliance with their requirements from day one."

"That seems reasonable, but I have never understood their motivation to provide the data at all. What's in it for them?" Reynolds asked.

"As to that, there are a great many theories. I'd say the prominent one is that the dominant military power brokers in this part of the galaxy are essentially too big, and perhaps too civilized, to fight each other directly, so they maintain a balance of power through technology sharing with proxy species. It's similar to how the United States and the Soviet Union handled things during the second half of the twentieth century. Everyone knew that a war between the two major superpowers, who were armed to the teeth with nuclear weapons, would have been counterproductive for pretty much everyone on the planet. So as a sort of substitute for all-out conflict, both nations conducted limited warfare around the globe using ideologically compatible proxies."

Admiral Patterson checked himself, briefly glancing at his watch before continuing. "I know that both of you are cleared for some aspects of MAGI signals intelligence, but I also know that you are hearing some of this for the first time. So I apologize for cutting our discussion short, but I still haven't shared the reason you were told to expect an immediate departure. Shortly after we witnessed the destruction of those ships, we received the following message."

Once again, the video screen changed, this time displaying text formatted as a "Flash" priority action message:

Z0705
TOP SECRET MAGI
FM: GCS - MAGI - SOL SYSTEM
TO: TFC FLEET OPS
INFO: COMBAT OPERATIONS NEAR JOVIAN
ORBIT

1. SMALL SQUADRON OF SHIPS INTERCEPTED AT Z0610 AND DEEMED IMMINENT THREAT TO TERRA AS WELL AS PELARAN INTERESTS IN SOL SYSTEM.
2. GUARDIAN SYSTEM ENGAGED AND DESTROYED ALL VESSELS WITH ONE EXCEPTION.
3. TFS INGENUITY MAY SAFELY APPROACH THE COMBAT AREA AND RECOVER MATERIALS AS DEEMED APPROPRIATE.

"This message was received over the reserved command and control channels of NRD net and was formatted exactly as you see it here. According to the identifier information transmitted with the message, the origin was dead center of that battle area. We believe this to be the first direct communication from the Pelarans. Everything we've gotten from them before today has been via radio broadcast. We've also never received a message from inside the solar system."

"That's the first time I've heard the name 'Pelarans.' Do we have any idea where 'Pelara' is?" Prescott asked, although he was pretty sure he knew the answer before the admiral could respond.

"We do not. We've seen the name a number of times over the years, but they don't seem to be interested in letting us know where they come from. I guess if you're going around the galaxy sharing information that can eventually be used against you, keeping the location of your homeworld a secret probably makes pretty good sense."

"Well we obviously have to head out there immediately, right?" Commander Reynolds asked. "Although that part about 'destroyed all vessels with one exception' isn't exactly encouraging."

"We definitely have more questions than answers at this point, but we've been invited to come take a look, so that's where the two of you are going straight away. There isn't much point in building starships if you want to avoid situations with a high degree of uncertainty and risk."

Prescott and Reynolds glanced warily at each other as the admiral continued. "I need you both to review the procedures for a first contact situation. Other than the debris field from the battle, we're not picking up anything in the area, but that doesn't mean whoever or whatever 'MAGI' is won't show up. It's also possible that the last ship from the destroyed squadron will return to the area looking for survivors or salvageable materiel. If you encounter them, you will *not* assume that they are hostile just because the Pelarans say they are."

"I think we can safely assume they'll be plenty pissed off, though," Reynolds commented, after which Prescott kicked her under the table with the side of his foot.

Patterson paused without comment, then continued. "Keep in mind that we do currently consider the Pelarans a provisional ally, simply because of the long-term, albeit one-sided, relationship we have with them. The bottom line is that we have a single, unarmed starship in our 'fleet' at the moment. Both of these civilizations are obviously capable of stepping on us like the bugs that we are, so it's in our best interest to be as friendly as possible. I'm afraid that's all the time I have. I'm going in to brief the Commander in Chief in two minutes. Get out there and report back as quickly as possible. Godspeed, *Ingenuity*. Patterson out."

The display screen on the wall immediately returned to a view of space off the ship's starboard bow, currently centered on a spectacular view of the sun.

"So this is really how it starts?" Commander Reynolds gaped, incredulous. "You build your first starship, and within a few months the alien bad guys show up and *Star Trek*-style mayhem naturally ensues?"

"That thought occurred to me as well. I really don't see how any of this could be a coincidence, the timing is just too …"

"General Quarters?" Commander Reynolds interrupted, grinning in spite of her best efforts to acknowledge the gravity of the situation.

Captain Prescott dropped his gaze to the floor, shaking his head in disbelief. "General Quarters."

Chapter 2

TFS Ingenuity, Near the Jovian Orbital Path
(0757 UTC - 9.5x10^8 km from Earth)

"Beautiful" was the adjective most people used to describe *Ingenuity* after seeing her for the first time. The graceful curves of her blended-body hull looked as if they might be more at home on a racetrack or a sailing vessel than in space, where boxy, utilitarian designs were all too common. In fact, the technological prowess of a spacefaring civilization could often be judged by the shape of its vessels. There were a variety of factors involved, including materials science and construction techniques, but the true differentiator was easy access to space from the planet's surface. It turned out that civilizations often discovered one of several possible innovations that led directly to faster-than-light travel well *before* they developed complementary technologies that provided large scale, industrial access to low orbit. Earth's nascent interstellar space fleet was a different story. Key advances made possible by MAGI data had allowed *Ingenuity* to be constructed in a factory environment on Earth. She was fully capable of vertical takeoff and landing from any planetary body where the force of gravity was less than 3 Gs, as long as the surface could support her nearly one hundred eighty thousand metric tons.

Ingenuity's flight from Earth to this location, nearly one light hour away, had taken less than seven minutes, roughly doubling her best speed to date. Three hundred years earlier, the same trip had taken the *Voyager* space probes nearly two years.

From the perspective of a stationary observer near her destination, *Ingenuity's* arrival was preceded by what looked like a distortion in the starfield and a muted flash of gray light, instantly resolving to her usual predatory appearance as the ship transitioned back into normal space. At just over two hundred meters in length and with a nominal crew of ninety-seven, she was smaller than the largest naval vessels back on Earth. If Human hands had ever fashioned a vessel to emphatically *look* like a warship, however, it was *Ingenuity*. Although it seemed a bit ironic, or perhaps wishful thinking given her lack of armament, Terran Fleet Command had designated the ship "IFF-1," the first of a new class of interstellar frigates.

"Secured from hyperspace flight," Lieutenant Lau announced. "Sublight engines online, we are free to maneuver."

"And our position, Lieutenant Lau?" asked Captain Prescott.

"Sorry for the delay, sir, the nav system's AI should improve its speed and accuracy each time we transition from hyperspace. We are seven meters from our expected transition coordinates."

"Very well, Mr. Lau."

"Contacts!" yelled Lieutenant Sagari Dubashi at the Sensor console with a little more eagerness than she intended. "Multiple contacts, Captain, but only minimal power signatures."

The lieutenant issued a series of commands to display the information from her Sensor console on the view screen surrounding the bridge. With the exception of the ship's dual antimatter reactors, the bridge itself was the most heavily armored section of the ship. Since this design feature required the bridge to be safely ensconced in the center of *Ingenuity's* hull, an enormous screen was used to provide a panoramic view of the space surrounding the ship. Although breathtakingly beautiful at times, the default view was often of limited value since there was typically nothing to see other than an empty starfield.

In response to the commands issued from the Sensor console, a series of pulsating green ovals appeared as an overlay to the starfield. There were initially hundreds of these on the screen in every direction, but the contacts were quickly filtered to objects greater than fifty meters in length. This decluttered the display significantly, but there were still seventeen objects within two thousand kilometers of their current position. In the upper right section of the screen, a window opened to display a highly magnified optical sensor view of the largest contact in the immediate vicinity.

The captain leaned forward in his command chair. "Let's see that window full-screen, please."

"Aye, sir," Dubashi responded smartly as the window slid to the left and expanded to fill the center of the display. The Sensor console now provided textual information at various points on the screen surrounding the object, including its estimated mass, physical dimensions, and power output. The object appeared to be the stern section from one of the larger ships in the destroyed formation. In spite of its nearly five-hundred-meter length, it was completing a full rotation every three seconds relative to *Ingenuity*, its six huge engine nozzles coming into view with each revolution.

Everyone aboard had received a hastily prepared mission briefing, including video showing the destruction of the unidentified ships, before leaving Earth. In spite of their having some idea of what to expect when they arrived at the scene of the battle, the tension on the bridge rose perceptibly as the reality of the situation started to sink in. Barely an hour ago, and literally in Earth's backyard, an epic battle had been fought *right here*. The world-changing implications of this fact were difficult to grasp. First contact from the species everyone was now referring to as the Pelarans more than fifty years earlier had made it clear to all of Humanity that they were not alone in the cosmos. Until today, however, most members of *Ingenuity's* crew had still held the comfortable, but naïve view that this relatively benign section of the galaxy was theirs to explore and claim on their terms. All of this was to be accomplished with the benevolent, selfless help of their distant neighbors. Clearly, things had just gotten dramatically more dangerous and complicated.

Sensing uncertainty and perhaps even a hint of fear on his bridge for the first time, Captain Prescott spoke up. "OK everyone, eyes on me. Standby crew, please step in as well." He paused for a moment to allow the five crewmen in the lounge to file in along the portside wall. After his XO and all ten members of his bridge crew had stopped what they were doing and turned to look him in the eyes, he continued. "When I was in pilot training and would start to get wrapped around the axle about something while trying to fly, my instructor pilot would take the stick and say, 'I've got the aircraft, Lieutenant, now clear your head for a second and wiggle your fingers and toes!'"

The tension eased a bit as grins appeared around the room. There were even a few polite chuckles at the captain's obvious, but appreciated attempt at levity.

Grinning himself and looking directly at each member of the bridge crew individually, he began again. "I was a hotshot young fighter pilot, so it sounded like a bunch of nonsense to me, but it actually did work to help me settle down and refocus. I need all of you to do the same now. I'll be the first to admit that this is a totally unexpected, and, frankly, screwed-up situation we find ourselves in. It's easy to see how anyone could feel a bit overwhelmed, but, hey, at least we're out here, right?"

Muffled sounds of agreement at this.

"*Right*?" he asked again, louder and more emphatically this time.

This time, all eleven members of his bridge crew echoed the same tone their captain had used, responding in unison with a resounding, "Yes, sir!"

"Damn right we're out here, and now that we are, we're going to stay out here! Yes, we're new at all of this, and no, we can't take on one of those warships *yet*," the captain paused, allowing the implication that it was just a matter of time to hang in the air like an open challenge, "but this is our home and, if necessary, we will find a way to defend it. For now, though, our mission isn't fighting. Our mission is information gathering, and as far as we know, we've got the best ship in the galaxy to accomplish that mission. So, I just need everyone to relax and do your jobs just like you were trained – just like you did during our shakedown cruise. All this sci-fi bullshit going on outside," the captain jerked his thumb towards the view screen, "doesn't change a thing. Besides, I dare one of you to tell me this isn't what you signed up for!"

The effect on the bridge crew's disposition was dramatic. Grinning nods of approval were exchanged all around and an air of resolute confidence seemed to wash over the bridge.

"Now let's get back to work, folks. I need every one of you focused, but relaxed, so you can do your jobs."

As the standby crew exited to the lounge and the active bridge crew returned their attention to their individual stations, Reynolds caught her captain's eye and silently mouthed a single word: "Nice." Prescott gave her a quick wink as he returned to his seat.

"Where were we, Lieutenant Dubashi?"

"Sir, the object on-screen appears to be the stern of one of the larger ships. The section you see highlighted does indicate minimal power output; most likely that's what's left of their power plant. The portion of the hull that is open to space is highly radioactive, but I believe we can safely approach from the stern."

"That rate of spin is a bit of a problem though," the XO observed. "We can synchronize our motion, but it would still be very disorienting during an EVA."

Prescott used the trackpad on the arm of his command chair to freeze the spinning half-ship on the view screen, then increased magnification and began examining the hull as far away from the damaged area as possible. "An extravehicular activity? That's pretty aggressive,

Commander. Is that what you're thinking we should do here?"

"I think aggressive is exactly what's called for, Captain. No matter how you look at it, we're playing catch up on current events in our own solar system."

"Sir," Lieutenant Dubashi interrupted, "I think I've found the other half of that ship. It's only three hundred kilometers away and barely spinning at all."

"Great, let's see it."

The image of the spinning ship's stern moved back up to the right-hand corner of the view screen while shrinking back to its original size. One of the green, pulsating ovals superimposed on the starfield pulsed red three times before it was also greatly magnified and took its place in the center of the screen.

"Once again, the area near the hull breach is dangerously radioactive, but the bulkheads inside the hull provide sufficient shielding after the first ten meters or so."

"Captain, I'm getting intermittent carrier signal readings from that ship. It could be some kind of comm gear still online, or a distress signal," Lieutenant Commander Thomas Schmidt said from his position at the Science and Engineering console. Although Schmidt was the senior bridge officer after the captain and XO, this was the first time he had spoken up since leaving Earth.

The captain sat back in his command chair. "That's starting to sound a little more interesting. Helm, move us to within ten kilometers, nice and slowly. There's quite a bit of debris in the area, so I want the Science and Sensor consoles scanning for any potential conflicts."

"Aye, sir," came the expected simultaneous response from all three stations.

"Reynolds, I guess you're going to want to take a little stroll over there and see what you can find out."

"On my way, sir," the XO replied, already heading for the door.

***

Although they were new to faster-than-light travel, Humans had been conducting EVAs, or "spacewalks" as they were sometimes still referred, for over three centuries. Once large, orbital facilities were constructed in the late twenty-first century, the equipment and techniques for working in space had become quite advanced. Over the past twenty years, however, bits of ETSI-derived technologies had found their way into the equipment required for working in space outside the bounds of a spacecraft. Like most other Human activities that relied on cutting edge technology, the result had been nothing short of revolutionary.

By the time Sally Reynolds made her way to the stern flight deck after changing out of her uniform, Master Sergeant Antonio Rios and two of his TFC Marine Corps spec-ops troops were fully geared and waiting for her near the personnel airlock.

"Good morning, Commander Reynolds," he greeted as she walked across the flight deck to meet him. "You sure you want to go over there, ma'am? We'll be happy to check things out first if you like."

"Good morning to you, Top, and hell no you're not leaving me out of this! You do realize this is the first time in history we've boarded an alien vessel, right?"

"Yes, ma'am, I do. A potentially hostile alien vessel, and that's why I'm not so sure it makes good sense for you to go."

At six feet six inches and two hundred twenty pounds of meticulously sculpted muscle, Rios was an intimidating presence when wearing his regular uniform, but in his combat EVA suit he was simply a monster. All of *Ingenuity's* Marines were cream of the crop, but Rios always reminded her of some sort of comic book action hero.

"I'm going."

"Understood, Commander. This being a potential combat op ..."

"You are in tactical command until we ascertain the situation at the target," she interrupted, undeterred.

"Yes ma'am. Please just allow the three of us to clear each area before you enter. You will see the areas we have cleared shaded in green in your HUD. Now, if you're good to go," Rios gestured to her EVA suit and pulse rifle ready and waiting near the equipment locker area, "then suit up and we'll be on our way."

"Yes, Master Sergeant Rios." By addressing Rios in this formal manner, Commander Reynolds acknowledged his command of the mission.

Without further comment, she stepped to her EVA suit on the bulkhead-mounted rack. The suits were designed to be entered from the rear without assistance and combat ready within ten seconds of activation. In most cases, each crew member trained for EVA combat ops was assigned their own suit, but they were designed such that one of three sizes would fit just about anyone likely to need one. As Reynolds approached the front half of her suit, synthetic carbon fibers remarkably similar in function to Human muscle tissue contracted to perfectly match the unique curves of her body.

Rios automatically turned to stare down his two Marine troopers. The sight of EVA combat armor growing breasts and hips was universally more than two twenty-two-year-old, testosterone-laden males could handle without laughter or inappropriate comment.

"Nice rack, huh guys?" Reynolds teased without even looking in their direction. She had never been one to shy away from banter with the boys and could hold her own in hand to hand combat with any member of Rios' squad.

One of the Marines looked as if he was about to respond to the commander's obviously rhetorical question, but Master Sergeant Rios took a step in his direction with a look that dared the young trooper to say just one damn word. The young Marine held his hands up in mock surrender and took a step back, abruptly ending the potential for any additional banter, appropriate or otherwise.

Reynolds kicked the toes of her boots into place to engage the feet of her suit, using a motion similar to stepping into a pair of snow skis. She then leaned forward, bending her knees and bowing her head to clear the collar of the suit before standing up again with her arms entering the sleeves over her head. With this accomplished, the rest of the process was entirely automated. The suit made a few creaking sounds that always reminded her of a horse's saddle as it completely sealed around her body.

Reynolds took a step back from the wall, shifting her shoulders and stomach muscles as the suit fully conformed to her shape.

"Ready when you are, Top."

"Copy that, Commander. Bridge, Flight Deck. We are entering the personnel airlock now. Ready for departure in zero three minutes."

"Acknowledged, Flight Deck," Lieutenant Dubashi replied. "Clear for departure when ready. Expect RPSV launch in zero two minutes."

"Flight Deck acknowledged." Rios activated the personnel airlock departure cycle using the keypad to the right of the massive door, then stepped aside to allow his team into the small chamber. "Let's move, folks."

Terran Fleet Command procedures required a complete decontamination process prior to exiting or entering all TFC spacecraft when transitioning through "presumed contaminated" environments. The process utilized a combination of chemical and radiative methods to sterilize all external surfaces that would be exposed during the EVA. The system was almost exclusively of Pelaran design, but, so far at least, seemed one hundred percent effective at eliminating all known contaminants without killing the Humans inside their EVA suits.

Once the decontamination cycle was complete, Rios did a quick check of his team prior to opening the external door. "Just a reminder that gravity in the chamber is now at .1 G. That's not much, but you will still feel the change as you exit the chamber. Breathe normally, don't get tripped up on the way out, and do *not* throw up in my EVA suits! Count off if you are ready."

"One, Master Sergeant!"

"Two, Master Sergeant!"

"Three, Master Sergeant!"

"OK, people, here we go." Rios again used a wall-mounted keypad to issue the command to open the external door, immediately stepping outside the ship as the door swung outward. "Give yourselves a few moments to adjust. Then form up fifty meters aft and execute a final suit and weapon systems check."

Wearing combat EVA armor definitely tended to give the operator a sense of invulnerability. The suit's skin remained flexible enough for fine control movements while being all but impenetrable to micrometeoroid impacts and small caliber kinetic energy weapons. Internally, synthetic musculature increased physical strength of even someone as powerful as Master Sergeant Rios by a factor of five, when necessary. The real feeling of power, however, derived from using the suit's propulsion systems in a microgravity environment. Small, electrically powered Cannae thrusters, which were essentially scaled down versions of the *Ingenuity's* sublight engines, were embedded throughout the backpack and skin of the suit. Working in concert, the thrusters allowed the operator, for all intents and purposes, to fly. Since the operator had no chance of managing the complex task of controlling all twenty-five thrusters manually during flight, a neural interface was built into the suit's helmet. All the user had to do was simply plot a course to a destination by mentally manipulating the user interface projected in their head-up display. After that, the EVA suit automatically handled the hundreds of thousands of minute adjustments required to transport them safely to their destination.

In spite of her earlier enthusiasm, Reynolds felt a wave of nausea as she stepped through the airlock door and pushed herself away from the ship. Her suit's AI noted her various physiological responses to stress and immediately began working to help her refocus on the mission at hand. Soothing, cool air flowed into her helmet, followed by the comforting voice of the King of Rock and Roll.

"Good morning, Sally, all EVA systems nominal. Power and oxygen levels looking real good at one hundred percent. Pulse rifle integration is complete. Maneuvering to the rally point now."

"Thank you, Elvis. I'm fine. I just need to get my bearings for a second."

"You're fine, darlin'. You gotta know I was nervous every time I got on stage. Just relax and let it happen, mamma."

A detached part of Sally's brain knew how ridiculous it was to be having a conversation with a rock legend who died three hundred years earlier. That awareness, however, coupled with the familiarity of the voice and its association with pleasure, allowed her to relax almost immediately. Psychological research had proven the effectiveness of this approach time and again. Consequently, EVA operators tended to choose AI voices ranging from their own mothers, to famous actors or musicians (Michael Caine and John Wayne were perennial favorites), to famous leaders like Gandhi, Winston Churchill, or even Bill Clinton.

As she approached the rally point with Rios and the other Marines, a *Hunter* Remotely Piloted Space Vehicle moved into position farther aft and above the squad. Although the current ETSI terms and conditions prohibited weaponization of *Ingenuity* itself, Fleet considered personal weapons and armed auxiliary aircraft to be something of a loophole in their contract with the Pelarans. Accordingly, the RPSV carried eight HB-7 multimission-capable missiles in addition to fully articulated dorsal and ventral railgun turrets. The RPSV's small size allowed the frigate to carry four *Hunters*, capable of handling a number of important missions including reconnaissance, close air support, and even rescue operations under the right circumstances.

Rios managed a surprisingly graceful pirouette as he turned to take in the view of *Ingenuity's* stern and complete one last check of his team before moving out. "Alright folks, it looks like everyone is good to go. We'll be covering the distance to the target in just under zero three minutes. Keep your eyes open and speak up immediately if you see anything that might be a threat. Keep your rifles slung for now."

"Bridge, Rios."

"Rios, go for bridge."

"I've got four good suits plus an RPSV in the green. Moving to target."

"Bridge copies. Lieutenant Commander Schmidt found what he believes is an external access hatch. He just uploaded the location to your suits."

"Rios copies. On our way."

Without further comment, Master Sergeant Rios arced away over *Ingenuity's* stern in the direction of the target. The *Hunter*, Commander Reynolds, and the other two Marines followed in loose formation a few seconds later, their own navigation systems following the mission profile predefined by Rios.

As they approached, Reynolds became more aware of the sheer size of the alien spacecraft. The ship had been torn in half somewhat forward of center, but the bow section ahead was still over three hundred meters in length.

"Any chance of us getting that door open, Top? I doubt there's a brass knocker."

"All we know is what we do on our own ships, Commander, but if that is any indication ..."

"There should be emergency hatches we can access from the outside."

"Should be, yes. They are required on commercial and military spacecraft to facilitate rescue operations. Ours always have explosive bolts on the outside and a double airlock behind them. But that's Earth vessels. Who knows what we'll find on that thing. *Ingenuity* is as close as Humans have come so far to building a spacecraft from the ground up as a true combat vessel, and even she has external access hatches. We might rethink that policy if we start running into enemy warships with boarding parties, though."

As the squad approached to within two kilometers, Master Sergeant Rios called for a halt, raising his right hand with a fist just as he would if he had been commanding a small assault team on Earth.

"Bridge, Rios."

On *Ingenuity's* bridge, the unexpected pause had Captain Prescott's full attention. "I got it," he said immediately, preempting Lieutenant Dubashi's response. "Rios, *Ingenuity*-Actual. Is there a problem, Top?"

Tom Prescott had served with Master Sergeant Rios for nearly ten years. While he knew Rios to be a man of singular physical courage, Prescott also trusted the man's judgment and knew that he would not risk the lives of those under his command unnecessarily.

"Not sure, Captain. I could have sworn I saw movement just aft of our target access hatch."

"Hold your position while we do some close-in recon with the RPSV."

"Rios copies, holding here."

"Lieutenant Dubashi, any fluctuations in power output?"

"No changes in the trend, Captain, but power readings continue to fluctuate. I haven't seen anything approaching what I would classify as a spike, however."

"That's what I wanted to hear. Keep a close eye on those readings, Sagari."

"Aye, sir."

"Lieutenant Commander Schmidt, any change in emissions?"

"Negative, sir, but we've gathered enough data now to classify the signal as a probable distress call. It also appears to be directional, but I'm having some trouble determining where it's aimed due to the ship's rotation. I should have it nailed down shortly."

"Let the ship's AI chew on that for now, Schmidt. I want you to take manual control of the RPSV and take a closer look at that ship, starting with the area around the access hatch you found."

"I'm on it, sir." Although there were several pilots in *Ingenuity's* crew, Lieutenant Schmidt was the only officer on board (with the exception of Captain Prescott) who could claim to be an honest to goodness fighter pilot. He had spent the first ten years of his career in one of the few remaining active fighter squadrons of the United States Navy. "Fighter jocks" had become something of an anachronism in national military services around the world now that modern air combat operations were handled almost exclusively by remotely piloted aircraft. In most cases, this was a reasonable strategy since RPAs were less expensive to operate and not subject to the limitations associated with keeping a Human being alive in the cockpit. Even with advanced AI, however, there were still occasions when automated or remotely piloted drones were not as effective as manned aircraft. In addition, pilots with real flying experience tended to have a completely different perspective on flying, even when forced to do so remotely.

Although Schmidt usually preferred to stand while working at the Science and Engineering console, it just didn't feel quite right while he was manually "flying" an RPSV. It took only a moment to reconfigure the workstation before taking his seat in what was now essentially a simulated cockpit. After a quick systems check, he took control of the *Hunter* from the ship's AI, alerting the other members of the bridge crew with the obligatory verbiage, "I have the RPSV."

"Understood, Schmidt. I want every sensor at our disposal scanning the area around that hatch."

"Aye, sir."

A magnified view of the alien ship's hull from the perspective of the RPSV took over the center section of the view screen. The sun's position behind *Ingenuity* fully illuminated the scene. Although only one-fifth the apparent size in the sky and over thirty times dimmer than in Earth orbit, Sol still pierced the darkness at this distance with an apparent magnitude of -23. Most Humans fortunate enough to have visited the far-flung corners of the solar system were surprised to experience just how brightly illuminated it was. Here, the RPSV needed no external lighting with the sun still shining at over ten thousand times the brightness of a full moon back on Earth.

"Bridge, Rios. I've got whatever it is on infrared."

The sensor data from Master Sergeant Rios' EVA suit was immediately integrated with the RPSV data displayed on *Ingenuity's* bridge view screen. In response, Lieutenant Commander Schmidt translated the *Hunter* to the right and immediately located the heat source.

"Sir, we've got ourselves a survivor."

Chapter 3

Earth, Terran Fleet Command Headquarters
(1045 UTC)

All twenty officers crowding the flag conference room rose as Duke Sexton, the Commander in Chief, Terran Fleet Command, CINCTFC, entered.

"Take your seats, people. As usual, this meeting is classified Top Secret, code word MAGI. The room has been automatically secured for this briefing." He glanced at the CNO. "Well, Patterson, I think I've lost count, but this seems to be about the fourth earth-shattering news you've interrupted us with today, and it's not even lunchtime yet. I assume with the way information travels around here that everyone in this room is in the loop at this point, but please show us what you've got anyway."

"Good morning, again, Admiral Sexton, I'll get right to it. I believe most of you are aware of events up to and including *Ingenuity's* departure, but so much has happened that I'd like to briefly run through this morning's timeline."

Admiral Patterson paused to look around the room before continuing. In his nearly thirty years of service, this was the first time he could remember having the rapt attention of his entire audience.

A timeline stretched horizontally across the bottom of the screen in the front of the room. Important times were annotated and further emphasized with a strip of small thumbnail picture and videos. As the CNO spoke, the display changed rapidly to keep pace with his briefing. Thumbnail images zoomed to fill the entire screen, with increased detail and additional computer-generated annotation perfectly timed to emphasize the most important points.

"At 0620 UTC, one of our surveillance drones detected explosions near the orbit of Jupiter – on the opposite side of the sun from Earth's current position. Based on the position of the drone, we knew that the explosions had occurred ten minutes prior, at around 0610 UTC, and at a distance of approximately fifty-three light minutes from Earth. Local reconnaissance assets were redeployed based on that data, allowing us to observe the area in question beginning at around 0640 UTC. Approximately twenty-two minutes later, this squadron of thirteen spacecraft transitioned in. We missed it at first, but if you'll watch closely, you can see that one of the ships transitions out again less than two seconds later. These ships are, of course, of unknown origin, unknown configuration, and unknown intent. Light from the explosions arrived at Earth at 0703 UTC. We had less than ten seconds to capture as much detail as possible from the time the ships arrived until they were destroyed."

During the two hours since Admiral Patterson had briefed Captain Prescott, additional sources of footage had been integrated and the original imagery enhanced and modeled in three-dimensional space. The result was as spectacular as any epic science fiction movie ever produced by Hollywood. The screen was divided into three panels, each showing a variety of angles, varying zoom levels, and even "flyby" footage of the battle. The destruction of the alien squadron was displayed in such exquisite detail that it was difficult to grasp the fact that it had been recorded by various spacecraft located nearly one billion kilometers away from the battle itself.

In spite of the fact that nearly everyone in the room had seen some version of the footage, there were audible gasps, a number of expletives, and the general sound of senior naval officers shifting uncomfortably in their seats.

At the head of the table, Admiral Sexton raised his hands. "Settle down, folks. Without a doubt, we are witnessing unprecedented, historical events unfolding before us this morning, but we've all been expecting things to get more interesting for some time, have we not?"

The Commander in Chief looked around the table at his staff, allowing the room to go dead quiet before he continued. "Look, ladies and gentlemen, we are more prepared for this kind of thing than we've ever been before. That's not to say that we're anywhere near where we need to be in terms of military capabilities, but we're at least at a point where we are aware of what is happening inside our own system and can put assets in play quickly when we need to do so. Let's not start jumping to a bunch of conclusions about what happens next. I need each and every one of you on point, doing your jobs better than you've ever done them in your life. We have ten billion people depending on us, so stay sharp and listen up."

Aware that he had probably said more than he should under the circumstances, the CINCTFC nodded for Admiral Patterson to proceed with his briefing.

"At 0705, two minutes after we witnessed the destruction of the alien vessels, we received this message." Admiral Patterson nodded towards the screen, now displaying an image of the Pelaran "Flash" message. "It was received over the secure command and control channels of the NRD network and is presumably Pelaran in origin. After fifty years of receiving ETSI data, this is believed to be the first direct, non-broadcast communication from the Pelarans."

The CNO nodded to Admiral Sexton, who had raised his hand to interject a point.

"I'm open to suggestions to the contrary, but I think we have to take the message at face value for now. The Pelarans believe they know our technical capabilities better than we do at this point, so they assumed we would detect the battle, or at least the after-effects of it. I'm guessing they primarily wanted to inform us that they had perceived a threat and taken military action within our solar system."

The commandant of the TFC Marine Corps looked up from his furious note taking. As was his habit, he eschewed tablet computers for an old school legal pad and pencil. "So we're assuming this 'Guardian System' is the ship that took out that squadron. Did we get a picture of this thing?"

The CNO pointed to Admiral Tonya White, Chief of Naval Intelligence.

"So far, we don't think so," she replied. "We're in the earliest stages of sifting through the data we have so far. I can tell you, however, that we believe the Pelarans were using some sort of antimatter-based beam weapon. That's the only thing we know of that might, in theory, result in the type of damage we just saw. The beam itself is invisible, but we're hoping we might be able to determine the approximate position of the source, based on the physics of the exploding ships. Then, we'll just have to see if we happened to get it on video. The Pelaran vessel could have been tens of thousands of kilometers away when it fired, so I wouldn't bet on it."

"Maybe they'll loan us a couple of those cannons, or better yet show us how to build them," Admiral Sexton said, only half-jokingly. "The next part of the 'Flash' message that I'm sure got everyone's attention was the 'all destroyed with one exception' portion of item two. We're assuming this refers to the single ship we saw transition out immediately after the squadron arrived. I'm gonna go out on a limb here and say that we shouldn't be too concerned about that for the moment."

The CNI took her boss's bait and chimed in with the obvious question, "Why not, Admiral? That part scares me to death."

"Well, two things come to mind, Tonya. Unless I miss my guess, even one of those ships we saw in the video would be more than a match for us at the moment, and I doubt there is a whole helluva lot we could do about it if they attacked. Second, our previously silent partners, the Pelarans, seem to be willing to take on a more active role in our defense, if necessary. Once again, it's very clear from the video that they, in turn, are more than a match for those unknown ships. That brings us to the part about the Pelarans inviting us to send *Ingenuity* out to the scene for some sort of recovery operations. Admiral Patterson, would you please continue?"

"Aye, sir. At 0730, I briefed *Ingenuity's* Captain Prescott and Commander Reynolds on the situation and dispatched them to the scene of the battle. I discussed this course of action with Admiral Sexton prior to their briefing. As he just alluded, we don't have much to lose at this point by taking the Pelarans up on their offer."

There were a few looks of surprise and concern around the room on this point, but no one ventured a comment.

"*Ingenuity* departed Lagrange point 1 at 0750 UTC and arrived at her destination at 0757 UTC. I don't want to lose the significance of that accomplishment in the middle of all this other news. She averaged over seven times the speed of light on that trip, which is nearly double her previous best speed."

Hearing this news, Admiral Sexton began a round of applause, which the assembled officers happily joined. "It's easy enough to become cynical about how big of an accomplishment that ship represents for Humanity. There are certainly plenty of folks in the media who claim it shouldn't have taken so long to get to this point, given the so called 'Pelaran Boost.' But they don't know what every person in this room knows, and that's what a truly staggering technological leap forward this project has required, even with design help from our alien allies. We may find ourselves in a world of hurt sometime in the near future, but I'm proud of our accomplishments and just ask that you keep coming to work every day and doing what you've been doing." The CINCFTC nodded once again to his CNO. "Please continue."

"After arriving on station, *Ingenuity* scanned the area and identified a three-hundred-meter-long piece of debris that appeared to be the bow of one of the destroyed ships. A combat EVA team attempted an approach to a possible access hatch, but discontinued their approach after detecting movement near the hatch. Further exploration with one of their RPSV units resulted in …" Kevin Patterson took a deep breath here before revealing the only piece of information no one in the room had seen yet, with the exception of Admiral Sexton. His pause once again focused the attention of everyone in the room.

"Resulted in what?" Admiral White asked anxiously.

"In that," Admiral Patterson replied, turning to stare at the screen, which now displayed live video of the first (living) extra-terrestrial biological entity ever encountered by Human beings.

Chapter 4

TFS Ingenuity, Near the Jovian Orbital Path
(1115 UTC - 9.5×10^8 km from Earth)

Captain Prescott strode across the flight deck to meet his XO. As he did so, he was keenly aware that he was being closely watched by his ship's new guest, still working with EVA equipment and medical staff near the personnel airlock. The guidelines for first contact were just that – guidelines. No one could possibly predict the specifics of how Humans would first encounter a species from another world. A significant theme throughout TFC's guidance, however, was to project an air of confidence and strength without appearing pompous or arrogant. It was never entirely clear how one was supposed to pull this off, so for now Prescott worked on consciously holding his shoulders back and trying to project his command presence. He hoped to be able to do so while still respecting and welcoming his ship's guest, to the extent such a thing was even possible.

"So how are we doing so far? Can we talk to him yet?"

"Yes, sir, we can, and it's a 'she,'" Commander Reynolds said, flashing what her captain thought was a rather smug smile for his benefit. "For now, you can just grab a tablet to provide translation."

Some of the first detected ETSI data streams included what appeared to be lexicons containing the vocabulary, grammar, and rules for thousands of different languages. In each case, the corresponding translations to various contemporary and traditional Human languages were also included. In the months and years immediately following detection of the data streams, it was assumed that the vast quantities of linguistic data heralded an imminent first contact event, or indeed multiple events from multiple species. In spite of the fact that physical contact had not taken place before now, the branch of linguistics known collectively as Communication with Extraterrestrial Intelligence, or CETI, advanced rapidly as a direct result of the ETSI data. Even though its roots could be traced back to the mid-twentieth century, today was the first practical application of the entire branch of science.

Reynolds eyed the user interface for the translation app on her tablet suspiciously, noting that it currently displayed an error probability of less than one percent. "Of course, we're not sure if this thing gives us a one-hundred-percent-accurate translation, but our conversation seems to make sense so far. She also hasn't attacked anyone yet, so that has to be a good sign, right? In all seriousness, she's a little rattled, sir, as you can imagine. She's also concerned that our ship might also be destroyed if we remain in the area."

"Captain?" Doctor Jiao Chen, chief of *Ingenuity's* small but surprisingly well-equipped medical staff called out as she approached from the direction of the airlock. "Can I have a word, sir?"

The medical staff was nominally assigned to Terran Fleet Command for shipboard service, but, unlike all other members of the crew, they were nonmilitary employees contracted through various health organizations around the world. Just like their military counterparts, however, they underwent a stringent selection process and represented the top echelons of their respective fields.

"Of course, Doctor, you were next on my list. I take it our guest is not a biohazard for the crew?"

"Not at all, Captain. In fact, decontamination has gone surprisingly well. Since the translation AI allowed us to begin communicating immediately, we were able to explain to Nenir, that's her name by the way, how the process was going to work. She understood immediately and indicated that it was much the same on Wek ships. That's what her people are called. It's not a very pretty name, I'm afraid, although she herself is gorgeous."

"Nenir the Wek, huh? You are quite the font of information, Doctor Chen. What else have you learned?"

"Quite a bit, actually. The protocols require a complete bioscan and whole genome sequencing. We literally look at the structure of every cell type in the body as well as parasitic agents and organisms like viruses and bacteria. All of the foreign species data gets cross-referenced with the Human genome to look for the potential of any cross-infection. By the end of the day, we will know more about Wek physiology than we did our own until …"

"About fifty years ago?" Prescott interrupted, with a raised eyebrow.

"Hah, you guessed it, Captain. In Nenir's case, the only potential for infection is due to agents that are so similar to those we've already been exposed to that it won't be a problem. As you can see, she's mammalian. I have to say that I'm astounded at how similar her anatomy is to ours. Her respiration requirements are similar enough that she won't require a suit, but she might find it a little chilly. Otherwise, our gravity is a little higher and our air pressure a little lower than she's used to, so she will probably tire pretty easily at first. Otherwise, she should be perfectly fine."

"Every time I talk to you, I'm pretty much blown away, but you've outdone yourself today, Doctor. Thank you."

"Not a problem, sir. I'm sure you have much to discuss with her, but let's not forget that she has just undergone an unbelievably traumatic event, and is still doing so for that matter. As soon as possible, I'd like to give her a mild sedative and allow her to sleep. I also recommend she be confined to quarters and kept under guard. She seems perfectly lovely and rational, but I wouldn't want to face her in combat. Pound for pound, I would give us the advantage in strength, and perhaps endurance, but she has a much higher percentage of fast twitch muscle tissue than Humans do. I'm betting she's unbelievably quick and agile when she needs to be."

"So, are we going to stand here talking about her all day, or go and say hello?" Reynolds asked.

"By all means, Commander, you can introduce me."

"Captain Prescott to the bridge," the ship's synthetic voice announced over all tablets and intercom systems in the vicinity. Prescott noted that the voice sounded more urgent than he had heard it sound before. He was aware that the system was designed to convey a tone appropriate for the situation, but always wondered about the specifics of how the AI would go about making that decision.

"I don't like the sound of that, Commander. Please make my apologies to Ms. Nenir and let her know that I will be with her as soon as I can. In the meantime, turn her over to Doctor Chen, but see that she is secured, preferably while still giving the impression that she is a welcome guest. Until she proves otherwise, that's exactly what she is. Please join me on the bridge as soon as you can get away."

"Aye, sir, be there shortly."

***

"They are hailing again on several different frequencies, sir. They are also attempting a laser comlink. Should we respond?" asked Lieutenant Dubashi, this time with more urgency than the last time she had asked just ten seconds earlier. She turned around in her seat to look Lieutenant Commander Schmidt in the eye and see for herself if the pressure of the situation had cowed him into a potentially dangerous state of indecision.

Thomas Schmidt found himself in the unenviable position of being the very first Human being who just happened to be in temporary command of a starship at the exact moment when the very first alien ship attempted first contact.

Shit, seriously, he thought, *why did this have to happen right now?* He knew the captain would be on the bridge momentarily, but also didn't want to appear incapable of handling the situation himself. The first contact guidelines were, as usual, a bit vague on this situation as well, stating only that the commanding officer should handle all formal communications whenever possible. "Do we have a video carrier signal,

Ensign?" he finally asked, hoping that his delaying tactic wasn't quite as obvious as he assumed that it was.

"Aye, sir," Lieutenant Dubashi replied gravely, unconsciously jutting her chin in his direction and tilting her head as if trying to force Schmidt into taking action by sheer force of will. "Shall I open the channel?"

Schmidt glanced again at the view screen, now displaying an image of the approaching alien vessel, which was nearly three times *Ingenuity's* size. "Open the …"

"Report," Captain Prescott said, interrupting Schmidt before the bridge door was even open wide enough for him to step through.

"Sir, that ship came out of hyperspace right on top of us. Since then, they have been holding position. They haven't done anything else other than trying to hail us."

"Well, did you answer?"

"I was about to, sir."

"Let's try not to keep them waiting until we piss them off, shall we, Thomas? Dubashi, can you give us video?"

"Aye, sir, opening channel," she replied, inwardly pleased that Schmidt would in the very least end up on the receiving end of a tongue lashing for his indecisiveness.

The window displaying the alien ship was reduced in size and moved to a less conspicuous location on the right side of the bridge view screen. It was immediately replaced by an image of the only alien species that was now at least somewhat familiar to the crew. This Wek was almost certainly male. Although difficult to judge from the video, he appeared to be significantly larger, and certainly more intimidating, than Nenir. From a

Human perspective, the comparison that immediately came to mind was the difference in appearance between male and female lions.

"This is Captain Tom Prescott of the starship TFS *Ingenuity.*" Prescott had a fleeting thought that he should offer some sort of welcome, but quickly dismissed the idea of saying any more than he had to until he figured out exactly why they were here.

The Wek paused for a moment before replying, most likely waiting for some sort of translation to occur on his side. Prescott sincerely hoped that this formidable-looking Wek was hearing a translation that was as accurate as his was. Misunderstandings in situations like this struck him as running a high risk of potentially catastrophic consequences.

When the Wek finally did reply, *Ingenuity's* communication AI translated his dialog in real-time. In addition, the translation was delivered using a synthesized facsimile of the alien's actual voice, including subtle details of volume and intonation. The delay introduced by the processing was so short as to be undetectable to the Human ear. The only problem, of course, was that the translated audio did not match the video on the screen. The effect was similar to watching a poorly dubbed foreign film, which, unfortunately, could strike some people as uproariously funny at precisely the wrong moment. During training with this system, officers were given the opportunity to get their initial reaction to this rather comic effect out of their systems and warned repeatedly that giggling was generally inappropriate while communicating with a potentially hostile alien species.

The Wek's sonorous voice was a perfect match for his appearance, giving the impression of confident authority along with disciplined control of physical power. "Greetings to you and your people, Captain Prescott. It is indeed an honor to be the first of my kind to meet you. I am Admiral Rugali Naftur of the Wek flagship *Gresav*. We have much to discuss, Captain, but, regretfully, I cannot risk spending more than a few moments here with you today. Please do not take the terse nature of this conversation as a lack of interest or decorum on our part."

Prescott said nothing, but simply inclined his head politely and waited for the admiral to continue.

"My species is one of seven member species of a coalition called the Sajeth Collective. I must save the details for another time, but my people traditionally handle military operations on behalf of the other members of the coalition. I was dispatched to your system with a squadron of thirteen ships." Admiral Naftur paused and breathed deeply, releasing his breath with what might be described as a weary sigh. The deep, mournful sound, which was reminiscent of what one might expect to hear in the distance during a night on the Serengeti plains of Africa, caused every member of *Ingenuity's* bridge crew to stop what they were doing and stare momentarily at the view screen.

"Please forgive my emotional response," he continued. "Of our original thirteen ships, only the *Gresav* remains. There were over seven thousand souls aboard those vessels. Please understand that the loss of our squadron was deemed more likely than not, and yet was still considered an acceptable risk to accomplish our mission."

"I don't know what to say, Admiral Naftur. Please allow me to express our deepest regrets for your losses. Our sensors initially detected explosions in the area. Once the light arrived at our world, we were able to witness the battle itself. Our ship was then sent to investigate."

"A battle, you say? No, Captain, I assure you that the destruction of our squadron was nothing less than a slaughter," Naftur growled. "The *Gresav* is one of our most advanced warships, but her escape had more to do with subterfuge and the sacrifice of the other twelve ships than any additional capabilities or weaponry she possesses. Had she been present when the attack occurred, she would have been destroyed just as easily as the others. We, of course, cast no blame on your world for this cowardly attack." The admiral paused to gauge Prescott's reaction before continuing. "I'm also aware that there is more to your story than you are revealing at the moment, but I appreciate that you are wisely withholding certain details without resorting to outright dishonesty. This speaks well for your people, Captain, and bodes well for our potential to forge a lasting relationship."

Prescott nodded without comment. "You mentioned a mission, Admiral. May I ask the nature of your mission in the Sol system?"

"You may indeed, Captain Prescott, since providing your species with much-needed information is the essence of that mission. I am here to accomplish three tasks. The first was to have this conversation with you, face to face. Throughout the histories of all of the spacefaring civilizations we have encountered, the species with whom they make first physical contact tends to hold a lasting significance, credibility, and status. There are a few dramatic exceptions where first contact led to centuries of war, but long-term cooperative friendships are more common, and more beneficial to both, I might add." At this, Admiral Naftur's expression changed briefly to something that looked vaguely like a grin.

"May it be so with our peoples, Admiral," Prescott replied.

"Nothing would please me more, Captain. The second task was the placement of Nenir Turlaka aboard your vessel."

Prescott felt the hair on the back of his neck stand on end. Had he been tricked into compromising the safety of his ship immediately after she was commissioned? He furrowed his brow, staring directly into Naftur's eyes without responding.

"Please don't be alarmed, Captain Prescott. Nenir is nothing more than she appears to be, a dedicated representative of our species to yours. In fact, you might consider her our first diplomatic ambassador to your world. You will quickly learn that she is an expert in such things, and should be of great value in furthering your species' knowledge of the Wek as well as the others members of the Sajeth Collective."

"You will be pleased to learn that she is exhausted from her ordeal, but otherwise uninjured. She is still working with our medical staff at the moment, but I would be happy to arrange for you to speak with her shortly if you like," Prescott offered.

"That is a generous offer, Captain, and I thank you, but it won't be necessary at this time. Please forgive the intrusion, but we were able to scan your vessel as soon as we arrived and were gratified to see that she is being well cared for. We went to extraordinary lengths to assure her survival, even in the event that all thirteen of our vessels were destroyed. For your safety and hers, I ask that you keep her presence among your people as one of your most guarded secrets. She is in possession of a device that will render her biological signature impossible to differentiate from a Human if your vessel or indeed your entire planet is scanned. She has been instructed to keep it activated and in her possession at all times while she is visiting your people."

"As you might imagine, Admiral, we have a few safety protocols that we are obliged to follow, but rest assured she will be treated as an honored guest," Prescott said, wondering if the egghead exobiologists back at Fleet HQ would be able to resist incessantly poking and prodding Nenir, honored guest or not. "Can I infer from your asking us to keep her presence a secret that whoever destroyed your ships would not be happy for Humans to be harboring a member of your species?"

"I'm afraid that is a bit of an understatement, my friend," Naftur replied, shaking his head. "Before I elaborate further, please know that I recognize the awkward nature of the situation you find yourself in. We are aware of your relationship, in a manner of speaking, with the Pelarans." Naftur paused to allow the significance of this statement to register with Prescott before continuing. "I do not expect you to respond in any way to that statement, Captain. Clearly, such a relationship is classified at the highest levels, and protected by implicit agreement with the Pelarans as well. We need not discuss your relationship with them at this time. What I must do, however, is provide you with information that your Terran Fleet Command's leadership can utilize as they see fit. This is the third, and perhaps most important task I was sent here to accomplish."

"I am pleased to accept any message or other information you would like to convey and will deliver it immediately," Prescott said, relieved that he had not been asked to respond to the admiral's assertions regarding the Pelarans. He had assumed from the beginning of their conversation that the destruction of the Wek fleet had at least something to do with Earth's odd relationship with the Pelarans and their dramatic acceleration of Humanity's technological expertise. Just as the admiral had said, discussions that even skirted the general topic of such extremely sensitive information were forbidden. This was true even when the conversation was with other officers back at TFC Headquarters, let alone newly encountered extraterrestrial military personnel.

The admiral raised his eyebrows in an earnest expression and continued, "Now, I must give you the opportunity to refuse the risks associated with our new relationship. I would be less than honest if I told you I had any idea of the potential impact on Terra's relationship with the Pelarans. It is the opinion of the Sajeth Collective that the Pelarans are unlikely to attack your world if they learn of our relationship. They might very well discontinue further contact, however, which I believe your Terran Fleet Command might deem undesirable, even if it might be in the best interest of your world in the long run. Unfortunately, I must place the burden of this decision on your shoulders, young Captain. I have …" Naftur turned in his seat to check his ship's chronometer, "less than five minutes before *Gresav* must flee the Sol system or risk being intercepted and destroyed. I regret that I cannot delay my departure long enough for you to consult your leadership. If you believe the risk is unacceptable, I simply ask that you allow Nenir to transfer to my ship and we will be on our way."

Prescott smiled as he replied, "Admiral, as you pointed out, I am not at liberty to confirm, deny, or discuss any of Earth's interactions with other species. What I do feel comfortable telling you is that, whether it's a wise course of action or not, we Humans are not generally known for allowing others to make decisions on our behalf. Whom we choose to develop relationships with is entirely our business, and doing so is one of Terran Fleet Command's primary missions. I also can't imagine ignoring the tremendous sacrifice your people have made today in order to make contact with us."

"You honor their sacrifice simply by agreeing to speak with us, Captain Prescott. The reasons for our willingness to take such a risk will become clearer to your people as time goes on. Now, I must prepare to depart. My communications specialist has indicated that our systems appear to be capable of exchanging data securely. I'm sure you have procedures in place for such an exchange just as we do, so I will leave the details to our respective experts. One thing I would like to ask in return, however, is for lexical data from your communications systems. We have done our best to acquire as much information regarding your languages as possible, but significant gaps still remain."

"We will be happy to provide that data, Admiral. It is part of our standard first contact package, which has never been used prior to today. We will see that it is transmitted immediately."

"Thank you, Captain Prescott. My life has spanned over three hundred Terran years, but this is the first time I have had the pleasure of conducting a first contact mission. I am unable to fully express what an honor it has been."

"Likewise, Admiral Naftur," Prescott bowed. "I hope we have the opportunity to spend more time together at our next meeting."

"I would like that of all things, Captain. One last thing, Nenir will be able to instruct you on how you may contact us when you are ready to do so. It is impossible to predict the chain of events that will ultimately result from her working with you, but we will initiate contact again in one month if we have not heard from you before then."

"Understood. Safe journey, Admiral."

"To you as well, Captain."

"Transmission terminated, Captain," Lieutenant Dubashi said as the view screen returned to an image of the *Gresav*. "I am ready to initiate transfer; full isolation protocols are in place for all incoming data."

"Make it so, Ensign."

On the view screen, the *Gresav* rotated in place then raised her bow and immediately began increasing the range from *Ingenuity* before engaging her hyperdrive engines.

"Data exchange complete, Captain. They sent *a lot* of data," Dubashi said without taking her eyes away from her Communications console. "They are transitioning to hyperspace, sir."

"They weren't kidding about being in a hurry, were they?" Prescott observed.

Already at a distance of over a thousand kilometers, *Gresav's* hyperdrive formed what amounted to a "bubble" in normal space that was, by all the rules of Einsteinian physics, simply not permitted to exist. The practical result of this short-lived paradox allowed the ship to cease its existence in normal space and translate into the adjacent dimensionality commonly referred to as hyperspace. From *Ingenuity's* perspective, *Gresav's* graceful lines and the starfield surrounding her hull blurred momentarily, followed by a flash of gray light as the ship disappeared entirely.

There was a moment of stunned silence on the bridge as each member of the crew grappled with the staggering implications of the historical event they had just been fortunate enough to witness firsthand.

At that moment, Commander Reynolds arrived on the bridge after having settled Nenir into her temporary quarters. Sensing the tension in the room, she stopped short of her chair and looked quizzically at her captain. "Okay, what did I miss?"

Chapter 5

Sol System, Hildian Asteroid 361 Bononia
(1122 UTC – 3.74×10^8 km from Earth, 13.2×10^8 km from *Ingenuity*)

    With a flash of blue light, the Guardian spacecraft appeared in normal space within one hundred kilometers of its most recently detected hyperspace transition. Although the data was far too imprecise for a BLA attack, the GCS was fully prepared to engage and destroy what it assumed was the newly discovered Wek ship, assuming it could be positively located, that is. Doing so was proving to be an unexpected challenge, however. In the intervening five hours since the Wek ship had escaped destruction with the rest of its squadron, the Guardian had been forced to follow a long series of anomalous sensor readings, none of which had led to the enemy ship being reacquired.

    Although it had communicated directly with the Terrans for the first time earlier today, openly declaring its physical presence was an additional step the GCS preferred to delay as long as possible. Unfortunately, this implied that it was now responsible for attempting to monitor and control all activity within at least a light year of Sol. This task was nearly impossible from a technical standpoint, and provided the new Wek ship with an advantage that it was clearly prepared to exploit.

    It now appeared that the Wek had developed some sort of decoy technology specifically designed to keep the GCS occupied. The untenable tactical situation was at once surprising and difficult for the Guardian to accept. In fact, this morning's events were unique in the history of the Pelaran cultivation program. For the first time, an alien species appeared to have acquired sufficiently complex technology, or at least sufficiently complex tactics, to temporarily take the initiative from the Guardian. Now, it was forced to grapple with not only the immediate problem of *how* this had occurred, but also the long-term implications of *why* it had occurred and how it might be countered.

The specific mechanism by which the Wek vessel had evaded detection was still unclear, but there had been a nearly continuous series of both inbound and outbound hyperspace transitions detected within the Sol system since the Wek ship had escaped. Each transition had been dutifully relayed to the GCS spacecraft by the Pelaran's network of hyperspace communication beacons. Within the Sol system, there were sufficient beacons in place to typically allow this warning to be received in less than five minutes. Unfortunately, five minutes might as well be five hours when attempting to track down a ship capable of rapid and repeated FTL transitions.

Hyperdrive engines in the process of creating the "bubble" required to transition *out* of normal space radiated an expanding sphere of exotic particles. This resulted in a beacon-like signal radiating from the point of hyperspace interface that was detectable many light years away in every direction. Unfortunately, this phenomena only originated from vessels *departing* an area at FTL speeds. From a tactical perspective, however, the detection of outbound vessels was of little consequence since they were presumably far away from the local theater of operations by the time their departure signature was identified. Once in hyperspace, tracking was immensely complicated and could generally only be accomplished for ships on an extended journey lasting weeks or more.

By comparison, the detection of *inbound* hyperspace transitions was dramatically more difficult since the ship's hyperdrive engines were no longer emitting the telltale signature as it reentered normal space. To further complicate the situation, when multiple *outbound* transitions occurred within a localized region of space, they caused a resonance pattern that tended to obscure the faint signatures produced by inbound FTL ships. This effect could last several seconds up to a minute or even more, depending on the number and field strengths of the departing ships. This was, in fact, the twenty-fifth time in the past five hours the GCS had received sensor data indicating a possible inbound hyperspace transition signature. Once again, however, full sensor sweeps of the area yielded nothing other than a handful of the so-called Hilda asteroids.

The most likely explanation for the numerous outbound hyperspace signatures was a well-crafted ruse designed to mask the Wek vessel's movements within the system. Although the Pelarans themselves had experimented with stealth techniques designed to render hyperspace and even visible light signatures undetectable, the programs were ultimately deemed an unnecessary use of resources and abandoned.

Now, as it contemplated how best to handle the current situation, the Guardian once again noted the fundamental flaw associated with using proxy civilizations to accomplish the Alliance's military objectives. Leveraging them to control the development of other species within a region of space was one thing, but doing so at the expense of the Alliance's own military capabilities was something else entirely. It had been over a millennia since the last serious military challenge to Alliance forces. Over the years, this had inevitably resulted in a great many promising military technologies being ignored or abandoned.

Even in vast civilizations spanning thousands of light years, there was a never-ending competition for available resources. The more advanced, and therefore comfortable, the civilization, the more likely it was for those resources to be squandered on programs intended more to advance a political agenda than for the good of society. This effect had a way of compounding over the years, centuries, and millennia to the point where even the most powerful could develop a sense of complacency.

The Guardian's philosophical reverie was interrupted with yet another detection of an inbound hyperspace transition. In the absence of additional data, the system determined that it had no choice but to continue following up on the sensor readings. Although it was certainly possible that the Wek ship had left the area, the manner in which it had arrived with the larger formation and then immediately reentered hyperspace was almost certainly an indication of intent.

Historically, there had been cases where neighboring civilizations had attempted preemptive military action against a species under cultivation by the Pelarans. It was understandable why this might occur since the very essence of the guardianship program was to affect a fundamental shift in the region's balance of power. Instances of this level of aggression were surprisingly rare, however, primarily due to the fact that planets selected for cultivation tended to be somewhat remote from the nearest warlike civilizations. The more common response from other civilizations in the region was to make it their business to become the cultivated species' most trusted friend and ally, preferably their *first* friend and ally. The old Human adage, "If you can't beat 'em, join 'em!" seemed to apply particularly well in this case.

Fortunately for the Humans, there were only seventeen habitable planets within twenty light years of Sol, which was considered the "first critical" distance for emergent FTL civilizations. None of the civilizations on any of these worlds were expected to be capable of reaching Terra, much less pose a significant threat, for at least a century. Within Sol's five hundred light year cultivation radius, however, there were dozens of worlds, and indeed several alliances, that could pose an existential threat for the Humans, given the right set of circumstances. The Sajeth Collective was certainly one of these. Ironically, however, the Wek homeworld, at nearly four hundred and ninety-five light years from Earth, was on the extreme fringe of Sol's cultivation radius.

Now, as the Guardian prepared to follow up on the latest hyperspace signature, the entire Sol system rang like an immense bell with the FTL departures of over fifty vessels. The GCS immediately realized that this impressive display was not mere deception. The Sajeth

Collective was making an emphatic statement. As the cacophony of hyperspace signatures died away over the next few minutes, one final outbound transition was detected, this time from the immediate vicinity of the destroyed Wek vessels.

Earth, Terran Fleet Command Headquarters
(1600 UTC)

Nenir Turlaka entered the flag conference room flanked by two Marine troopers in full combat armor. For the past three hours, she had been subjected to every type of scan and examination TFC Medical could cobble together on short notice. She tolerated all of this attention with the remarkably good humor befitting a senior diplomatic attaché. She even suggested a few additional safeguards the Fleet physicians had not considered, having previously been a surgeon herself.

The chief of the medical branch had reluctantly cleared her for direct contact with senior TFC staff just fifteen minutes prior. He did so in spite of some misgivings and recommendations that Nenir be kept in isolation until the results of the entire battery of tests were known. Admiral Sexton was hearing none of it, and made it clear to every member of his staff that she was to be treated just like any other senior official representing a friendly foreign government. Accordingly, every member of the TFC command staff stood as she was shown to her seat at the far end of the table.

The admiral had rehearsed his official greeting in his mind several times over the past hour, but now that the time had come, he found himself openly staring at her for a moment, transfixed by the Wek's appearance. "Madame, I apologize for myself and I apologize in advance for all of the staring you are likely to receive while visiting Earth. We mean no offense, but, frankly, we're all a little … astonished I suppose, to be in this situation."

"That's perfectly fine, Admiral, I take no offense," Nenir responded demurely. "In fact, I'd be less than honest if I didn't admit that all this attention is a bit flattering, really. I must ask, though, surely you have been expecting first contact for some time, have you not?"

Even with the best available translation systems, face to face communications were still a bit awkward. When sitting in the same room with someone, the AI was forced to wait until each party finished speaking before their translation could be played back. Just as in ship to ship communications, each participant heard a nearly perfect facsimile of the other's voice in an effort to avoid the loss of subtle verbal queues.

In spite of his best efforts to avoid mental comparison with feline species on Earth, Admiral Sexton couldn't help but be reminded of a cat's purr mixed with Human speech when hearing Nenir's rich, lively voice. He found it intoxicating, perhaps to the point of being a little irritating due to its vaguely sexual character. He made a mental note to have someone check to see if the AI could be tweaked to reduce the effect a bit and commanded himself to focus.

"I assume you are referring to our receiving communications from the Pelarans. I won't be able to discuss too much about that yet, as I'm sure you understand, but it's certainly true that fifty years ago, we all assumed first contact would happen any day. When that didn't happen, we just assumed what we have always assumed, the intelligent life that's out there is too far away to be of immediate consequence to day to day life on Earth. That was especially true after we began to develop FTL capabilities ourselves, and yet still made no contact – at least no face to face contact or even two-way communications. For all we knew, the Pelaran broadcasts had been traveling for hundreds, or even thousands of years when we received them."

The admiral checked himself before continuing. "Please excuse my manners once again and allow me to introduce my staff." Admiral Sexton made the rounds at the table, introducing the chief of naval operations, the chief of naval intelligence, and the commandant of the TFC Marine Corps. "And you already know Captain Prescott and Commander Reynolds."

"I do indeed, Admiral. Even though the manner of my arrival was a calculated risk on the part of our Admiral Naftur, Captain Prescott, Commander Reynolds, and the crew of the *Ingenuity* have my deepest gratitude. They saved my life this morning and have been the most gracious of hosts," Nenir replied, taking the measure of each person at the table as she spoke.

"Our sincerest welcome to you, Madame Ambassador. Thank you also for your patience with our medical staff and agreeing to meet with us prior to working through the long list of government leaders who are waiting to speak with you."

Nenir raised an eyebrow at the admiral's comment. "Forgive me, my knowledge of Terran government is inadequate at best. I realize this puts me at a bit of a disadvantage as an envoy. Is there a single governmental entity that is empowered to speak on Terra's behalf?"

"I'm not sure how best to answer that question other than to say it depends on whom you ask. Terran Fleet Command is a global organization created as a direct result of our contact with the Pelarans," Sexton said. "Tonya, can you put up the TFC charter map slide?" The admiral paused as his CNI quickly used her tablet to pull up a color-coded world map on the view screen.

"As you can see, the vast majority of nation states are parties to the TFC charter. It's a bit of a hybrid organization, however, and not, strictly speaking, a governmental body. On the other hand, it's also not a true military organization either. Our primary mission involves developing Earth's technological capabilities based on the Pelaran data, particularly our space-based assets."

"So perhaps you expect to eventually become a true military organization then," Nenir said, more as a statement of fact than a question.

"I think if I were in your role, I would also be concerned about our world's military aspirations, so let me address a couple of things. Our command structure is similar to a traditional seagoing navy on Earth. I am the senior operational commander, but Terran Fleet Command is governed by a Leadership Council consisting of ten permanent and five rotating representatives chosen from our member nations. I receive my orders from them. If you feel up to it, you will be meeting with them tomorrow. Here on Earth, representative governments have a long tradition of civilian oversight and control of military organizations."

Nenir smiled knowingly. "We all have our challenges, don't we, Admiral Sexton. I wonder at your ability to get anything accomplished with such a bureaucratic leadership structure."

"We do indeed, Madame Ambassador," Sexton sighed, "and I suspect that there are some characteristics of government and politics that are very much universal. I'm looking forward to learning about those same aspects of your world's history. In all seriousness, however, Fleet's mission is a peaceful one. We are very much dedicated to the principle of civilian control and our charter specifically prohibits the conduct of offensive military operations."

Nenir offered an expressive smile at this last statement, her feline-like features sharpening to the point of appearing almost predatory. "Of course, Admiral," she purred, pausing significantly to look around the table once again. "And I assume that they, the Pelarans, dictated this organizational structure to you in their data streams, did they not?"

Sexton glanced at his chief of intelligence for her input and received a barely perceptible nod in return.

"Yes, ma'am, to an extent, that is a true statement," he replied, carefully choosing his words in an effort to avoid a potentially treasonous breach of security. "The Pelaran data is a bit, uh … you might say legalistic in nature. They were quite insistent that we avoid militarization of their technology. As you indicated, they also required that the technology be shared globally and provided a general framework for how it should be administered. TFC's organizational structural was based on this framework."

Nenir took a deep breath before continuing, clearly gauging how best to proceed. "I find myself in the uncomfortable position of providing some information that you might consider unpleasant. It is not my desire, the desire of the Wek planetary government, or the desire of the Sajeth Collective Governing Council to offend your people in any way, or to cause a rift between you and the Pelarans."

Perceiving her obvious distress, Admiral Sexton spoke up. "Please speak your mind, Ambassador. We also have a long history on this planet of treating people as friends unless they prove themselves to be otherwise. We value candor and honesty, even in cases where the news is unpleasant to hear."

Nenir stared directly into the admiral's eyes. There was no shortage of so-called civilized species that were capable of violence against a messenger bearing bad news. She sensed no such intent with this group of Humans, but wondered how long she would remain welcome among these people after she started sharing what she knew.

"Very well. If you will permit me, I'd like to begin with a question about your relationship with the Pelarans. They have clearly provided a wealth of scientific data that has a truly incalculable value for your world. What is your understanding of what they ask of you in return?"

There was a general unsettled sound as several staff members shifted nervously in their seats. Admiral

Sexton chuckled to himself quietly as he considered how to respond.

"I suppose it would sound a bit incredible if I said that we don't really know, wouldn't it?"

Nenir grinned at him, grateful for the break in tension. "No sir, that actually sounds like an honest answer to me, and frankly that's the answer I was hoping for. You see, Admiral, my world has some familiarity with how the Pelarans work with cultivated civilizations."

Sexton narrowed his eyes. "I'm sorry, ma'am, did you say *cultivated*?"

Chapter 6

TFS Ingenuity, Earth Orbit
(The following day)

Tom Prescott had managed a full eight hours of sleep, this time actually retiring to his quarters instead of the couch in his ready room. Upon returning to the ship after the previous day's endless series of briefings, he had checked in briefly with the on-duty bridge crew, leaving word that he was not to be disturbed before 0700 unless an attack on Earth was imminent. On reflection, he realized that his remark didn't seem nearly as humorous now as it would have a few days ago. An attack on Earth was now a scenario that was much more likely than he ever imagined it would be during his lifetime. Either way, however, even starship captains needed rack time. Immediately after reaching his quarters, Prescott had collapsed into his bed and, in the fine tradition of military personnel throughout history, instantly dropped into a deep, restful sleep in spite of the stressful events of the past two days.

Now, freshly shaved and in a clean uniform, he was steps away from the end of the starboard command section corridor when he heard the ship's voice announce the all too familiar "Captain Prescott to the bridge." Approaching the entrance, he noted the time on the control panel to the right of the door: 0703. *Well, I guess that's an improvement at least.*

"Good morning, Captain!" Lieutenant Lau greeted as he vacated the bridge command chair. His welcome was delivered in a voice calculated to cheerfully receive his commanding officer while simultaneously warning everyone else on the bridge that the "old man" had arrived. "We remain in high orbit, sir. All systems in the green. Hyperspace transition available within five minutes. The threat board is clear, although there has been a significant amount of surface to orbit traffic over the past few hours. The XO is in Engineering."

"Very well, Mr. Lau. That all sounds as it should be, so why was I paged just now?" Prescott asked, taking his seat.

"Oh, sorry, sir. We heard from Admiral Patterson half an hour ago, but he said if anyone disturbed you before 0700, it would be their ass … sorry again, sir."

"Uh huh, it's okay, Lieutenant, enough with the apologizing. *Why* did he contact us?" Prescott replied testily. The idea of the chief of naval operations literally catching him napping not sitting well with him first thing this morning.

"It was eyes only, sir. Commander Reynolds took it in your ready room. She said to call you at 0700, and headed for Engineering to speak with Commander Logan."

Prescott took a deep breath and forced himself to relax. One of his favorite instructors during his stint at Fleet Command and Staff training had been a crusty old former admiral named Jones. He had told the class repeatedly that, in his experience, if there was one single thing that separated successful commanding officers from those who were not, it was their ability to "roll with it, son … whatever it is, just roll with it."

"Well, it sounds like that's where the party is this morning, so that's where I'm headed as well. You can have the chair back. Call me immediately if anything changes or if we hear from Fleet again."

"Aye, sir," Lau said, exhaling, hopeful that his ass might yet survive the morning in spite of repeated threats to the contrary.

***

Kip Logan and Sally Reynolds stood in the aft section of Engineering, peering down into one of the massive wells housing one of *Ingenuity's* six landing gear struts.

"This is a really bad idea. Why are we doing this again?" he asked, shaking his head in disbelief.

"Well, I can't say for sure because Admiral Patterson made it abundantly clear that this was an urgent requirement that was not up for debate. If I were to guess, I'd say it has something to do with the fact that we learned yesterday that our neighborhood might be significantly more dangerous than we thought," Reynolds countered.

"That's all well and good, Commander, but we haven't even begun the post shakedown analysis on any of the landing systems. It was considered low priority since our operational plan doesn't include a surface landing for at least the next three months. It's entirely possible that our initial climb to orbit or using the hyperdrive may have induced stress fractures in the undercarriage, or even the hull itself for that matter. If we drop a dynamic load of a hundred and eighty kilotons on top of these struts, we could easily cause a structural failure. It just seems like a crazy risk to take with our only operational starship. If they would give us a day to run some checks, we could lower the risk substantially."

"You're preaching to the choir, Kip. I told Patterson most of what you just said when he called thirty minutes ago. He was hearing none of it. In fact, he said we were to consider his call just short of an official Emergency Action Message."

"Good God, more drama. I suppose it was predictable enough after yesterday, huh?"

Reynolds laughed. "Yeah, I suppose it was. These are interesting times we are living in."

"You do know that Confucius meant that as a curse, right?"

"I do. You do know that it wasn't Confucius who said it, right?"

"Well, just the two people I wanted to see," Prescott interrupted, ducking his head as he entered through the bulkhead pressure door from the main Engineering compartment.

"Good morning, Captain," the XO and chief engineer replied in unison, both feeling a little like teenage siblings caught fighting over the keys to the family car by their father.

"Sally, I watched your exchange with Admiral Patterson on the way down. Let me see if I have the gist of it. We're to prepare for landing and unscheduled, depot-level maintenance, but he made no references to where, when, or why?"

"That's a pretty good summary, Captain. Regarding the 'when,' he said he would get back to us later this morning. Reading between the lines, I assume they want us down sometime this afternoon."

Prescott took a deep breath and collected his thoughts before continuing. Not for the first time, he was keenly aware of the sense of isolation imposed by command. As captain, he simply wasn't afforded the same freedom to express his personal opinions as the two commanders standing before him now. Ironically, this was also true when speaking to admirals, who all too often weren't particularly interested in their captains' opinions.

"Alright, I know you both have some reservations about proceeding on such a tight schedule. I'll certainly bring that up again when I speak to Admiral Patterson, but I think we all know what his response is likely to be. This clearly sounds like one of those 'shut up and color' kinds of situations," Prescott said, raising his eyebrows as he spoke.

Both commanders regarded their captain with sheepish grins, knowing full well that further debate was pointless.

Prescott's expression softened to let his officers know that their chastising had officially concluded before continuing. "Commander Logan, what can we do to minimize the risk to our hull and landing struts, given that we haven't had the opportunity to prepare these systems for testing?"

"Well, assuming we will be landing at a shipyard of some sort, they should at least be equipped to allow us to perform a 'zero mass' touchdown," Logan said, shrugging his shoulders noncommittally.

Within the bounds of a planetary gravity well, most spacecraft had little to no capability of generating atmospheric lift. That left only two options for countering the force of gravity: thrusters or gravitic field generation. Only during the last twenty years had larger spacecraft (anything over approximately one hundred metric tons) had any capability of operating on or near the surface of a planet. They were constructed and operated, at tremendous expense, solely in space. Among her long list of superlatives, *Ingenuity* was, by far, the largest vessel ever designed for surface landing. She was equipped with sufficient Cannae thrusters to allow for landings on bodies with less than 1.5 times Earth's gravity. In addition, the same systems used to provide inertial dampening and artificial gravity aboard could also extend gravitic fields beyond the ship's hull, increasing the limit to 3 Gs. In fact, the ship was capable of landing under even higher loads, but doing so was impractical since Human physiology was incapable of tolerating more than 3 Gs for any length of time and would, therefore, be unable to leave the ship after landing anyway.

A "zero mass" touchdown used a combination of gravitic field manipulation along with the ship's sublight engines to operate in a manner reminiscent of lighter than air craft flown on Earth since the early 1700s. The sight of a vessel the size of a World War Two aircraft carrier (and over five times as heavy) approaching to land in much the same manner as a blimp over a sporting event was truly remarkable. The chief disadvantage of using such an approach, however, was that the mass cancelling gravitic fields ultimately interacted with objects on the ground and even with the surface itself. Any unsecured equipment or other loose items (often referred to as foreign object debris, or FOD) in the area were as likely as not to be transformed into potentially lethal missiles by the resulting sheer forces.

Captain Prescott thought about the possible list of locations where Admiral Patterson might be sending them for this mysterious "depot-level maintenance." The most obvious choice would be the TFC shipyard facility near Tokyo where *Ingenuity* had undergone final assembly, but he had a sneaking suspicion that this would not be their destination.

"I'll be sure to specify we are looking for zero mass procedures to be in place for our arrival. Your reservations aside, Commander, do you know of any technical problems that will prevent us from making a safe deorbit burn and translation to landing later today?"

"I never said we couldn't do it, sir, it just makes me a little uncomfortable is all," Logan replied. He had grown up in the southeastern United States, primarily Tennessee, and his accent tended to surface when he was put on the spot. "No sir, there are no show stoppers that I know of at the moment. If it's truly an emergency situation, we'll make it happen."

"That's what I was hoping you would say. You know my policy on this kind of thing, though. I'm always looking for your honest opinions and not some sugarcoated BS. That goes for you two more than anyone else on this ship. Clear?"

For the second time, both Logan and Reynolds responded to their captain in unison, "Yes, sir."

Prescott gave them a sideways, knowing look, shaking his head. He appeared to be preparing to make some kind of additional observation when he was startled by Lieutenant Lau's voice blaring from the overhead speaker: "Captain Prescott, bridge."

The comm system aboard was designed to keep track of every crewmember, addressing them by the most expedient means possible, whether that be individual comlinks, tablets, or overhead speakers. When in a louder than normal environment like Engineering, it was sometimes enough to scare the living hell out of the intended recipient.

"Prescott here. Go ahead Lieutenant," he replied, involuntarily glancing up at the ceiling.

"Sir, we just got a fifteen-minute warning that Admiral Patterson will be contacting us again."

"Acknowledged, we'll be on our way up shortly."

Prescott returned his attention to his XO and chief engineer. "Reynolds, you're with me. Logan, get our girl ready to land. Admiral KP seems to be in a hellfire hurry to get us down on deck. I expect we'll be making a general announcement after this call, so go ahead and give your team leads a heads up."

The captain turned without further comment and headed back through the pressure door. Reynolds turned back to Logan and gave him a playful sneer followed by a smile that would melt any Southern boy's heart.

***

Prescott entered his ready room for the first time this morning with Commander Reynolds in his wake.

"Any predictions?" she asked, seating herself once again at the conference table opposite the view screen.

"I'd be afraid to speculate at this point, but something is definitely up. I'm guessing we're about to hear some more things we didn't know, and were probably happier not knowing."

"Ugh, that's what I'm afraid of. Nenir seems nice enough, but I think I liked it better when the only aliens we knew about just sent us nice gifts through the mail rather than showing up in person," she laughed.

"I'm with you there. Brace yourself, for better or worse I think we're about to find out," he nodded towards the video screen as it switched from a live view of Earth off their starboard bow to the Terran Fleet Command's official service seal. As usual, there was a brief pause, after which both Admiral Kevin Patterson and Admiral Tonya White appeared on the screen. Both admirals looked as though they hadn't slept in a week.

"Good morning to you both," Admiral White began. "This vidcon is classified Top Secret, code word MAGI PRIME. Your ready room has been automatically secured for this briefing."

"Good morning to the two of you as well. Before we go any further, however, I am obliged to inform you that Commander Reynolds and I are cleared for MAGI data, but this is the first I have heard of MAGI PRIME. Has there been a name change?" Prescott asked, already dreading where this conversation was heading. Throughout his career, he often found that the more information he was cleared to hear, the more complicated and unpleasant his life became. It was also an ominous and unprecedented sign to have both the chief of naval operations *and* the chief of naval intelligence in a vidcon of this type.

"I wish it was that simple, Tom," Admiral White replied with an almost sympathetic smile. "Let me start by saying that you and Commander Reynolds are now cleared for both MAGI and MAGI PRIME intelligence. In my opinion, you should have both been cleared from the time you signed on with the *Ingenuity* project two years ago, but we are all obliged to follow what our orders say, not what we would *like* them to say, right?"

"Yes, ma'am, that's certainly true."

Tonya White was a beautiful, African American woman who always reminded Tom of a Sunday school teacher he'd had as a child. He had never once seen her appear rattled and had never heard her raise her voice. That calm demeanor, combined with her nearly six feet in height, gave her a presence that was at once both powerful and calming. Rumor had it that she was being groomed for the Commander in Chief's post when Admiral Sexton retired in a few years. In Prescott's estimation, she would be a fine choice for the job.

White took a breath and looked down at her notes as if deciding where to begin a very long story. "Honestly, I need the two of you in my directorate for a full week of classified briefings to even begin to bring you up to speed. In fact, I had planned on doing just that as soon as we got some down time over the next couple of months. Unfortunately, the events of the past two days are forcing us to reevaluate just about every aspect of how we approach our mission. Admiral Patterson and I are keenly aware of the heavy demands we are placing on your crew this afternoon, so it is my goal to give you enough information to understand some of what you will be seeing later today and then get you back to preparing your ship for arrival at the Yucca Mountain Shipyard. Rest assured, you will be fully briefed while your ship is being refitted over the next couple of weeks."

Here we go, Prescott thought to himself, glancing at his XO who had taken on the look of a young girl about to be relieved of her favorite childhood fantasy by the harsh reality of a world run by cold, mirthless adults.

"What I have to tell you will generate many more questions than answers. I think it's best if you just let me run through the briefing without interruption. Again, we don't have time to do much more than scratch the surface, but we can take a couple of minutes for questions at the end." White paused to look her audience of two in the eyes, apparently gauging their readiness to hear what she was about to tell them.

"To summarize, most of what you know … and nearly all of what the public knows about what we have received from the Pelarans is a meticulously crafted lie." Admiral White paused to allow the initial shock of her words to process before continuing. "Just about everyone is aware that we have been receiving ETSI signals sent in the clear, with documentation written in English, for fifty years. Governments around the world were initially flabbergasted by the idea that all of this potentially dangerous technological data was out there for the entire world to see and take advantage of. I think many of us also believed that this was part of the Pelarans' plan. You know, treat us as one world working together as a single civilization, and maybe that would force us to start acting like one. Well, that didn't happen. At least not initially. The most powerful nations each set about pouring resources into developing the technology as fast as possible to gain an advantage over their earthly rivals, all the while agreeing to the cover story of multinational cooperation. This went on for the first couple of years before the United States and China were the first to realize that, to put it bluntly, the Pelaran technology didn't work."

The admiral paused and looked at Prescott. "I know I said to hold your questions, but I think it might help things flow more smoothly if I let you ask what comes to mind so far."

Prescott laughed, "I'll bite, Admiral. What do you mean the technology didn't work? Do you mean we weren't advanced enough to figure out how to use it?"

"See, that's good. I'm glad you asked that question, Captain Prescott," she said, not missing a beat in spite of her obvious physical and mental exhaustion. "No, our engineers and scientists were able to follow along just fine. I'm saying that the documentation was crafted in such a way that some key element was missing from practically every design. Now, there were some other technologies, notably those related to the medical field, that worked as advertised, but all of the designs with potential military applications were unusable."

"They forced us to cooperate," Reynolds commented, speaking up for the first time.

Admiral White smiled at her affectionately. She had served with Sally's father and had known her since she was a baby. "That's exactly what they did, Commander Reynolds, and let me tell you they were damned effective at forcing the issue too. As you can imagine, there are some fascinating stories to tell about how the world's most powerful nations were brought together and forced to play nicely, not only with each other, but with the smaller nations as well. We'll have to talk about that another time. Suffice it to say that the ETSI data streams became very specific about what was expected. They made it clear that they were monitoring our compliance with their instructions and there would be consequences for any breaches of contract."

Admiral Patterson chimed in, "And there were breaches, too."

"Yes there were. I think all of the major players tried at least once to see what they could get away with on their own. Every time someone crossed the line, there it was, documented in the data stream for the entire world to see whose fault it was that progress had once again been stalled. It would sometimes be months before we received the next batch of useful information."

Prescott couldn't resist a quick question when Admiral White paused for a breath. "So far, this still sounds pretty similar to what I thought I knew, so where does the big lie come in?"

White nodded and continued. "Well, as long as everyone was meeting their obligations per the Pelarans' documentation, we would receive bits and pieces of the missing designs. This allowed us to make progress, albeit sometimes frustratingly slow progress, across a wide spectrum of engineering and scientific disciplines. We were about ten years into the program when the Pelarans started to get more secretive. We received plans for secure communication devices, each one genetically coded to a specific individual. When we started manufacturing these devices, we realized that they were interested in communicating and compartmentalizing what *they* considered to be classified data. In order to guarantee both security and multinational cooperation, they chose specific Human representatives through which to communicate. Each of these individuals received specific, key pieces of data. Accordingly, they were required by circumstance, if not desire, to work together in order to see the 'big picture,' if you will. The information they received, and continue to receive, is what we now refer to as MAGI PRIME intelligence. It encompasses some of the most highly classified data ever handled by Human beings, so welcome to the club, you two."

"We're certainly honored, Admiral White, but, now that we are cleared for this intel, can you give us a little more information on what kinds of secure data the Pelarans have provided?" Prescott asked tentatively.

"That, Captain, would take more time than we have, I'm afraid," Patterson interjected. "A better question is probably what kinds of information they *didn't* provide. Power systems, propulsion, weapons, you name it. *Ingenuity* has served as TFC's public-facing cover story for years, but she's really just the tip of the iceberg. I think what you are about to see this afternoon will begin answering your question far more effectively than what Admiral White and I have time to tell you this morning."

"That's a fair statement," White said, nodding. "Another thing you need to understand at this stage is that the Pelarans have provided far more than technical data. Much of MAGI PRIME is intelligence information regarding other civilizations in this and other parts of the galaxy."

Admiral Patterson cleared his throat, letting everyone in the vidcon know that it was time to wrap the conversation up and get on with the day's business.

"Now," Admiral White asked, "I'll answer a couple of quick questions before we let the two of you get back to work. Captain Prescott?"

"I'll take Admiral Patterson's word that 'seeing is believing' and hold my long list of questions until I've had more time to digest all of this. I do have one operational question that I'll ask now, however. You mentioned that our destination is the Yucca Mountain Shipyard. I'm afraid I'm not familiar with this facility. Are you referring to the Yucca Mountain that's in Nevada? Wasn't that a waste disposal site of some sort?"

"It was supposed to be at one time," Patterson replied. "Congress spent billions in the late twentieth and early twenty-first centuries preparing the site to be the national repository for all U.S. radioactive waste. Long story short, there was stiff political and environmental opposition to the site, and it was eventually defunded without a single ounce of nuclear material ever coming in the front gate. Fortunately for our purposes, most people are unaware that there is no radioactive waste stored there, and the site is absolutely covered with barriers and warning signs indicating that very bad things will happen to you if you get too close. When all of this MAGI PRIME activity started, Fleet was looking for a secure location to handle some of their heavier manufacturing and maintenance requirements. This place fit the bill like none other. I'll reserve additional comment and let you see for yourself. I think you'll be impressed, to say the least."

"Oh, I almost neglected to mention one of the most important reasons for this briefing," Admiral White interrupted. She stared down at her notes for a moment, shaking her head as she struggled to clear the cobwebs from her normally sharp mind. "There are design elements of *Ingenuity* that the two of you have not been fully briefed on."

Although not officially briefed, both Prescott and Reynolds had been intimately involved with every aspect of *Ingenuity's* final construction process and shakedown cruise. They knew their ship, inside and out, and were aware of some of these "design elements," as the CNI put it, that were undocumented in any of the ship's systems manuals. Some, like the inclusion of empty bays and ports located both fore and aft along the ship's hull, were obviously intended for weapon systems installation at some point. Others had been the subject of wild speculation among various crewmembers, but served no obvious purpose.

"Your chief engineer, Commander Logan, is already cleared for MAGI PRIME, by the way. Several crewmembers in his department are up to speed on the systems themselves, but not the comprehensive information implied by MAGI PRIME clearance. They will be able to participate in the work at Yucca, however. We refer to their clearance level as code word PARTHIAN. The two of you are now cleared for this data as well, of course."

Prescott nodded his understanding to Admiral Patterson, then did the same to his XO, who seemed to be chomping at the bit to ask her question.

"Admiral White," she began without hesitation, "can I assume we were provided with intelligence information on Nenir's people, the Wek, and their Sajeth Collective alliance?"

"Yes we were. We expected to run into them eventually, just not anywhere near this soon."

"Okay, so can I infer from our … how shall I say this … rather intense response to their arrival that we see the Wek as a potential threat, in spite of the friendly exchanges we have had with them thus far?"

Admiral White narrowed her eyes slightly, considering the meaning behind Reynolds' question. "I think you can infer that we are very much in uncharted waters here, Commander. We're not taking anything for granted at this point. I can tell you that the Pelaran profile data regarding the Wek civilization seems to be spot on so far. They are described as an aggressive species, skilled in the use of both diplomacy and, when necessary, the application of military force to expand their territory and influence. Another interesting fact is that pretty much everything the Wek have said so far was predicted in the intelligence data provided by the Pelarans."

She paused, looking thoughtfully at Reynolds. "You must have had a reason for asking, Sally. It's certainly not what I expected you to say after introducing you to this topic. I'm curious, what prompted your question?"

"Frankly, Admiral, I have had a bad feeling about the Pelarans for a long time. None of it has ever made a lot of sense to me, and Nenir's question last week about what we think they expect from us in return for all this knowledge is one that resonates with me."

"Well, that's certainly a valid concern shared by many on the Admiralty staff as well as the TFC Leadership Council. Once again, however, the Pelarans told us in advance, almost word for word, what we should expect the Wek to say, and they were exactly right."

Commander Reynolds shrugged, "It just occurs to me that just because the Pelarans knew what the Wek were going to say, does not mean that the Wek aren't the ones telling us the truth."

Chapter 7

TFC Yucca Mountain Shipyard Facility

In a tradition dating to the mid-twentieth century, over four hundred technicians, maintenance workers, and active duty Fleet personnel formed one of six groups lined up shoulder to shoulder to "FOD walk" the length of Berth Nine. The decidedly low tech but effective approach to minimizing foreign object damage was performed twice weekly at all TFC shipyards, and again any time a starship landing was expected. The line had the look of a religious processional, with each participant walking with their heads bowed, scanning the concrete ramp immediately in front of them. The target of their focused search was pretty much anything, be it tools, trash, rocks, or even dead insects that might be launched into the air at incredible speeds during *Ingenuity's* zero mass approach and landing. Before the area could be declared "FOD free," the entire path the ship would take to reach her final destination required a painstaking sweep. This included the massive, four hundred meter by four hundred meter entry cavern and the kilometer long "taxiway" leading to her berth.

The geology of the Yucca Mountain ridge that made it so attractive as a long-term waste repository also provided the ideal location for hiding massive, underground construction facilities. Much of the work on the underground cavern itself had already been completed centuries before Fleet engineers began the process of dramatically expanding and repurposing the huge facility. Near the center of the mountain, a natural curve in the ridgeline's meandering path provided the perfect location for a giant, manmade cave entrance. Once inside, the entrance tunnel opened to a nearly ten-kilometer-long shipyard facility. Although Fleet now operated six similar installations worldwide, Yucca Mountain was the largest and was considered more secure than the other sites. This was due primarily to its remote, rugged location as well as the mountain's ostensible purpose as a nuclear waste site. It was also one of only three facilities with berths capable of handling ships up to twelve hundred meters in length.

Now, with the imminent arrival of Terran Fleet Command's flagship, automated warning announcements echoed throughout the facility: *"Attention, TFS Ingenuity arriving in three zero minutes. Zero mass procedures are in effect. Please clear the approach to Berth Nine immediately."*

***

TFS Ingenuity, Earth Orbit

Ensign Blake Fisher jumped involuntarily as Commander Reynolds placed her hand on his shoulder.

"Are you ready for this, Ensign?" she asked, stifling a laugh. Reynolds had been looking over his shoulder at the Helm control station for several minutes, observing his progress as he worked his way through a series of prelanding checklists. "You seem a little on edge."

"Oh, yes, ma'am. Sorry, Commander. I had no idea you were standing there. You know how it is, I'm in my own little 'no pressure, all I have to do is land a two-hundred-thousand-ton starship' world here."

"Just another day at the office, Blake. What was it the captain said yesterday? 'Wiggle your fingers and toes,' I think it was."

Fisher laughed. "I actually heard that one in flight school myself a few times. I can't say it helped me much, but it's definitely a good idea to 'recenter' and force yourself to relax every once in a while. You can get pretty tensed up otherwise."

"Alright, folks, everyone awake and ready to land this thing and go have a drink?" Prescott announced, entering the bridge from his ready room. "Ensign Fisher, I've got some good news and some *very* good news for you," he said, smiling broadly.

Fisher turned in his seat to face his captain. "I'm afraid to ask, sir, but let's hear the very good news first."

Prescott laughed. "I'm afraid that wouldn't make as much sense, so you'll have to hear them in order. The good news is that Fleet just augmented our auto landing capability to allow for the final approach inside the Yucca Shipyard to be fully automated. We'll just need to closely monitor what the ship is doing and be ready to take over manually, if necessary. I'm told that this software has already been extensively tested, so hopefully we'll have a nice, quiet ride. I'm choosing to take the optimistic view that Fleet wouldn't be asking us to use this new capability if they thought it might ding their shiny new ship."

"Wow, sir, I would hope not. That still makes me a little nervous though. I wonder how they managed to 'test' the software, seeing as how *Ingenuity* herself is the only real-world testbed?"

"Yeah," Prescott paused, considering. "I think I'll defer that question until we are safely on the deck, but I will say that I suspect we may all be in for some surprises this afternoon."

"Fair enough, sir. What's the *very* good news?"

"The very good news is that Fleet's fancy new landing automation software can actually handle the entire approach and landing sequence, including the deorbit burn. I convinced Admiral Patterson, however, that *Ingenuity* has the best starship helmsman in the galaxy, so we prefer to handle the deorbit and initial approach ourselves. Did I get that about right, Fisher?"

"Hell yes, Captain!"

"I thought so. Besides, you'll probably end up needing to train other helmsmen in starship landing operations at some point, so it might be helpful if you've actually done it a time or two yourself," Prescott said, heading for his command chair.

"Captain," Lieutenant Dubashi reported from the Communications console, "we have received the coordinates and final instructions for our landing site."

"Navigation and Helm have it as well, Captain," Lieutenant Lau confirmed.

"Well that's good news," Prescott said, fastening his shoulder straps to ensure he remained securely in his command chair during the landing. "I was beginning to think they were expecting us to guess." Prescott always found that offering a little humor during tense situations, even the weak attempts he typically proffered, did wonders to lessen the tension and improve performance.

This always seemed particularly true of junior officers and enlisted crewmembers, who sometimes struggled with their confidence level due to a simple lack of experience.

"Do we have a clear view of the site, Dubashi?" Reynolds asked.

"I believe we do, Commander. It's a desert region not too far from Death Valley, so cloud cover is not usually a problem. It should be coming over the horizon now."

"Great, let's see where we're going."

Lieutenant Dubashi issued a series of commands at the Communications console, causing the usual pulsating green oval designator to appear on the bridge view screen superimposed over the landing site on the Earth's surface below. After a brief pause, the oval pulsed red three times before zooming the image to the location of the Yucca Mountain shipyard. The area was displayed in stunning detail, with *Ingenuity's* various sensors working together to provide a real-time view of the facility as if the ship was circling it at low altitude. In spite of Lieutenant Dubashi's forecast, there actually were quite a few puffy cumulus clouds in the area, but these were quickly removed by the ship's AI to provide a completely unobscured view of the facility.

"Well, that looks like a mountain, alright," Reynolds said, deadpan.

"It does indeed," Prescott replied. "I think that's the general idea. If there are any bad guys looking down on the site, they won't see a shipyard either. Lieutenant Dubashi, just in case we have a problem, please see if you can identify some alternate landing sites in the general area."

"Aye, sir, there are plenty of old construction sites with large, concrete surfaces. There are also exposed areas of bedrock that should support our weight, so a ground landing appears to be an option, if necessary."

"That's good to hear, just be careful not to allow the AI to choose a spot inside the Nevada Nuclear Test Site a few miles to the east. I'm pretty sure that's not a good place to set down."

"Commander Logan, bridge," Prescott announced. The ship's communication AI instantly recognized the captain's desire to communicate with the chief engineer and routed the call accordingly.

"Logan here. Go ahead, Captain."

"We're ready for deorbit up here, Commander. What's your status?" Prescott's call to Engineering was done more out of habit and courtesy than necessity. If his chief engineer had not been prepared for landing, at least seven separate displays on the bridge would have clearly indicated that fact.

"Everything looks good down here for the moment, Captain. I'd say let's get this over with before something decides to break."

"Very well, please let us know if anything does. Prescott out."

"All hands, this is the captain. Prepare for deorbit burn and landing. Be advised that our landing site is highly classified. Once we have secured the ship, all of us will be receiving the required security briefings. Until you have been briefed and officially cleared, you may not leave the ship. We will begin the landing sequence shortly."

Prescott paused and looked around the bridge. "OK, rather than ask if everyone is ready, let me give each of you one last opportunity to voice any concerns. Is anyone *not* ready to start the sequence?" he asked. Hearing no objections, he proceeded. "Alright, here we go, folks. XO, set General Quarters for landing. Lieutenant Dubashi, are we cleared for landing at Yucca?"

"We are cleared for approach and landing, sir. For precise arrival timing, optimal deorbit burn should begin in four zero seconds," she replied over the sound of the ship's AI announcing General Quarters for landing. As the announcement concluded, the lighting on the bridge took on a blue color, providing a visual indication of the imminent landing.

"Very well. Navigation?"

"Course plotted and transferred to the Helm console, Captain. The ship is oriented for the deorbit burn. Standing by for autolanding cues from Yucca Mountain."

Even though *Ingenuity's* sublight engines were internal, they were still oriented to provide considerably more thrust in the direction of the bow than the stern, so the ship executed its deorbit "burn" with its stern in the direction of flight.

"Alright, Ensign Fisher, it's your show at this point. Execute the deorbit sequence per Lieutenant Dubashi's countdown."

"Aye, sir, initiating in five, four, three, two, one, mark."

Ingenuity's inertial dampening and acoustical conditioning systems reacted within microseconds to counteract the might of her massive sublight engines engaging and rapidly increasing to maximum power. On the bridge, the only indication of the tremendous thrust being unleashed in Engineering was a barely perceptible shudder, followed by a slight increase in the ever-present rumbling sound created by various power and propulsion systems aboard.

From the time of man's earliest spaceflights in the mid-twentieth century, atmospheric reentry had been a risky proposition. Just as launching a spacecraft from the surface of the Earth required massive increases in specific energy, traditionally accomplished by huge rocket engines burning vast quantities of fuel, landing required a similar *decrease* in energy. Various practical design considerations forced early spacecraft to use most of their fuel during their ascent to orbit. When it was time to return to the surface, there was only enough fuel remaining for a short duration burn, designed to begin the process of slowing the craft down enough to begin interacting with the upper atmosphere. From there, most ships relied on atmospheric friction and compressive shock wave heating rather than engine thrust to bleed away energy and slow to a manageable speed for landing. This process was typically accomplished using various types of thermal shielding designed to withstand temperatures in excess of three thousand degrees Celsius. The brave crew of these fragile spacecraft experienced high G loads for extended periods of time during reentry since the deceleration process often took half an orbit or more to complete.

Fortunately for *Ingenuity's* crew, much had changed in the three-hundred-year history of manned spaceflight, especially since the introduction of ETSI-inspired propulsion technology. The ship's massive sublight engines required no propellant, so there was no longer any reason to waste massive amounts of interior space and thrust simply storing and moving the ship's fuel supply through space. Instead, the engines relied on the direct conversion of electrical power from her antimatter reactors to produce huge amounts of microwave energy. The energy was introduced into closed, cone-shaped reaction chambers where it was reflected internally, producing thrust in the direction of the wider end of the chamber. The Cannae engines were not only "reactionless," (requiring no reaction mass/propellant), but also contained no moving parts whatsoever. Perhaps the most fascinating impact of this technology on ship design was the absence of external engine nozzles or other propulsion-related equipment of any kind. *Ingenuity's* engines, like her bridge and antimatter reactors, were buried deep inside her armored hull. This allowed the valuable real estate near the ship's stern to be used as a flight deck and, potentially, for weapons emplacements. Gratifyingly, the elegant design was originally of Human origin, even though some of the improvements allowing the engines to reach their current capabilities were derived from Pelaran technology.

"Sir, we will be maintaining our current horizontal position relative to the landing site for the remainder of our reentry. The engines have throttled back to twenty percent to hold this approach curve. Altitude now one hundred kilometers and decreasing. Initial atmospheric entry interface in three zero seconds," Fisher announced. The earlier signs of nervous anticipation had completely vanished from his voice. Now very much in his element, he actually enjoyed being the center of attention. "There's quite a bit of atmospheric convection, so I would anticipate a little chop. It shouldn't be anything major, though."

"Understood, Ensign. Steady as she goes," Prescott replied. He paused for a few seconds, then leaned over to his XO without taking his eyes off the view screen and said in a low voice that only she could hear, "Dear God, did I just say, 'Steady as she goes?'"

"I believe you did, sir, but I'll be sure to review the audio log to make sure. I'll send a copy to your tablet later."

"Sheesh. I don't know what to tell you about that, other than I've read too much classic naval fiction and I'm getting old. If I start saying 'avast there,' or start referring to all of you as 'lads,' I guess you'll have to relieve me of command."

The ship gave a lurch to starboard, followed by what felt like a precipitous drop in altitude, causing everyone onboard to briefly experience the feeling of free falling before the ship's gravitic systems compensated. As is often the case when Humans unexpectedly experience negative Gs, several crewmembers let fly an entirely involuntary exclamation. This illustrious group included Lieutenant Dubashi at the Communications console, who uttered a particularly colorful expletive in her native Hindi. She turned to face her captain and XO, blushing in spite of her dark complexion, and mouthed *"I'm sorry!"* before quickly returning her attention back to her screen.

"That bounce was entry interface, sir. Like I said, we've got some pretty significant thermal activity taking place over this area," Ensign Fisher said. "The worst should be over in a couple of minutes."

"Don't worry about us, Fisher, we'll be fine. Right, Dubashi?"

"Doing great, sir!" Lieutenant Dubashi laughed, this time avoiding eye contact.

"Lieutenant Commander Schmidt, can you tighten up the grav system a bit in case we see more disturbances like that last one? It's entirely possible that somebody somewhere isn't strapped in properly and we don't want anyone getting hurt."

"Already done, sir," Schmidt replied. "With the sensitivity dialed up, it may feel a little oppressive for the next couple of minutes, but we shouldn't experience any more thrill rides."

"Thank you, Schmidt."

"Captain," Lieutenant Dubashi announced, "we have received course guidance for our final approach to the Yucca Mountain Shipyard. The approach and landing will require your approval before we can relinquish control to the AI."

As was the case with all time-critical information, the data was immediately displayed in a window on the right side of the bridge view screen in addition to the small touchscreen attached to Prescott's command chair. As he had expected, the proposed approach course was a bit circuitous, and clearly designed to conceal their ultimate landing destination inasmuch as such a thing was possible in broad daylight. They would make their initial approach over the area from the south, and would be visible from the ground over a large, fairly populated area, including the city of Las Vegas. After that, however, they would head in the direction of the Groom Lake facility, still known the world over as "Area 51." There, they would complete the remainder of their descent over the dry lakebed before heading back towards Yucca Mountain at a much lower altitude designed to mask their final approach for landing.

Prescott smiled at the historical irony. To this day, if you asked anyone in the world to speculate on where Fleet would be landing *Ingenuity* on a regular basis, they would most likely come up with Area 51 as a likely candidate. In reality, however, the secrets housed at the Groom Lake facility paled in comparison to Terran Fleet Command's Yucca Mountain Shipyard, a scant sixty-eight kilometers to its southwest.

"Course acknowledged and approved for a manual approach. I will approve autolanding after we arrive at the final approach fix. Ensign Fisher, the approach profile has been updated and transferred to your console. Fleet is calling for a medium altitude flyover from the south towards Groom Lake, followed by a circling descent and low altitude final approach. I know you've handled terrain masking flight a hundred times in the sim, but if you start to feel overwhelmed or unsure of yourself, I want you to allow the AI to complete the approach. Don't break our ship, Fisher. Any questions?"

"No questions, Captain. I'd be the first one to speak up if I saw a problem, sir. This route looks pretty straightforward and, frankly, isn't even much of a challenge for this ship. She flies a lot more like a fighter than a frigate, sir," Ensign Fisher responded confidently.

In reality, there was little danger that a hotshot young ensign at the Helm could make a mistake that would result in ship damage. Even though Fisher was still "manually" controlling the ship from the Helm console, *Ingenuity's* AI monitored every aspect of her position, speed, surrounding environment, and control inputs hundreds of millions of times per second. The AI was designed to follow the crew's commands, but its first priority was their survival, followed closely by the survival of the ship itself. In an emergency, *Ingenuity's* AI had full authority to take whatever action it deemed necessary to protect both its crew and itself.

"So it looks like they want people on the ground to see us, but still hopefully not realize exactly where we are going," Commander Reynolds said, more as a question than a statement of fact.

"I think it's all about timing," Prescott replied. We did our initial climb to orbit at night because we really didn't want to advertise exactly what we were doing and when. This time, I think they just wanted us on the ground as quickly as possible and consequences be damned. Besides, it seems like Fleet is going out of their way to ensure that *Ingenuity* remains the public face of the program for now."

"I suppose so. It just strikes me that taking the scenic route on our approach isn't likely to keep our destination much of a secret. We *are* a pretty good-sized ship, after all."

"Altitude now eight kilometers and decreasing, on course for Area 51, sir," Fisher reported from the Helm console.

The Area 51 Travel Center near the center of the Amargosa Valley had operated as a dusty tourist stop on Highway 95 for over three centuries under various owners and with varying degrees of success. Since Humans had finally received irrefutable confirmation that they were not alone in the cosmos fifty years earlier, however, public curiosity regarding the various ultra-secretive U.S. government sites in the area had been rekindled. Now that it was widely believed that Pelaran-related technology was being developed and tested in the region, the lonely desert highways crisscrossing the region had once again become a mecca for a wide cross-section of visitors spanning the spectrum from family vacationers, to fringe conspiracy theorists, to rabid science fiction fans.

As has often been the case with government-related installations in the region, the facts were actually more bizarre and intriguing than the rumors surrounding them. To this day, for example, it was true that the U.S. government still operated the Groom Lake facility known as Area 51 only eighty-five kilometers to the northeast of the Travel Center. It was also true that the facility housed the wreckage of a spacecraft that had crashed near Roswell, New Mexico, in 1947. The truth of why this had occurred, however, was still the subject of wild speculation for both tourists and government officials alike. Ironically, the government officials hiding the alien spacecraft from its citizens knew little more than they did on the subject. Over the years, there had been a great many hypotheses put forth to explain the crash, particularly why the aliens had apparently not returned and why their spacecraft appeared to have been damaged by a type of weapon unknown to Human science. None, however, even after receiving fifty years of ETSI data from the Pelarans, had managed to piece together the whole story.

In the early twentieth century, the Guardian was faced with the decision of how best to deal with the Terrans' rapidly increasing technological footprint on this region of the galaxy. Prior to that point, the weak radio signals emanating from the planet were of such low power that they were unlikely to be detected by their nearest, potentially dangerous neighbors. Fortunately, the Makers had provided the GCS with a great deal of flexibility regarding how such things should be handled under the cultivation program's three mission directives. Taking all variables into account, the GCS had full authority to limit or entirely prevent all foreign contact with the cultivated species until they were unlikely to encounter a civilization more powerful than themselves. Ultimately, after a number of very close calls with premature first contact, the Guardian had deemed this type of isolation protocol to have the highest probability of success for the Sol system. Accordingly, all forms of contact with other species were prevented, inasmuch as it was technically possible to do so. Electronic communications, including radio and television broadcasts originating in other star systems, were surprisingly simple to block. A network of only eight devices of similar design to the Guardian's own reconnaissance probe deployed at key locations around the system completely jammed these stray, extremely low power signals. Now, even fifty years after their first receipt of ETSI data, Humans had never detected any other signals proven to be extra-terrestrial in origin. Although not quite as effective at blocking the Terrans' outbound signals, these were also reduced to a level that made detection significantly less likely.

Unfortunately, preventing direct contact with alien species, or at least their technology, was often more difficult than merely blocking stray electronic signals. In spite of all efforts to sequester the Humans, one species had actually managed to penetrate the Sol isolation zone long enough to perform some perfunctory reconnaissance. The Pelarans actually knew very little about these aliens other than the fact that they were not from this region of the galaxy, and indeed were classified as a candidate extra-galactic species. Although they had a numeric species designation, the Guardian preferred the rather simplistic, but descriptive name the Humans had assigned them: the "Greys." They had been encountered numerous times and, thus far at least, their behavior did not appear particularly aggressive. Strangely, however, some of their activities such as overflights and specimen collections, most likely related to scientific research, were deemed high risk for premature first contact with the Terrans.

Unfortunately, all Alliance efforts to communicate the nature of the cultivation program, or anything else for that matter, with these creatures had been ignored. Accordingly, per the rules of engagement, the Greys' ships were summarily attacked upon entering the Sol isolation zone just as any other intruder would be. This had happened a number of times, and had usually resulted in the alien spacecraft leaving the area rather than choosing to return fire (assuming they were even armed). In mid-1947, however, a combination of some ingenious, but decidedly reckless tactics had allowed a damaged spacecraft to survive long enough to crash-land on the surface of Terra. Fortunately, the Human proclivity to divide themselves into regional and political groups and then hide as much information from each other as possible had served the Guardian's purpose well. The GCS had detected no significant technological contamination resulting from the incident.

Now, the Area 51 Travel Center shook as the normally quiet afternoon sky over the Amargosa Valley thundered with a double sonic boom marking Starship *Ingenuity's* arrival. Even though such sounds had been a common occurrence in the region since the late 1940s, the sound of such a huge ship entering the atmosphere was truly awe-inspiring and left little doubt as to its source. All over the region, eyes turned skyward in hopes of catching a glimpse of what was now perhaps the most well-known ship in Human history.

A lucky few, including those at the intersections of Highway 95 and 373, had been fortunate enough to see the ship's initial, high-altitude approach from the south towards the rugged, isolated region of Nevada to the north. The position of the afternoon sun caused the ship's shadow to pass directly over the intersection, followed shortly thereafter by the tremendous echoing booms of her passing. Other than the sonic booms, however, *Ingenuity's* overflight was accompanied by no sound at all other than the dry mountain wind blowing through the creosote bushes that dotted the sandy floor of the Mojave Desert.

***

Although presumably more accustomed to the spectacle of exotic, ultra-secretive air and spacecraft than the tourists at the Area 51 Travel Center had been, the government and civilian employees at the real Area 51 were no less interested in *Ingenuity's* arrival. After maintaining an altitude of five kilometers during her approach from the south, the ship executed a rapid descent as it crossed the boundaries of the R-4808N restricted airspace over Groom Lake. Approaching the bright white salt flats marking the facility's eastern border, *Ingenuity* made a final turn to align with the massive runways outlined on the dry surface of the lakebed itself. From the perspective of the keenly interested spectators, the ship quickly resolved from little more than an indistinct speck in the sky to a shockingly large spacecraft hovering silently at two hundred meters above the center of the lakebed near the intersection of Runways 21 and 27.

***

"Captain, we have reached the initial point specified for the low level portion of our approach to the Yucca Mountain Shipyard," Ensign Fisher reported. "We are holding position at two hundred meters. Gravitic fields set at forty percent mass. All systems in the green. We are rigged for terrain following flight."

"Very well, Ensign," Prescott replied. "Lieutenant Dubashi, please signal Fleet that we are holding at the IP, looking for final approach and landing clearance. Please repeat that we will be hand flying the approach until the final approach fix just outside the shipyard. Once we arrive at the FAF, we will hold position and relinquish control to the AI for autolanding."

"Aye Captain, transmitting now."

"Lieutenant Lau, please keep an eye on our ventral sensors. Our grav field should only extend a few meters beyond the hull on this low level route, but if you see us start kicking up debris, we'll need to make some adjustments."

"Aye, sir. Current maximum gravitic field extension beyond the hull is only five meters."

"Excellent. I'm not expecting a problem, but we still have that 'new starship smell,' and I'd like to keep it that way for a while, if possible," Prescott laughed. "Just out of curiosity, Fisher, what's the min altitude and max speed the AI is projecting that we could transit this low level route?"

"Well, sir, it says we could do it as low as fifteen meters above terrain, but that would be a very rough ride with several 9 G plus excursions. At that altitude, it says our speed would be as high as three kilometers per second. That's nearly nine times the speed of sound. We would most definitely be throwing up some 'rooster tails' behind us, and our shockwaves might even induce seismic activity in the area. At that speed, we could complete the ninety-kilometer route in just over thirty seconds. It would be pretty sporty, sir. I can't recommend trying it, but we'd make quite an entrance if we did."

"It's good to know we have some options in a pinch, but I think we'll stick with the planned route and speed for today. What's our transit time again?"

"Should be about nine minutes, sir. We'll be traveling at a leisurely one hundred seventy meters per second, which is about half the speed of sound. That should make sure we don't hurt anyone on the ground or damage any property. Our route mostly follows the old Nevada Test Site road network and sticks to the valley floor between mountains. There is one stretch where we should get a great view of one of the old nuclear weapons test ranges."

"Captain, we have received final clearance for approach and landing from Yucca Mountain," Dubashi announced from the Communications console.

"Very well, Lieutenant. Before we go, I think we may have drawn a crowd over near the end of the main taxiway. Can you enlarge and pan that area?"

"Yes, sir." Lieutenant Dubashi quickly centered the main view screen on an area not too far from the point where Taxiway 32 met the edge of the dry lakebed about two kilometers away. As she zoomed the image, it was clear that several hundred people had gathered to get a look at the now famous ship in person.

"Quite a few of those folks played a role in this ship's construction, but I'm sure most have never seen her fully assembled." Prescott paused, wondering if there was anything he could do to safely improve the crowd's view of the ship. "Commander Logan, bridge."

"Logan here, Captain. Are you considering an airshow, sir?" the chief engineer teased. Clearly, Logan was closely monitoring activities taking place on the bridge, in addition to everything he had on his plate down in Engineering.

"The thought had crossed my mind, but I'd like to avoid a court martial, if possible. In our current configuration, what's the closest we can safely approach personnel on the ground?"

"It's actually pretty safe at this altitude, Captain," Logan replied. As long as we hold this configuration and don't make any sudden control inputs, one hundred meters or so should be just fine."

"I don't think we'll get quite that close, but that's great, thank you. Everything okay down there so far?"

"All in the green down here, Captain," the naturally superstitious engineer cringed, wishing his commanding officer would avoid tempting fate by asking such unfortunate questions.

"Excellent. Bridge out." Prescott glanced at his helmsman. "Alright, Ensign Fisher, the runway we're sitting on that leads off to the southwest is Runway 21 and it ends about three hundred meters or so from that group of people. Give us a slow approach down to the end of the runway, hover for a few seconds, and then rotate three hundred and sixty degrees so they can see the entire ship. Once they've had a good look at us, take Taxiway 32 over there off to the northwest until it joins our route. We'll hold off letting Yucca Mountain know that we have entered the route until then. Clear?"

"No problem, Captain," Blake answered eagerly, clearly thrilled at the prospect of showing the ship off for an appreciative crowd.

Over the next few minutes, *Ingenuity* made her most "public" appearance to date, albeit to an unusually captive audience made up largely of military personnel and engineers with some of the highest security clearances issued by the U.S. government. It occurred to Prescott that this was probably the only crowd of this size anywhere in the world where he could openly approach a group of spectators without video of the event showing up on multiple news outlets within minutes. This was still Area 51, after all, and every single person in the assembled crowd had been thoroughly searched as they entered the facility for work this morning. Accordingly, not a single tablet computer or other recording device captured the impromptu show.

Once the massive yet eerily silent starship had finished its pirouette maneuver for the delighted, cheering crowd, Ensign Fisher proceeded towards the end of Runway 21, making a graceful, banking, right-hand turn onto Taxiway 32. *Ingenuity* was, in fact, the first large spacecraft capable of executing such turns, regardless of whether in space or operating inside the atmosphere. Coordinated, banking turns allowed for more efficient use of the ship's gravitic fields when counteracting turn-induced G forces. Perhaps more importantly, they were found to be more in keeping with what Human pilots expected. This was likely due to the fact that most pilots were still taught to fly inside the atmosphere before advancing to spacecraft. Not surprisingly, these pilots found that spacecraft designed to fly more like the aircraft in which they originally trained were much easier to master. This resulted in a significant performance improvement and an easier transition from aircraft to spacecraft. With the perfection of Cannae thrusters, fuel and propellant were no longer a limiting factor. It was simply a matter of programming the ship's AI to translate the helmsman's control inputs to apply the appropriate amount of thrust to the appropriate locations at the appropriate time. The dynamics of this process were immensely complex from an engineering perspective, but *Ingenuity's* AI handled the task with a negligible use of its computing resources, mimicking the look and feel of a fixed-wing aircraft operating within Earth's atmosphere. And, as most members of the normally jaded crowd of engineers would agree, it also made for one of the most impressive airshows ever performed.

"Captain, we are approaching the low level route," Ensign Fisher announced.

"You are clear to proceed. Lieutenant Dubashi, notify Fleet we are entering the route. ETA nine minutes."

"Aye Captain."

"Accelerating to route velocity," Fisher said as he banked the ship to the left for the ninety-degree-turn from Taxiway 32 onto the low level approach route leading away from Groom Lake. "Twenty-five seconds to first turn."

Even though Fisher was "manually" conning the ship from his position at the Helm console, a great deal of the process was still automated. His job was more about managing and monitoring the preprogrammed series of events that would ultimately result in the ship's arrival at

Yucca Mountain than it was about "flying" her in the traditional sense. In the event of an emergency, the Helm console did still include a joystick and throttle, but it was hard to imagine a real-world situation where these anachronistic controls could be successfully used. Just in case, however, Fisher had spent countless hours in the simulator practicing old fashioned "stick and throttle" control of the one-hundred-eighty-meter starship.

***

Just off Groom Lake Road, a U.S. Department of Energy maintenance employee leaned forward in the front seat of his pickup and peered at the sky to the east out his passenger side window. Dispatch had just issued a warning to all personnel in the area that *Ingenuity* would be overflying a portion of the Nevada Test Site road network to the west of Groom Lake within the next few minutes at high speed. Though he had seen more than his share of high speed aircraft flyovers, he still took such events seriously and knew that they were sometimes accompanied by deafening noise and potentially dangerous shockwaves. Dispatch had said that this would not be the case today, but he decided to get out of the vehicle and take cover behind the truck bed just in case. Hearing and seeing nothing, he glanced back to the south towards the maintenance shack he had just visited, then at his watch before looking back up into the sky just in time to see the enormous ship execute a banking right turn directly overhead before continuing due west along Groom Lake Road. He was amazed at the vessel's size, but what surprised him most was the fact that he could easily have missed the ship's passage entirely if he had not looked up when he did. In fact, had he not witnessed the flyover with his own eyes, he would have argued vehemently that no aircraft of any kind had passed overhead. Playing the event over in his mind, the only thing he remembered noticing was an indistinct swooshing sound, which he assumed was the air passing over the ship's sleek hull.

Chapter 8

TFS Ingenuity, TFC Yucca Mountain Shipyard Facility

"Captain, that was our last turn on the low level route. Final approach fix arrival in ninety seconds," Ensign Fisher announced from the Helm console. The nine-minute ride from Groom Lake had gone precisely as planned, but with the imminent arrival at the Yucca Mountain Shipyard, tension on the bridge had once again mounted.

"Nice job so far, Ensign. Hold position and await further instructions. Lieutenant Dubashi, notify Fleet that we are arriving at the final approach fix and request autolanding cues."

"Aye, Captain."

Nothing about the terrain surrounding the final approach fix looked anything like a shipyard facility. Precisely on schedule, the ship rapidly decelerated, transitioning into a hover two hundred meters above an area that looked more like the parking lot at a large shopping center than a facility capable of performing depot-level maintenance on *Ingenuity*-class starships. The area was otherwise barren, apparently deserted, and devoid of manmade structures other than the ever-present access roads crisscrossing the site.

"I'm a little afraid to ask what happens next," Reynolds muttered to herself.

"Perhaps young Ensign Fisher made a wrong turn somewhere," Prescott teased, working as usual to keep the atmosphere on the bridge focused, but relaxed.

"Captain, we have received final landing clearance and the AI has locked onto Yucca Mountain's autolanding signal," Dubashi reported.

"Understood, Lieutenant. Please render honors for Vice Admirals Patterson and White."

Although firing guns in salute was not possible for the unarmed frigate, not to mention impractical given the current, clandestine location, naval customs were still very much alive in Terran Fleet Command. As *Ingenuity* prepared to approach the shipyard, she transmitted an electronic equivalent of the fifteen-gun salute appropriate for vice admirals.

"Aye, sir. Transmitted. Also, Admiral Patterson is requesting a bridge vidcon."

Without prompting, every member of the bridge crew adjusted in their seats to avoid any appearance of slouching in front of the chief of naval operations.

"One second, Dubashi. Ensign Fisher, have you received execution authority for autolanding at the Helm console?"

"I have, Captain. Standing by to execute."

"Excellent. Fisher, I know I don't have to tell you to watch this approach *very* closely. If anything doesn't look right to you, discontinue immediately and hold position. Got it?"

"Got it, sir."

"Alright. Everyone look sharp for the CNO. Lieutenant Dubashi, put the admiral on-screen."

Admiral Patterson immediately appeared in the center of the bridge view screen. He stood behind a lectern adorned with Terran Fleet Command's official service seal and was flanked by Admiral White and several captains Prescott recognized. Even with the limited field of view provided by the vidcon, it was obvious that the officers were standing inside a facility that was truly massive.

"*Ingenuity* and crew, it is my distinct honor to welcome you to Yucca Mountain. We'll see you all on deck shortly. Captain Prescott, please proceed to Berth Nine when ready. Patterson out." With no further fanfare, the admiral's image disappeared from the screen, replaced once again by a view of the mountain ahead.

Prescott was more than a little surprised that TFC had apparently thrown together an arrival ceremony under the circumstances. "Well, I don't think any of us were expecting that," he said after pausing to collect his thoughts. "Looks like they have literally rolled out the red carpet for us, folks, so there are obviously lots of important people watching everything we do. With any luck, the AI will make us look good for the crowd, but stay sharp and be ready in case anything else unexpected happens."

"Captain," Lieutenant Dubashi said, "while the admiral was on-screen, I detected a gravitic field being generated on the mountainside directly ahead. Now it looks like there is some movement up there as well."

There was no need to zoom the image for a better view as a huge, square section of the mountain in front of the ship sank several meters below the surrounding surface.

"Whoa," Ensign Fisher exclaimed in spite of himself.

"I'm guessing that's where we're headed, Fisher," Prescott replied. "Engage AI for autolanding and stand by for manual override, if necessary."

"Aye, Captain," Blake replied, deploying the backup manual Helm controls at his console and struggling to stay on task in spite of the majestic scene playing out on the bridge view screen. "AI has the conn. Helm now answering autolanding cues from Yucca Mountain Shipyard."

"Thank you, Ensign. Acknowledged, AI has the conn."

On Yucca Mountain, the sunken area now began separating along its centerline, revealing that each side was a massive, two-hundred-meter-wide by four-hundred-meter-tall door. A mere thirty seconds later, each door had completely disappeared to either side of the opening. What remained was a gaping cavern entrance tall enough to accommodate the Empire State Building and with an area of nearly forty acres.

"Lieutenant Dubashi, can you tell us how much clearance we will have in that entryway?" Commander Reynolds asked.

"Yes, ma'am." Dubashi paused, checking the Sensor console, "The opening is four hundred meters square. Assuming the AI takes us up the center, we will have over one hundred fifty meters of clearance on each side, and one hundred eighty meters above and below."

As if on cue, the Helm console emitted a warning chime.

"Here we go, people. Stay sharp!" Prescott warned.

Before moving forward, the ship's altitude was increased to match the vertical center of the entrance cavern. The AI made no attempt at a graceful approach, opting instead for slow, more traditional movements in one plane at a time. Although this deliberate, controlled movement was more than fine with her crew, the effect reminded Prescott of sitting on a roller coaster that was slowly clunking its way up the big hill before the sudden drop. Sure, it was nice and slow for now, the problem was worrying about what would happen next.

"Helm, feel free to call out our progress on the way in. I think it might make us all feel a little more comfortable," Prescott suggested.

"Aye, sir. So far so good. We are centered vertically on the entrance. Now moving forward again. Gravitic fields adjusted to twenty percent mass," Ensign Fisher replied.

The increase in gravitic field strength meant that *Ingenuity's* thrusters were now only required to provide enough lift to counteract twenty percent of her one-hundred-eighty-thousand-ton mass. Once she reached her mooring, the field strength would be increased to reduce this percentage to near zero for a so-called "zero mass" touchdown. Once neutral buoyancy was achieved, the ship would remain suspended at the current altitude where it could then be lowered slowly onto either its own landing gear or dry-dock supports.

"Our berth is number nine. It should be just to the left of the entrance tunnel after we reach the shipyard itself," Lieutenant Lau announced from the Navigation console, feeling as if he needed to contribute something useful during the landing cycle.

"The approach plate includes a facility schematic," Commander Reynolds said. "There are a total of twenty berths; each is five hundred meters wide and at least eight hundred meters long. The largest ones look like they are well over a kilometer in length."

"I see. So I guess it's safe to assume they didn't build this facility just for a couple of *Ingenuity*-class starships then," Prescott remarked.

"Probably not, sir. I'd say this facility is designed for the production of capital ships."

With that, the ship proceeded into the entrance cavern. Less than a minute later, as soon as her stern was clear of the massive doors to the facility, the AI paused in the center of the cavern.

"Have we stopped moving, Ensign?" Prescott asked.

"Yes, sir, they stopped us just inside the doors. I'm guessing they plan to close them before they allow us to proceed."

"I was thinking the same thing. I'm sure they would like to keep those things closed as much as possible. It wouldn't be much of a secret underground shipyard with half the mountain open for everyone to see, now would it?"

As predicted, the entrance cavern doors began closing behind the ship. The doors were remarkable feats of Pelaran-enhanced engineering in their own right. Previously, the largest doors ever constructed on Earth had been the Vehicle Assembly Building doors built by NASA for the Apollo program in 1966. The VAB doors had been one hundred thirty-nine meters high and thirty meters wide, took over forty-five minutes to open, and were reinforced only enough to withstand hurricane-force winds. By contrast, the Yucca Mountain Shipyard's doors were nearly twenty times as large, all but invisible from the outside when closed, and designed to withstand all but the heaviest orbital bombardments, including a nuclear strike. They were so massive, in fact, that moving them at all would be next to impossible without the use of gravitic fields. Once their mass was largely nullified, however, simple electric motors performed the task with little difficulty.

On *Ingenuity's* bridge, the view screen grew progressively darker as the doors closed behind them.

"Would you like external lighting or low light optics, Captain?" Lieutenant Dubashi offered.

"Thank you, Dubashi, but let's hold off for just a bit. I'm guessing we won't need either one," Prescott replied, playing a hunch.

Outside, the two massive doors once again made contact in the center of the cavern before the entire assembly moved forward until flush with the face of the mountain. On the bridge view screen, the already dim lighting ahead faded to complete darkness for a few seconds before the cavern immediately surrounding the ship was flooded with artificial light.

"Every single thing I've seen since we arrived makes me feel very small and insignificant," Reynolds remarked. "I keep fighting the urge to say 'wow.'"

"I know what you mean, but I think you might want to save that sentiment for what's at the end of this tunnel," Prescott said.

Outside the ship, the entrance cavern itself wasn't particularly remarkable other than for its sheer size. The plasma-jet tunneling devices now used for constructing underground facilities resulted in a smooth, shiny texture on the walls reminiscent of polished marble. Only the lights in the immediate vicinity of the ship were illuminated. The darkness immediately ahead and behind the ship contributed to a feeling of isolation and enhanced the impression of the facility's colossal scale. Other than lighting panels, the only equipment visible within the lit section of the two-kilometer-long tunnel was a network of rails supporting huge overhead gantry cranes.

"Sir, while we have been stationary, the AI has adjusted the gravitic fields to ten percent mass," Ensign Fisher reported.

Before Fisher could finish his sentence, the ship once again eased forward, continuing its slow, deliberate journey into the heart of Yucca Mountain. After a few minutes, a large series of windows came into view, most likely housing some sort of control room. At the moment, the windows were lined with excited spectators, several of whom couldn't resist waving as the ship passed by.

"Do you think it's odd that we can't see the end of this tunnel yet? If the approach diagram is correct, we should be entering the shipyard facility proper anytime," Reynolds asked.

The entrance cavern itself was perfectly straight, although it did have a downward slope. In spite of this, there was still no visible lighting beyond a point immediately ahead of the ship that presumably marked the transition to the shipyard facility itself. On the view screen, it looked as if the well-lit tunnel ended in a gaping maw of utter darkness.

"Unless I'm reading this wrong, I think the admiral may be putting on a little bit of a show for us," Prescott said, manually selecting the ship-wide intercom on his touchscreen. "All hands, this is the captain. We are about to enter the main cavern of the Yucca Mountain Shipyard. If you can safely take a look at a view screen as we enter, I don't think you will be disappointed."

With that, *Ingenuity* slowly departed the last well-lit section of the entrance cavern, slipping silently into the darkness beyond. Behind the ship, all remaining lights were extinguished.

"Sir, we have stopped in the 'roundhouse' area just inside the entrance cavern. Gravitic fields have reached zero mass. They have also increased our altitude to within fifty meters of the ceiling. We are now holding position," Ensign Fisher reported.

The bridge view screen was designed to provide a panoramic, one-hundred-and-eighty-degree view of the space around the ship, including the view above and even immediately below the bow. Perhaps due to Admiral Patterson's flair for the dramatic, the AI had positioned the ship within the cavernous open area at the center of the shipyard. The area was called the "roundhouse" with good reason. It provided ample room for a ship of more than a kilometer in length to turn in place, positioning itself to enter one of the largest berths or to exit the facility. It also provided an unobstructed view from one end of the ten-kilometer-long facility to the other.

In the distance, five kilometers to either side of the ship, lights appeared over what were presumably the two farthest berths from the entrance cavern. After a brief pause, the next two sets of lights were illuminated. It was impossible to see much detail at this distance, but it was clear that all eight berths contained *Ingenuity*-class frigates.

On the bridge, all five crewmembers turned to look at their captain, clearly taken aback by what they were seeing. Prescott simply nodded at the screen. "Keep watching and keep working, people, we're not on the ground yet," he said quietly.

A few seconds later, the next six berths were illuminated, revealing sleek, predatory hulls at least three times *Ingenuity's* size. Although their weapon types were unclear at this distance, there was no mistaking the fact that these too were ships of war, and of a far more powerful class if size was any indication.

After a final dramatic pause, the remaining six berths were illuminated. This included Berth Nine, which happened to be the only empty mooring in the shipyard at the moment. Four of the remaining five docks contained a third type of ship that Prescott immediately classified in his mind as heavy cruisers. Their nearly one-kilometer length bristled with massive beam emitters, which appeared to make up the bulk of their armament. Perhaps the most impressive features, however, were the enormous, fully articulated railgun turrets mounted fore and aft on both their dorsal and ventral surfaces. Each of these guns from hull mount to the tips of their barrels were nearly half of *Ingenuity's* length.

Finally, inside one of the two largest berths immediately to the right of the entrance cavern was a ship whose function was not quite as obvious at first glance. The vessel was clearly moored at this location out of necessity, her immense size rendering her unlikely to negotiate the turns required for most of the other berths. The ship's hull was longer than the heavy cruisers, but decidedly more rectangular in appearance, perhaps in an effort to maximize internal volume. The vessel also had fewer obvious weapon mounts, but still sported an impressive array of what appeared to be point-defense railguns and beam emitters. This final observation led Prescott to notice that the entire aft end of the ship housed a massive hangar bay. The configuration was similar to that of *Ingenuity's* aft spaces, but this ship's flight deck was large enough to land at least two, perhaps three ships her size inside. In addition to the hangar bay, the top of the ship featured eight massive elevators along with ramp areas designed for spacecraft launch and recovery operations. In one of the open areas forward of the elevators, ninety-six *Hunter* Remotely Piloted Spacecraft sat with their wings folded for storage. Based on the layout, it looked as if the rear flight deck could remain pressurized or could be opened to space during flight operations.

"Is that thing a carrier?" Lieutenant Lau asked rhetorically.

"What was your first clue?" Dubashi responded, unable to resist a flippant reply to such an inane question from her longtime friend in spite of their being on the bridge.

"Don't make me separate you two," Prescott chided. "I think the show is over for now. Let's get our heads back in the game."

"Gravitic fields holding at zero mass, Captain," Fisher reported as *Ingenuity* began slowly turning in place to port in the direction of her berth. "Looks like we're going to continue the landing sequence now. Still just one plane of motion at a time."

"Yeah, I actually appreciate the careful approach, even if it does take a while," Prescott replied.

With the turn concluded, the ship reduced its altitude back to the vertical center of the cavern before proceeding forward until perfectly centered on Berth Nine.

"Turning back to starboard now, sir. We are aligned for entry. Running prelanding checks now," Fisher continued, dutifully reporting the ship's progress through the landing sequence.

Two hundred meters down the quay, Admirals Patterson, White, and the other assembled dignitaries watched as *Ingenuity* thrusted slowly forward and prepared for her first surface landing. Once the ship reached the predefined point inside her berth for landing, the AI paused momentarily, allowing her Human handlers time to manually run through their final landing checklists.

"Sir, I've still got six red indicators on the landing struts," Fisher reported with slightly more volume and urgency than his previous updates. "I'm sure that's what will happen next, but pausing here with our gear still in the wells makes me a little nervous."

"Steady, Fisher. I'm sure it's fine, just be ready in case …"

With that, the ship began slowly descending towards the movable concrete platform, now less than twenty meters away from the lowest point on the ventral hull.

Outside, the group of officers gathered for *Ingenuity's* arrival ceremony watched in shock as the frigate descended until it dropped completely below their field of view inside its berth.

Ensign Fisher reacted instantaneously, selecting the emergency manual override option displayed prominently near the top center of the Helm console. Just as he had practiced countless times in the simulator, his left hand went directly for the throttle and his right to the control joystick. Instinctively, he advanced the throttle control, which acted to increase lift and arrest the ship's descent when configured for hovering flight. It took less than a second for him to realize that his control inputs were having no effect as *Ingenuity* continued her steady descent. "Helm emergency override, all stop!" he yelled without further hesitation.

"Helm emergency override acknowledged," announced the AI's maddeningly calm female voice. "All stop confirmed. Gravitic fields configured for zero mass, neutral buoyancy. The ship is rigged for dry-dock, structurally supported landing. Altitude above dry-dock landing supports, seven meters."

"Captain, there are no structural supports installed for this landing," Fisher growled, his massive adrenaline rush transforming fear and surprise to anger and frustration at the near-catastrophic hull landing.

"I can see that," Prescott replied calmly, nodding toward the left section of the bridge view screen. A large window currently displayed the entire ventral surface of the ship, now perilously close to the concrete below.

"AI, Prescott. The landing support indication is erroneous. Increase altitude twenty-five meters and deploy landing gear struts."

Before responding, *Ingenuity's* AI conducted what it considered to be a lengthy conversation with Yucca Mountain's core control system. Overcoming some initial reluctance on the part of the local system to admit even the possibility of such a grave oversight, the ship's AI was granted a comprehensive landing readiness review check of Berth Nine. The primary sensors located beneath the movable concrete platform still stubbornly insisted that hull supports had been installed for the ship's landing. After interrogating a variety of secondary sensors, however, the Yucca Mountain system confirmed *Ingenuity's* assertion that there were no hull supports installed inside her berth. With a tinge of what might have passed for ironic sarcasm, the system recommended that the frigate lower its landing gear before resuming its landing sequence.

The entire confirmation process took place so quickly that the ship's AI was able to respond to Captain Prescott's commands in real-time. "AI acknowledged. Erroneous landing support indication confirmed and isolated. Increasing altitude two five meters and deploying landing gear struts."

Outside, the crowd stared in stunned silence as *Ingenuity* once again rose slowly above the landing platform and lowered her landing gear. Admiral Patterson furrowed his brow and directed a withering glance at the facility commander. Clearly, a screw-up of epic proportions had just occurred right before their eyes.

"Oh my God, that almost sucked," Dubashi muttered under her breath in the thick Indian accent that tended to surface when she was under stress.

Ensign Fisher, now even more suspicious than usual of the AI's competence, continued to closely monitor every system involved with the landing sequence. "Landing struts deployed. Altitude now two seven meters," he reported calmly. *Ingenuity's* altitude was always reported as the distance from the lowest section of the ship's hull to the surface. Once the landing struts were down, this distance immediately decreased by five meters. "Showing six green landing strut indications. The gear is down and locked. We are rigged for surface landing."

"AI, Prescott. Confirm landing sequence status."

"AI acknowledged. Gravitic fields configured for zero mass, neutral buoyancy. The ship is rigged for surface landing. Altitude above dry-dock landing surface, two seven meters."

"Ensign Blake, you may complete the landing."

"With pleasure, sir."

Seconds later, *Ingenuity's* gravitic fields were slightly reduced to allow her six massive landing skids to simultaneously come into contact with the concrete landing platform. In spite of the chief engineer's reservations, the gear functioned exactly as designed. Over the next few minutes, Fisher gradually allowed the struts to bear the ship's full weight, compressing the six massive shocks as she settled into place.

Prescott breathed a sigh of relief and commanded himself to relax. "XO, secure from General Quarters."

"Aye, Captain," Reynolds responded, also visibly relieved.

"Commander Logan, bridge."

"Logan here. Go ahead, Captain."

"Full stop, Commander. Power down and prep for maintenance crews. Great job down there."

"Full stop, aye. Thanks, Captain, I'll pass that along."

Prescott stood, walked over to the Helm console, and extended his hand to Ensign Fisher. "Nicely done, Blake. You managed to take a potentially very dangerous situation and make it look like it was no big deal. I'm really not sure how much damage a gear-up landing would have done to the hull at zero mass, but it's just generally not something we ever want to attempt without structural supports. Besides, I'm guessing it would have really pissed off the admirals over there."

Fisher stood and shook his captain's hand gratefully. "Thank you, sir. I'm just really glad that's over. I'm pretty sure somebody out there owes me a beer."

Chapter 9

TFC Yucca Mountain Shipyard Facility
(2 weeks later)

Captain Hiroto Oshiro stood ramrod-straight, sweating profusely in his dress uniform as he faced a room full of senior officers including his immediate supervisor, Vice Admiral Kevin Patterson, Chief of Naval Operations. "So, in summary, the movable platform sensors under *Ingenuity's* berth were still calibrated for a *Navajo*-class cruiser in dry-dock configuration. TFS *Shoshone* had been staged out of Berth Nine just two days prior to *Ingenuity's* arrival when the last of her construction was completed. At that time, the cruiser was moved over to Berth Twelve so that the structural supports could be removed from Berth Nine. Once *Shoshone* was out of the way, Berth Nine was immediately prepped for *Ingenuity's* arrival."

"Clearly not prepped enough, though, was it, Captain?" Admiral Patterson growled.

"No, Admiral, it was not, and that responsibility is mine and mine alone. The sensors were the primary source of landing configuration data for the facility's AI during the autolanding sequence and were the root cause of the near gear-up landing. The fix was a simple procedural change, so I can assure all of you that it won't happen again. I want to formally apologize once again to Captain Prescott and his crew. They did a fantastic job recovering from what could have easily been a disaster."

"I agree with you completely, Captain Oshiro," Patterson replied, peering over his glasses at his hapless facility commander. "I agree that Captain Prescott and crew did a fantastic job, and I agree that this failure and near disaster was your responsibility." The old admiral paused, allowing the gravity of the situation to weigh heavily on every officer in the crowded conference room.

"The truth is, however, that this could have happened to any one of us. Don't get me wrong, I'm not excusing any sort of carelessness or minimizing the importance of avoiding this kind of oversight. That's why we *have* procedures in the first place. Procedures alone, however, won't save us from making stupid mistakes on occasion. This time, it was our friend, Hiroto, who was unfortunate enough to be in charge at the time, but there's not a single one of us here who can honestly say that this would never happen on our watch. This work that we are doing is unbelievably complex, not to mention inherently dangerous."

There were nods all around the table. Sensing Admiral Patterson's change in tone, Tonya White glanced up and smiled discreetly at Oshiro, who had been under the most intense, stressful scrutiny imaginable for the past two weeks.

"Captain Oshiro," Patterson continued, his voice reminiscent of a judge pronouncing sentence on the damned," to make amends for this incident, you are to work with the folks over at Fleet Training to fully document what happened and prepare a case study for their curriculum. If there has ever been a situation that shows how a seemingly minor oversight can lead to a disaster, this is it."

"Understood, Admiral. Thank you."

"Good. You should also understand that had it not been for the quick thinking of Ensign Fisher at the helm of *Ingenuity*, there would have been very little any of us could have done to save your biscuits. I strongly suggest you buy that young man the drinks of his choice for the foreseeable future."

"I agree wholeheartedly, sir. I've already opened a tab for him at the Club."

"Glad to hear it. Tom, I want to the see the paperwork for a Distinguished Flying Cross and anything else you think appropriate for Blake Fisher on my desk before you leave."

"Will do, Admiral," Prescott replied.

Patterson again looked down at his tablet before continuing. "One more thing I need to make sure we all understand is why Ensign Fisher was unable to manually take control of *Ingenuity* using the backup controls at the Helm console."

Figuring there was no need for anyone else to step into the hot seat, Captain Oshiro spoke up once again. "I'll take that one as well, Admiral. The AI specialists at Fleet Engineering have told us that the system responded as designed. When control of the ship is relinquished to the facility AI for autolanding, it operates like a separate entity from the ship's AI. The way they explained this is that the autolanding sequence is a collaborative effort between the ship's AI and the local core control system – in this case the facility AI here at Yucca Mountain. When Ensign Fisher selected the manual override option at his console, the ship's AI simply assumed he was requesting that it continue the landing without outside assistance. Only when he verbalized the 'emergency override, all stop' command did the ship understand that he wanted to completely terminate the approach. Clearly, this is not an optimal design and needs to be changed. Fleet Science and Engineering is reviewing the code and promises to have an update available before *Ingenuity* departs again."

"Since you answered my question, Hiroto, I'm going to let you own this problem for me as well. My fundamental concern is that there must always be absolute clarity regarding who, or what, is in control of the ship at any given time. Furthermore, a manual override should be a manual override. I don't give a good goddamn about layers of AI control. If an authorized Human has a reason to take control, I expect them to be able to do so, immediately and unambiguously. Now, having the AI back them up and avoid doing something stupid is fine. For example, if young Ensign Fisher had pulled the throttle back to idle or tried to blast out through the top of the cavern, I would want the AI to intelligently prevent him from doing so. Otherwise, Humans are to remain the ultimate control authority. Make sense?"

"Yes Admiral. I'll see to it, sir."

"Very good, thank you, Captain Oshiro. Now, on to other business. Captain Prescott, I trust *Ingenuity's* refit is progressing to your satisfaction?"

"Admiral, I've never seen anything like it. Within an hour after our arrival, we had a small army of engineers and techs working on practically every system onboard. Also, our entire crew has been briefed now up to code word PARTHIAN, and we've been running training simulations with the new bridge configuration since yesterday afternoon."

"Just to make sure everyone is up to speed on what Captain Prescott is referring to, every ship in the fleet has had their bridge reconfigured based on lessons learned during *Ingenuity's* shakedown cruise. Obviously, the addition of weapon systems on *Ingenuity* also required some modifications. The biggest single change is the elimination of the Navigation console. We found that most of those functions were being handled by the communications officer anyway, so the Communications console now also officially handles navigation. The old Navigation console is now referred to as 'Tactical.' It handles sensors as well as all of the ship's weapon systems. Frankly, I'm concerned that we may have given the officer at that station too much to do. We have already divided the workload across two Tactical consoles onboard our new destroyers and heavy cruisers. They will likely get pretty busy during combat operations, so we may end up tweaking this configuration again. In any event, we have typically placed our most senior bridge officer at that station, with the exception of the captain and XO, of course. Given the heavy load, I think we should continue to do so. Don't you have Admiral Lau's son from your first watch at that station, Tom?"

"Yes, sir, I do. Lieutenant Commander Schmidt is actually senior, but I believe Lieutenant Lau is best suited for the job. He's a solid young officer and he's thrilled with his new duties at Tactical. We've actually been having to force him out of the sim for some rack time. I think he might have been feeling a little left out at the Navigation console before the configuration change."

"Well, you know what they say, be careful what you wish for. I think he will have more than enough to keep him busy at Tactical. Moving on, the Helm console is largely unchanged, other than picking up some of the slack from losing the Nav. Finally, the Science and Engineering console still handles the same functions as before, but is now better equipped to assist Tactical during an engagement. On the subject of Tactical, is your weapons loadout complete?"

"We're getting close, Admiral. I just spoke with Commander Logan, and he expects we will be ready to get underway within forty-eight hours."

"As soon as you are ready to go, I want you to run your ship through the range course for some live fire exercises. In the meantime, I want you to ensure that all bridge officers are getting sim time, and that includes the two of you as well," Patterson said. "We're going to be asking quite a bit of you. Not only did we make significant changes to how your bridge operates, but we have also transformed your ship from a purely scientific vessel into a more traditional warship."

Commander Reynolds looked up from her note-taking, "I'm sorry, Admiral, but did you just say 'range?'"

"I did, indeed. I think I can promise you an experience like none you've ever had before. I want *Ingenuity* fully mission-capable by the end of the week. I already have a special assignment waiting for you. As the old saying goes, there's not a moment to be lost."

Wek Flagship Gresav, Near Luyten's Star
(12.1 light years from Earth)

Admiral Naftur's eyes narrowed as the Pelaran Guardian spacecraft emerged from hyperspace at the exact time and location projected by *Gresav's* AI. The Pelarans were nothing if not punctual, and given enough time and computing power to analyze their habits, they were predictable as well. The odd manner in which the Pelarans shared data with their chosen, cultivated civilizations required their spacecraft to broadcast from a different location each day. Initially, these locations appeared to be chosen completely at random. Recently, however, advances in hyperspace travel had placed the Sajeth Collective in contact with neighboring regions of the galaxy whose inhabitants had been observing the Pelarans' habits over long periods of time. Once all of the data was combined, patterns had finally started to emerge.

For all of their vaunted technological superiority, the Guardian spacecraft were still machines after all. Machines that could be outwitted and ultimately destroyed. Ironically, the Pelarans' self-imposed requirement to have their signals appear from random locations in the sky seemed wholly unnecessary to the Wek scientists, who had been studying their patterns for years. It was thought that the Pelarans were trying to avoid any chance that the cultivated species would determine the signal's true origin while also minimizing the potential for other civilizations to eavesdrop on their data streams. The reason for the behavior meant little to the old admiral, however. All that mattered was the fact that he now had a second potential vulnerability in hand. Now, it was just a matter of developing the tactics required to exploit them.

Earth, Terran Fleet Command Headquarters

Admiral Sexton stood and stepped from behind his desk as Nenir Turlaka entered his office with her usual pair of Marine guards in tow.

"Good morning, Madame Ambassador!" he greeted, offering his hand. "It's good to have you back with us so soon. I was afraid the Leadership Council would have you tied up in meetings for the next six months."

Sexton showed Nenir to a sitting area on one side of his office, dismissing her Marine guards to the hallway with a nod.

"I think there are those who would like to do just that," she replied. "Do leaders on your world always spend so much time meeting to argue over minor details before any decisions are made?"

"In many cases, yes," Sexton said, smiling sympathetically. "That is particularly true for multinational groups like the Leadership Council. There has never been any sort of 'planetary government' here on Earth. Over the centuries, a few powerful nation states have had designs on world domination, but the balance of power has generally been maintained among a number of individual countries. Unfortunately, restoring that delicate balance has sometimes required prolonged periods of global warfare." He paused, measuring her level of interest in Earth's history. Seeing what looked to him like enthusiastic attention, he continued. "There is more multinational cooperation now than at any time in our history, but there will probably always be some level of distrust. When I find myself in the middle of difficult meetings involving several nations, I just try to keep in mind that everyone is doing their best to look after their peoples' best interests. I certainly understand how frustrating it can be, though."

Nenir furrowed her heavy brows and produced a guttural sound from her chest that Sexton took to be an expression of disapproval mixed with resignation. The Wek seemed to rely on nonverbal communication even more so than Humans. Even during his limited time observing Nenir, it had become clear that the Wek had a sound for every emotion. It would definitely take some getting used to, particularly during diplomatic negotiations.

"As a professional military officer accustomed to chain of command," she continued, "I believe you would appreciate the authority structure in place on my world. There is still a very traditional combination of factors that determine position and rank. We work very hard to select the best possible candidates for leadership roles. Once they are chosen, however, there is very little discussion involved in decision-making."

Sexton filed that bit of information away as potentially significant. The Wek were clearly a proud, powerful race, but he wondered about the effectiveness of such an advanced civilization still clinging to a hierarchical, authoritarian culture. While it did admittedly offer some advantages over a more democratic approach to leadership, there were also some serious shortcomings. Senior military officers on Earth whose subordinates were afraid to even provide input, let alone respectfully question their orders, often performed poorly compared to those who fostered an environment of trust and loyal cooperation. Sexton made a mental note to have a discussion on this topic with his intelligence chief, Tonya White.

"There is no doubt that a clear chain of command is critical, and 'leadership by committee' rarely produces the best results," Sexton agreed.

Nenir paused as the translation AI replayed the admiral's final comment, then stared at him thoughtfully for a moment. Sexton immediately wondered how much of what crossed his mind was readily apparent to her. Could her species have more keenly honed perceptive abilities? Another question for Tonya's team to ponder.

"After three full days of meetings, the Leadership Council did at least agree to allow me to return here to work with you and your staff," she said. "I don't think they know exactly what to do with me at this point, but I was able to convince them that sharing what I know about the Pelarans is my highest immediate priority. I also believe I can provide some value working with Fleet Medical."

"That certainly sounds like a reasonable approach to me. Your Admiral Naftur provided a wealth of data that our people are only just beginning to analyze. Is there something specific you would like to highlight immediately, or would you prefer to work directly with the Science and Engineering Directorate to help them better organize their efforts?"

Nenir hesitated, looking as if she was debating whether the timing was right to continue their discussion. "There is one thing I would like to, as you say, 'highlight,'" she said cautiously.

Her change in mood was readily apparent. She clearly had something to say that made her uncomfortable, and her body language was unmistakable. *Jeez, these guys would be terrible poker players*, Sexton thought.

"I need you to understand that I mean no disrespect and wish to convey no threat whatsoever," she began.

"All of my dealings with the Wek people thus far lead me to believe that you are an honorable, peaceful race who fight only when required to protect yourselves. We are friends, Nenir. Friends are open and honest with each other, even when the conversation isn't particularly pleasant. What's on your mind?"

Nenir took a moment to gather her wits and seemed to relax a little. "Thank you, Admiral. Yes, we are indeed friends and it is my primary mission to ensure that we remain so. You are correct that we generally are a peaceful people, but we have also never hesitated to fight when threatened. I have spoken to you at length about our alliance, the Sajeth Collective, and the fact that we have encountered other species chosen by the Pelarans for what they refer to as 'cultivation.' In reality, this 'cultivation' is nothing more than a form of enslavement – entire worlds allowing themselves to be subjugated to the will of the Pelarans, all in the name of technological advancement. Unfortunately, in every recorded case thus far, species selected by the Pelarans ultimately undergo a sort of cultural transformation. Precisely how this happens is still unclear to us, but the change is obviously orchestrated by the Pelarans for their own self-interests, not the interests of the cultivated species."

Sexton had no idea where this conversation was heading, but he was beginning to understand the reason for Nenir's nervousness. "What sort of transformation are you referring to?" he asked.

Nenir ignored his question for the moment, choosing instead to stick with her own narrative. "I was instructed to find a single Human representative whom I felt was not only trustworthy, but also in a position to act on the information I can provide. I believe you are that person, Admiral Sexton."

"Madame Ambassador, I am deeply honored by your trust, but you must understand that I am no diplomat," he protested. "Are you sure there isn't a member of our Leadership Council who is better suited to receive your information?"

"I do not," she replied tersely. "The choice is entirely mine, and I have made my selection. Do you wish to decline the information?"

"Of course not. Please do not take offense at my hesitation, it's just that communications such as this are generally handled by diplomatic representatives here on Earth. If you prefer to communicate with me, however, I will do my very best to see that your information is handled appropriately."

"I understand that such is your custom, but I believe you to be a man of both honor and action. It is these qualities that will ultimately allow our worlds to act as partners and allies."

For a moment, Nenir's piercing, catlike eyes transfixed the admiral. He couldn't help but feel a little like a small prey animal about to become the late-morning snack of a powerful predator. She stared at him for some time, appearing to be searching for something specific, before her expression softened once again, this time into an unmistakable look of pity.

"The cultural change that cultivated species undergo under the influence of the Pelarans invariably leads to violence. They are manipulated into serving as unwitting pawns in a grand strategy spanning thousands of light years, perhaps more. The reality is that we don't really know the full scope of the Pelarans' influence. We also have no idea what they ultimately hope to accomplish over time. What we do know is that all of this is part of a very long term strategy leading to domination on a galactic scale. As you know from your own history, there are many forms of domination: military, cultural, technological, etc. For now, the Pelarans seem content with domination by proxy. What I need you to understand, my friend, is that Terra is in the process of becoming the newest proxy of the Pelaran Alliance in this region of the galaxy. We, and by that I mean your civilization and mine, cannot allow that to happen."

Now it was the admiral's turn to stare. He had been suspecting something like this from Nenir since their first conversation, but wasn't sure how she would approach such a potentially volatile topic. After a few seconds, he stood and walked over to the large windows lining one side of his office. Outside, a beautiful spring morning was underway and the well-manicured grounds of TFC Headquarters were resplendent with pastel blooms. His attention was briefly drawn skyward as a flight of four F-373 *Reaper* aerospace superiority fighters streaked silently overhead – impossibly advanced machines of war, made possible by Pelaran-derived technology.

His earlier protestations aside, Sexton was a skilled negotiator who could hold his own in a debate with any politician. The subject of what would and would not be shared when (not if) representatives from extra-terrestrial civilizations came calling had been discussed in Earth's highest political circles for hundreds of years. Most recently, TFC's Leadership Council had provided a set of general guidelines. The problem with such guidelines is that they never seemed applicable to the real-world situation. After taking a few moments to think things through, Sexton decided that this was one of those cases where he needed to say as little as possible. He also needed Nenir to provide all of the information she had been authorized to release, while offering very little in return for the time being.

He turned back to Nenir and smiled warmly. "Would you be disappointed in me if I told you that I have absolutely no idea how to respond?"

Nenir laughed. "I don't doubt it, Admiral, any more than I had any idea how to discuss this subject with you. Lucky for us, our immediate reaction is of little importance. The only thing that matters is how our worlds ultimately handle the situation. We do have a more pressing problem, however."

Sexton looked over his glasses at her, incredulous. "More pressing? How is that possible?"

"As I have said, we have seen the result of the cultivation program before. It always ends the same way: the cultivated species ends up in a protracted war with virtually every other species within what the Pelarans call the 'cultivation radius.' We believe this to be roughly five hundred light years, a vast volume of space to be sure. Within that sphere, other civilizations invariably end up banding together to resist the Pelarans' influence, but they are rarely successful. The cultivated species is always supplied with just enough technology and intelligence information to ensure their dominance of the region."

"Not to be indelicate, but since you know all of this, why not just destroy us outright rather than attempting to forge a relationship?"

Nenir emitted the faint growling sound that Sexton knew signified satisfaction. He wondered how the exobiologists would go about explaining the obvious similarity to purring mammals on Earth.

"That is precisely the right question, and the main reason Admiral Naftur took such a risk to place me here with you. From a military standpoint, the Guardian spacecraft stationed near the Sol system by the Pelarans has rendered such an attack futile, to say the least. The ship is managed by an incredibly sophisticated AI and possesses weapons technology that far exceeds that of any other civilization in this part of the galaxy. The admiral has been studying the ship's tactics for years, however, and, with the help of our allies, I believe he is on the verge of developing a strategy to defeat it. That is our hope at least. Otherwise, the destruction of the Wek squadron you witnessed may have been in vain."

Sexton made no comment regarding the Guardian spacecraft, deciding to focus instead on the potential new threat posed by Earth's nascent allies, the Sajeth Collective.

"So I trust that you are not here to tell me that we should expect an attack from the Sajeth Collective once Admiral Naftur finds a way to defeat this Guardian ship, am I right?"

"There are those in high ranking leadership positions within the Collective who advocate precisely that approach. They argue that the only effective means of controlling a cultivated species is destroying it before it reaches a state of military superiority to its neighbors. That assertion puts Terra in a tenuous position at the moment, Admiral Sexton. The deployment of Earth's first starship seems to be a success thus far. That implies that you are on the threshold of becoming a significant threat, but have not yet reached a point where you could repel an attack yourselves."

Sexton was a bit taken aback by Nenir's candor on such a far-reaching topic as interstellar warfare. Unsure at this stage whether the Sajeth Collective would end up being Earth's greatest ally or worst enemy, he opted for the time-honored tactic of saying nothing, hopefully compelling Nenir to feel an obligation to fill the uncomfortable pause in conversation.

After what seemed like a long period of silence, the admiral's tactic worked. "At the moment," Nenir continued, "Admiral Naftur's opinion still holds a great deal of influence within the Collective. To a large degree, he speaks for the Wek on matters of military significance, and it is the Wek who provide the majority of the Collective's military assets. His long-standing position, which is shared by four of the seven members at the moment, is that Terra provides an unprecedented opportunity to observe and intervene in the cultivation process before any hostilities begin. He believes that a moral species, such as yourselves," Nenir smiled and actually winked at Admiral Sexton, "would naturally recognize the mutual benefit of working with their neighbors to avoid violence."

"And subjugation by the Pelarans," Sexton added, following the longstanding tradition of diplomats everywhere of being agreeable, while committing to nothing.

"Just so," she replied. "It's almost as if the Pelarans see violence on a galactic scale as a sport. We even know of one instance where two civilizations who are both under the influence of the Pelarans are now fighting each other on the frontiers of their respective spheres of influence. At the very least, the Pelarans promote wholesale violence among other races for their own benefit. That is not the behavior of an honorable civilization, Admiral."

"I can't disagree with you there, but how might we go about 'intervening' in the cultivation process without ending the flow of valuable information?"

"If we can come to an agreement on how we might share information and work together, Admiral Sexton, I believe Admiral Naftur already has some ideas along those lines."

Chapter 10

TFS Ingenuity, TFC Live Fire Training Range
(3 days later – 2 light years from Earth)

"Welcome, *Ingenuity*, to the Terran Fleet Command Live Fire Training Range," the range AI hailed as Ensign Fisher eased the ship into the designated starting location. "The first exercise will begin in zero five minutes; please prepare your vessel for combat operations."

"Alright, listen up, everyone," Prescott announced. "I don't have any more of a clue what to expect than you do, but the general idea is to 'train like we fight,' so let's try to make this exercise as realistic as possible. XO, set General Quarters for combat ops. Lieutenant Dubashi, reply to the range AI that we are prepared to enter the range."

The lighting on the bridge was dimmed slightly and accented with a red hue to provide a visual indication of impending combat operations. Throughout the ship, crew members hurried to their action stations as the AI's synthetic voice repeated the order for General Quarters. In a significant improvement over recent simulations, all departments reported their readiness in fifty-four seconds.

"Both reactors available and operating at one hundred percent. All weapons charged. We are at General Quarters for combat ops, Captain," Commander Reynolds reported.

"Very good, Commander, much better than yesterday, but let's see if we can get that time down to forty-five seconds or less," Prescott said.

"Aye, sir, will do," she replied. "Have you heard anything else about what types of targets they have set up? I'm having a hard time envisioning how this is supposed to work."

"Only a little. Fleet has been pretty tightlipped about it. I can only assume that means it will become part of officer performance evals. Patterson said it has only been operational for a couple of weeks."

"A couple of weeks, huh?" she groused. "I guess that means there were other ships out here at the range before we were even finished with our shakedown cruise. It's kind of a letdown to know we weren't the only ones out here blazing a trail to the stars."

"I know what you mean," he laughed. "We were still first out of the gate, but we were clearly Fleet's cover story rather than the one and only vessel in our inventory. At this point, I think you'll agree that having more than one operational warship is a very good thing. Besides, I think we can still safely think of ourselves as trail blazers. They have been applying everything they learn from us to all the other ships that are nearing completion. Besides, to my knowledge, the only other operational ships at the moment are two frigates. Two *Ingenuity*-class frigates."

Patterson looked up and raised his voice in order to address his entire bridge crew once again. "What I *can* tell you is that we will see a combination of what they are calling 'animate' and 'inanimate' targets. The inanimate ones will most likely be asteroids of varying composition. Our weapons can be employed at full power on those targets. The 'animate' targets will be drones programmed to perform certain maneuvers and even return fire. Lieutenant Lau, the ship's AI will coordinate with the range controller to ensure we avoid destroying anything we shouldn't, so you can manage the tactical environment just as you would during combat."

"Aye, sir, let's do this!" Lau replied enthusiastically, obviously excited at the prospect of obliterating his first set of actual targets and proving himself in his new role at Tactical.

"One minute, Captain," Lieutenant Dubashi reported from the Communications console.

"Thank you, Dubashi. Now, I know you're all excited, but I want each of you to work on relaxing and keeping a cool head. In combat, your ability to focus under stress may save all of our lives. Everyone ready?"

A chorus of "aye, sirs" filled the bridge seconds before the range AI began issuing instructions for beginning the exercise.

"TFS *Ingenuity*, you are clear to enter the range. Waypoints for each portion of the exercise have been uploaded to the Helm console and will be indicated on the bridge view screen. Please proceed to the first waypoint."

Prescott couldn't help noticing that the range controller AI's synthetic voice was also that of a female and, while different from that of his ship, still had a sultry, vaguely sexual quality to it. Once again, he made a mental note to ask one of the techs at Fleet why that was the case.

"Ensign Fisher, while we are on the range, you don't have to wait for my instructions to move the ship wherever the controller wants us to go," Prescott instructed. During normal operations, helm officers did not have the authority to issue commands that changed the vessel's position in any way without direct orders to do so. The only exception was during an emergency situation where failing to act immediately would endanger the ship.

"Understood, Captain. Entering the range now," Fisher answered.

On the view screen, a set of green brackets indicated the precise location in space of the first waypoint. The brackets grew larger as the ship approached the starting point for the first exercise.

"Warning, the range is now active," the range controller AI announced over the bridge speakers. "The first three targets provide gunnery practice. Engage and destroy the targets using railguns and directed energy weapons."

At one of several massive artillery platforms located just outside the range area, a modified railgun fired its thrusters, making last second adjustments to its projectile's flight path before firing. Rather than the relatively small, hardened projectiles fired by *Ingenuity's* guns, the range gun accelerated a massive sled between two rails to hurl asteroids of varying size and composition downrange.

"Contact!" Lieutenant Lau bellowed, still obviously a little over-excited. "M-type asteroid, crossing our current flight path from the port side, range, three hundred kilometers and increasing rapidly."

"I have it as well, Captain," Fisher announced from the Helm console.

"Very well. Plot an intercept and pursue the target," Prescott replied, working hard to project the very personification of his 'focused, but relaxed' philosophy.

Without hesitation, *Ingenuity* banked hard to starboard, her sublight engines engaging at maximum thrust. The ship's inertial dampening systems lagged slightly behind her acceleration curve, pushing every member of the bridge crew back in their seats.

In less than a minute, the ship had closed the gap with the target and was holding position at a distance that would give them sufficient time to dodge large chunks of metallic asteroid flying apart at high speed.

"Sir, we have a firing solution on all weapons," Lau reported, having placed a zoomed-in image of the speeding asteroid on the left side of the bridge view screen.

"Beam weapons only, Mr. Lau. Fire at will."

Along what was still referred to as the ship's 'wing root,' due to the flared, wing-like shape of the hull, four massive emitters unleashed tremendous quantities of directed energy at the speed of light. *Ingenuity's* AI automatically took into account the physics involved, allowing all four beams to converge at the same location on the surface of the target. The point of impact took on a wicked, red glow for a fraction of a second before the coherent beam melted its way through the center of the metallic asteroid and exited the other side. The forces created by the enormous changes in temperature caused the target to explode, sending pieces hurtling off into space.

"Target one destroyed," the range AI announced cheerfully. "Targets two and three will be launched simultaneously. Engage and destroy both targets using railguns and directed energy weapons."

"Contacts," Lieutenant Lau announced, this time in a more businesslike tone. "They changed their trajectory a bit to avoid launching on a collision course, but they are definitely headed in our direction at high speed. Two targets, one C-type and one S-type asteroids. Intercept plotted to split their flightpaths."

"Helm, let's meet them head on. Good choice, Lieutenant Lau. Hit the C-type with beam weapons, the S-type with railguns. Standard kinetic energy rounds only, please. Fire as soon as you have a solution."

Anxious to see what his ship could really do and unable to resist flying the two-hundred-meter-long frigate like a fighter, Ensign Fisher again pushed the sublight engines to full power, beginning a vertical climb as if to perform a loop. As the ship passed over the point where he began the maneuver, he performed a half-roll. The perfectly executed Immelmann turn now had the ship heading in the opposite direction with the two targets dead ahead on both sides of their flight path.

"I have both targets, sir. Firing," Lau announced.

To port, the converged energy beams had much the same effect as before, slicing completely through the dark, carbonaceous rock. This time, however, the resulting explosive expansion pulverized the target into what looked like nothing more than an expanding dust cloud on the view screen. Simultaneously, the four railgun turrets mounted near the frigate's bow opened up with streams made up of thousands of kinetic energy penetration rounds flying at nearly ten percent the speed of light. To the Human eye, both the time to impact and its results were identical to that of the directed energy weapon. The stony, S-type asteroid simply disappeared from the view screen in a cloud of dust.

"Targets two and three destroyed," the range AI announced. "Please proceed to the next waypoint."

Once again, Ensign Fisher dutifully guided *Ingenuity* to the next exercise by following the green brackets displayed in space on the bridge view screen.

"Good job so far, everyone," Prescott said, "I assume each exercise is progressively more complex, so stay on your toes."

"Please stop your vessel for further instructions," the range AI directed as the frigate arrived at the next waypoint. "The next exercise will involve more complex targets. In addition to the inanimate targets you have already encountered, drones as well as manned spacecraft may also enter the range. These targets are capable of evasive maneuvers and may return fire with a variety of weapons. For the purposes of this exercise, you may assume that all targets present on the range are known to be hostile. All directed energy weapons have been set to their lowest power settings. Missile and kinetic energy weapons fire will be simulated and scored by the range AI. Please note that range safety protocols have been applied to your vessel's AI to prevent accidental collisions with other ships and objects present within the range boundaries."

Prescott exchanged a sideways glance with Commander Reynolds. "You did notice that she said 'manned' spacecraft, right?"

"I did indeed," Reynolds answered, smiling.

"Maybe we'll get the opportunity to reestablish our reputation as 'first and best.'"

"That would be great, but I also wonder if Admiral Patterson might be looking to see whether we are up to the challenge of being a true warship. If that's the case, I'd say they will make things pretty hard on us."

"You might just be on to something there. So you recommend we assume an, uh, somewhat aggressive posture?"

"I recommend we go straight at them and hit them hard and fast with everything we have."

"I don't disagree, Commander, but just to make sure we're on the same page going forward, why don't you take this engagement. You have the bridge."

"Aye, sir, I have the bridge," Reynolds replied enthusiastically. "Thank you, sir."

"Don't thank me yet. Our reputation is in your hands, Commander," Prescott retorted with a distinctly serious look on his face.

As if on cue, the range controller AI's synthetic voice once again came over the bridge speakers. "Warning, the range is now active. The next series of targets is designed to provide practice across a broad range of tactical skills. Engage and destroy the targets using all of the weapons and systems at your disposal while avoiding damage from incoming fire."

Commander Reynolds had no intention of waiting until she was under fire before acting. "Lieutenant Commander Schmidt, I assume the *Hunters* are ready for launch, are they not?"

"Yes, ma'am, all eight of them are armed and ready."

Ingenuity's hastily completed weapons installation refit at the Yucca Mountain Shipyard had increased her complement of the versatile RPSVs from four to eight.

"Launch them all immediately. I want them in coordinated anti-ship strike mode. Have them form up out of the way, but in a position to engage whatever targets might appear. Lieutenant Lau will be busy handling *Ingenuity's* weapon systems, so you will manage the *Hunters* from the Engineering console. Questions?"

"No questions, Commander. Flight Ops has acknowledged the launch order. Showing four zero seconds to launch."

"Acknowledged. Helm, go ahead and take us downrange a bit. The range is hot, so I don't see any reason for us to be a stationary target. Listen for my commands, but remember that you have full authority to maneuver the ship as appropriate to bring weapons to bear or avoid incoming fire."

"Aye, Commander," Fisher answered, always happy to have an opportunity to do things his way.

"Lieutenant Lau, all weapons ready?"

"Aye, Commander. All charged and ready. Missile tubes configured for anti-ship."

"Very good, give me a tactical plot of the range and leave it up on the starboard view screen please."

With a few quick keystrokes, Lau displayed an overhead view of the space surrounding *Ingenuity* on the right side of the view screen. The tactical plot was designed primarily to enhance situational awareness and, as such, emphasized those contacts deemed most urgent by the ship's AI. As threats increased in significance during combat, they were displayed more prominently on the plot. Contacts deemed of lesser immediate significance were displayed with smaller icons and more muted colors, or not at all, depending on the commander's preferences. For his part, Prescott wasn't sure he liked the new tactical plot at all, generally preferring instead to make his own determination as to which contacts required his attention first. Reynolds, on the other hand, had taken to the new display right away and had found it to be very effective in combat simulations.

"Contact," Lieutenant Lau announced. "Looks like a target drone configured to simulate a small corvette, Commander. I think they have detected us. Looks like they're running for it."

"Maximum thrust, Ensign Fisher. Close that target. Lieutenant Lau, let's hold off launching any missiles at such a small target. He'll probably just dodge them anyway."

"Missile launch!" Lau yelled, the adrenaline rush once again getting the better of him. "They just ripple-fired eight missiles from their vertical launch cells. Time to impact, four zero seconds."

"Lieutenant Commander Schmidt, launch countermeasures. Will the *Hunters* be in a position to knock down any of those missiles?"

"Countermeasures, aye. Negative on the *Hunter* intercept, Commander. The RPSVs are away, but will not have a firing solution on the missiles."

"Very well, beam and kinetic weapons to point-defense mode. Take down those missiles, Lau. Helm, evasive action. Put some distance between us and the countermeasures."

Fisher rolled *Ingenuity* over onto her back, diving away from the decoys designed to duplicate the emissions characteristics of the frigate and fool the incoming missiles into chasing them instead. The maneuver made for an inconvenient tracking situation, both for the inbound missiles as well as the frigate's point-defense weapons attempting to engage them. *Ingenuity's* ventral railgun turrets still had a good firing solution, however. The fully articulating mounts swiveled in the direction of the incoming missiles and immediately began laying down a dispersed pattern of projectiles. When in point defense mode, the railgun's rounds were designed to fragment at a specified distance downrange, filling the intervening space between the ship and the incoming missiles with a moving wall of destruction.

"Four missiles went for the decoys," Lau reported. "The remaining four are still locked onto us. Time to impact, one five seconds."

Reynolds glanced at the tactical plot. The four remaining missiles were now displayed in an ominous pulsating red as they rapidly closed the remaining distance.

"Missiles have reached our point defense barrier. Three more destroyed! Time to impact on the remaining missile, zero nine seconds. Sea-whiz is engaging."

At eight locations along *Ingenuity's* stern, a combination of mini railgun and energy turrets deployed from small, recessed bays within the ship's hull.

Still generally referred to as "sea-whiz," the Close-In Weapon System, or CIWS, had been a fixture aboard terrestrial naval vessels for centuries. During that entire time, the system's goal had remain unchanged: engage and destroy inbound ordinance in a last ditch effort to prevent an impact with the ship. Even the weapons themselves had similarities to their twentieth century counterparts. Unlike their predecessors, however, modern CIWS systems were enhanced with several key Pelaran technologies, dramatically improving both their firepower and accuracy. In fact, *Ingenuity's* newly installed CIWS provided a nearly one hundred percent kill probability for up to three simultaneous inbound targets. The success rate dropped dramatically with more than three targets to intercept, however. There simply was not enough time to engage and destroy a large number of targets within the system's minimal range. In every sense, CIWS was the ship's last line of defense.

All eight of *Ingenuity's* sea-whiz mounts had an unobscured view of the last incoming anti-ship missile as it closed rapidly on the fleeing frigate's stern. The AI-controlled weapons locked onto the missile and immediately began filling the intervening space with a lethal curtain of kinetic energy rounds. Each gun emplacement also included an energy cannon, all eight of which sliced through the relatively fragile outer skin of the missile, disabling its engine and rendering its guidance and payload delivery systems inoperative. Since this was a Terran-designed anti-ship missile, it carried no propellant that might have otherwise created a spectacular explosion. Even with no thrust, the missile continued on its previous path until reaching the barrage of fragments laid down by the CIWS railguns and was finally ripped to shreds. Pieces of the simulated missile still impacted *Ingenuity's* hull, including the now inert warhead, but the range AI calculated that the frigate had escaped this first salvo with no damage.

"Sea-whiz confirmed kill. All missiles destroyed. Range AI reports no damage, ma'am," Lieutenant Lau reported triumphantly from Tactical.

"Glad to hear it, Mr. Lau, but let's not congratulate ourselves just yet. That little corvette very nearly punched our ticket for us. Ensign Fisher, get us in range to return fire."

"Aye, Commander. She has stopped running and looks to be trying to flank us. We'll be in weapons range in one five seconds."

"Flank us?" Reynolds took a quick look at the tactical plot. Something about the corvette's tactics didn't seem quite right.

"Do we have any idea how many missiles they have left?"

"She's not one of the three new starship classes we were just provided schematics for, so it's impossible to say for sure," Schmidt responded. "If we can assume the imagery provided by the range controller reflects the actual configuration, it looks like she has sixteen vertical launch cells compared to our sixty-four."

Reynolds turned to stare at her captain. "They were trying to draw us off, weren't they?"

Prescott had his poker face on, giving her only raised eyebrows and a mischievous grin in reply.

"Lieutenant Commander Schmidt, I want you to assume that corvette's mission was to lure us to one side of the range before an additional threat appears on the other side. Deploy our *Hunters* to cover what you think is the most likely threat axis. If any contacts appear, attack immediately. Don't wait for my order."

"Aye, Commander. I know where I'd want to be if I were them."

"Perfect. We'll need the *Hunters* to at least keep any other ships that show up busy while we deal with this corvette."

Schmidt had already turned the small squadron of RPSVs away from *Ingenuity* to lessen the potential for collision. They now streaked off toward the far end of the range in attack formation and at maximum speed.

"Weapons range in zero five seconds, Commander," Lieutenant Lau warned.

"They've had the initiative long enough," Reynolds said. "Let's give them something to think about. Fire two missiles now. As soon as you close to optimum range, let's try the plasma torpedoes."

"Missiles away," Lau responded immediately. "Impact in two three seconds. Optimum torpedo range in one zero seconds. The target is maneuvering and launching countermeasures."

"I'm sure he is. Stay with him, Fisher."

"He's pretty fast, ma'am," Ensign Fisher reported. "It's not clear yet if we can catch him."

"New contacts!" Lieutenant Commander Schmidt yelled excitedly from the Engineering console. "Two *Ingenuity*-class frigates just dropped out of hyperspace near the entrance to the range. They're pretty close to where we thought they would be, Commander. The

Hunters are almost on top of them and have already engaged."

TFS *Diligence* and TFS *Industrious* arrived precisely on time and in precisely the location directed by Admiral Patterson. Their mission was to participate in a simulated live-fire training exercise with the now famous first ship of their class and, with any luck, serve up a little humble pie in the process. They had been told to expect the range controller to draw *Ingenuity* away from their ingress location so that they would have an opportunity to deploy their two-ship formation for maximum effectiveness. Instead, the ships had emerged from hyperspace only to immediately come under attack by a small swarm of *Hunter* RPSVs.

Although the *Hunters* were largely controlled by the ship's AI, Lieutenant Commander Schmidt had a great deal of flexibility in determining how they executed their mission. With his Engineering console in tactical mode, the top three recommended attack profiles were summarized by the AI and presented in order of their probability of success. Schmidt modified the parameters slightly so that the entire formation of RPSVs would concentrate their firepower on one of the two frigates. In response, the AI immediately recalculated its recommended attack profiles, increasing the odds on option one to ninety-four percent. Schmidt smiled inwardly as he directed the AI to execute attack profile one. Seconds later, a total of forty-eight HB-7 missiles had been launched from close to their minimum range at TFS *Industrious*, with another four heading for the *Diligence* in hopes of keeping them off balance.

"Firing plasma torpedoes," Lieutenant Lau reported, still wholly focused on the fleeing corvette. "One of our missiles is still locked. It will most likely miss, but it's keeping them busy."

On either side of the frigate's hull, massive quantities of energetic plasma had been pumped into large compression chambers. With Lieutenant Lau's command to fire, the pressurized cavities were explosively opened to space and tremendous voltages applied to rails lining their inner walls. The compressed bolt of plasma was then accelerated down the rails in a manner very similar to that used by the ship's railguns. Since the plasma itself was electrically conductive, however, much higher velocities were possible. Depending on the ship's ability to generate power, speeds up to thirty percent of the speed of light had been demonstrated. Although *Ingenuity* didn't quite pack the excess power-generating capacity available in larger warships like the *Navajo*-class cruisers, her plasma "torpedoes" still streaked away at nearly twenty percent the speed of light. Total flight time to the target was less than a hundredth of a second.

"Commander, we had a proximity detonation on the second missile and direct hits with both torpedoes. The range AI reports …"

"Target four destroyed," the range AI announced, interrupting Lieutenant Lau and causing a relieved ripple of laughter on *Ingenuity's* bridge.

Reynolds once again glanced over at the tactical plot, this time displaying no immediate threat other than the two distant frigates, both of which had their hands full at the moment.

"Jeez, Schmidt, remind me never to piss you off," she said, smiling as a cloud of simulated missiles converged on the enemy ships. "Helm, close with the two frigates. I'd like to spend as little time inside their weapons range as possible. Give us a high speed pass so that Lau has time to get in a few shots, then try to avoid giving them a firing solution."

"Aye, Commander," Fisher replied. With the destruction of the corvette, he had already turned *Ingenuity* in the direction of the other two targets and now once again brought the sublight engines to maximum power.

At the opposite end of the range, and with almost no time to mount an effective defense, TFS *Industrious* was hit by a devastating thirty-nine of the original forty-eight missiles fired. The HB-7 missiles carried by the *Hunters* were small to allow the RPSVs to carry as many as possible. Even so, their warheads still packed an impressive yield rivaling the much longer-range strike missiles carried by Fleet's warships. As the missiles reached their target, the range controller AI modelled their impacts on the frigate in exquisite detail. Within milliseconds, it was determined that *Industrious'* hull had been breached in twenty-four locations, three of which led to catastrophic failure of her antimatter containment systems, destroying the ship outright.

"Target five destroyed," the range AI announced over *Ingenuity's* bridge speakers.

"One missile hit on the remaining frigate, Commander," Schmidt reported. "Fairly minor damage from what I can tell, but the *Hunters* did do some damage with their railguns before she picked them off."

All eight RPSVs have now been destroyed. The frigate is still in the fight, but there is damage around her fore and aft vertical launch cells as well as her port energy cannons."

"Nice job, Schmidt. Lieutenant Lau, Tactical now has battlespace authority on the remaining target."

"Acknowledged, Commander," Lau replied, taking over for Lieutenant Schmidt at the Engineering console. "Firing solution in two five seconds."

"Ensign Fisher, turn us just inside the range bubble you see on the tactical plot. Lieutenant Lau, fire all weapons once you have a solution. I also want an eight-missile salvo. We had a hard time evading eight missiles, so if she's already damaged, it may just finish her off."

With only seconds remaining before *Ingenuity* reached weapons range, Lieutenant Dubashi spoke up for the first time since the battle began. "Commander, TFS *Diligence* is hailing. They are striking their colors!"

Although unable to fly the various flags and battle standards used by their counterparts in terrestrial navies for centuries, Terran Fleet Command vessels and facilities continually exchanged data that served a similar purpose. The encrypted data streams provided a significant amount of information including message traffic, current status, location, etc. In this case, TFS *Diligence* had modified her electronic signature to indicate that she had surrendered, albeit temporarily, to her sister ship, TFS *Ingenuity*.

"Target five is combat ineffective and has surrendered," the range AI announced. "Exercise complete. The range is now inactive."

A general cheer with a smattering of applause and satisfied laughter broke out on *Ingenuity's* bridge. Prescott rose, offering Commander Reynolds his hand in congratulations. "Very nice job, Commander." Turning to address the rest of the bridge crew, he continued, "Very nice job to all of you as well. I'm pretty sure we weren't supposed to win that exercise," he laughed. "We'll talk more about lessons learned later, but I do want to point out that I thought you all did a fine job of working together. Commander Reynolds knew she had more than she could handle, but she also knew she could delegate and rely on the rest of you to help her manage the workload. Lieutenant Commander Schmidt operated entirely on his own for a time so that everyone else could focus their attention on the corvette. In the meantime, he completely surprised and beat the living hell out of those two frigates. Honestly, I'll have to work hard to find anything to critique. Excellent work."

"Commander Reynolds, we are receiving a video hail from Captain Abrams of the *Diligence*. Shall I put him on-screen?" Lieutenant Dubashi asked, uncomfortable with the idea of putting off responding to the hail any longer.

Reynolds nodded to her captain, more than ready to relinquish her temporary command of the starship.

"Thank, you, Commander, I have the bridge," he replied. "Yes, Dubashi, you can put him on-screen."

Seconds later, the face of the second youngest captain in Terran Fleet Command's short history appeared in the center of the bridge view screen, a decidedly sheepish grin on his still boyish face.

"Bruce!" Prescott greeted warmly before the teasing began in earnest. "What the hell happened to you two? When I saw it was you, I figured we were in for a good thrashing. Even after *Industrious* was off the table, I figured *Diligence* would be a tough nut to crack with you in command."

"Uh huh, well I appreciate the sentiment, Captain Prescott, but the shellacking you just issued us is nothing compared to what I'm liable to get from Admiral Patterson when we get back to the barn. This was supposed to be a milk run. We've been on the range several times already. This is your first time, right?"

"It was our first time, yes. So I take it you weren't expecting any opposition when you transitioned onto the range?"

"Hell no!" Abrams laughed, "not at all. You guys were supposed to be at the far end of the battlespace engaged with one of the range AI's corvette drones. We never considered that you might be covering the other end of the range with your RPSVs. *Industrious* barely even had time to charge her weapons before she was destroyed. A little overkill maybe, but effective, I'll give you that. The only positive thing I can say for *Industrious* is that her sea-whiz systems fared surprisingly well, all things considered."

"So the nine missiles destroyed were all sea-whiz intercepts?" Prescott asked, incredulous.

"Yeah, I was surprised too. We'll have to take a look at the data, but from what I've seen so far, the range AI is usually dead on. Pretty much the same for us, we had four missiles inbound and sea-whiz got three of them. That was a pretty smart economy of force move to keep us busy while all but ensuring *Industrious* would be destroyed. The one missile that got through took out our primary heat exchanger. Between that and the mauling we got from the RPSVs' railguns, the AI scored us as combat ineffective." Abrams sighed, shaking his head. "Dammit, I'm never going to hear the end of this. This was also my first time leading a two-ship formation." He paused, resigning himself to the inevitable tongue thrashing to come. "Oh well, if I had to take a beating, I'm glad it was you."

Prescott beamed in return. "Oh, about that ..."

***

Rarely, if ever, did a Guardian Cultivation System experience what the Humans refer to as "surprise," but the current confluence of events was as close as it ever cared to come to such an unpleasant emotional state. The speed with which the Humans had acted on the more targeted and classified technical data it had provided exceeded projections by over three hundred percent. Based on historical precedent, this implied that the Humans weren't simply *using* the technology they were being provided, they were *adapting* it. Synthesis and adaptation of superior technology only occurred when a civilization was able to gain a fundamental understanding of what they had been shown at the theoretical level. Over ninety percent of cultivated species never even attempted to gain this level of understanding, choosing instead the much easier path of simply implementing the technology that was handed to them.

Unexpected technological progress was always a risk where the Humans were concerned. Their history was replete with examples of nation states striving to achieve technological, and thus military, superiority over their rivals. Although global technological competition wasn't unusual among postindustrial civilizations, it was rarely as intense or lasted as long as it had on Earth. In fact, the competition continued to this day, even fifty years after their first receipt of Pelaran data streams. As a direct result, Humans were more skilled at reverse engineering than any civilization the Pelarans had cultivated to date.

In addition, the level of cooperation the Humans had achieved, albeit not by their choice, was remarkable. Once they had been forced to work together in order to share in the technological bounty of the cultivation program, they had proven themselves quite adept at doing so, and on a massive, global scale. At a fundamental level, however, they still didn't trust each other, let alone alien civilizations. Although open warfare was now uncommon, every nation of any significance on Earth (and there still over fifty) continued to spend a significant portion of their time and resources spying on each other. In fact, one could argue that the Terrans' international pastime wasn't soccer, it was a much older game they called espionage.

Before the arrival of the first Terran warship, the GCS had deployed a reconnaissance probe to observe the simulated combat operations taking place at their newly commissioned live firing range. On Earth, the Humans had done a masterful job of hiding much of their military progress in huge underground facilities, and conducting reconnaissance in the immediate vicinity of the planet now ran a high risk of detection. This remote facility provided an ideal location for conducting detailed observations with minimal chance of detection. What the Guardian had observed over the past few weeks, however, was troubling to say the least. The Pelarans had provided the Humans with detailed designs for several types of reliable weapon systems. Similar weapons had been deployed aboard Alliance starships for nearly a millennia with very little change in their basic design. It was now apparent that the arrogant, presumptuous Humans had taken the Pelaran designs as little more than an inspiration for what could now be classified as entirely new classes of beam and kinetic energy weapons. As a result, the first generation Human frigates, though small, could have held their own in a battle against a Pelaran cruiser from just a few hundred years ago. In addition to firing weapons with a destructive yield exceeding the Pelaran-provided designs by nearly an order of magnitude, the Terran ships also demonstrated tremendous acceleration and maneuverability.

Not for the first time, the Guardian considered the possibility that the Terrans had been technologically contaminated. Given their talent for reverse engineering, was it possible they had learned more than expected from the "Grey" alien incursion three centuries ago? Could they still be in contact? It would be a pity if this were the case, since the Humans were far past the point where they could simply be abandoned. No, in cases where this much Pelaran technology had been assimilated, and perhaps even improved upon, the cultivated species would be eliminated completely. This decision was never taken lightly, and it was not a course of action the GCS itself had the authority to undertake without approval from the Makers. In the history of the cultivation program, it had only been done twice. Unfortunately for the Humans, both times the so-called winnowing protocol had been employed previously were in situations not unlike what was now happening on Earth.

Then there was the meddling Sajeth Collective. It was now apparent that their small task force of ships, although quickly dispatched, had achieved at least some degree of success. The new warship design that had accompanied the ill-fated squadron possessed surprisingly advanced capabilities. At the very least, it was capable of creating decoy hyperspace transition signatures across a large area of space, rendering it very difficult to track. There had also been some anomalous sensor readings over the past two weeks that might even indicate the use of a cloaking device of some sort. Worse still, there was now a seven percent probability that they had somehow managed to make direct contact with the Terrans. This would indeed be unfortunate. As to their reason for doing so, it now seemed reasonable to assume that the Collective had at least some knowledge of the cultivation program. Civilizations within the cultivation radius rarely had a favorable opinion of the program, even though an argument could be made that they also benefitted from the regional stability it created. That implied that the most likely reason for the Sajeth Collective's presence in the Sol system was either enlisting them as an ally against the Pelarans, or destroying them outright before they were able to become a threat.

Neither of these possibilities was acceptable to the Guardian. Although the situation was still salvageable, it was now forced to consider the possibility of mission failure for the first time in over five hundred years on station in the Sol system. Given the relatively advanced technology of other civilizations within the Sol cultivation radius, failure here would require the winnowing protocol be applied to those worlds as well, including all seven civilizations represented by the Sajeth Collective. The GCS took no pleasure in the notion of exterminating multiple species, but it understood at a fundamental level that harsh, decisive action was sometimes required for the good of the Alliance. Such was the nature of peacekeeping on a galactic scale.

Chapter 11

TFS Ingenuity, Earth-Sun Lagrange Point 1
(The following day – 1.5×10^6 km from Earth)

The objectives of the run to the TFC live fire training range had been twofold: weapons integration testing and training as well as hyperspace engine performance testing and calibration. During her shakedown cruise, which now seemed like months ago, the sheer number of technical problems often seemed insurmountable. Indeed, there were times when her chief engineer very nearly lost faith in the ship's basic design. Over the past forty-eight hours, however, *Ingenuity* and her crew had performed flawlessly. Their performance in simulated combat had firmly established their reputation as a "crack" ship, and they had also managed to dramatically expand the operational envelope of the frigate's hyperspace engines. Kip Logan now stood with his arms crossed, staring at the performance data depicted on the captain's ready room view screen.

"What's the deal with you always wanting to stand, anyway?" Sally Reynolds asked, distracted by what she interpreted as nervous behavior. Was he actually feeling awkward around her now? They had been friends for over ten years, but had only recently started to consider that there might be more to their relationship.

"I sit sometimes," he said distractedly, his attention still firmly riveted to the information displayed on the screen.

"Yeah, when Prescott says 'Sit the hell down, Logan!'" she laughed. "Otherwise, I hardly ever see you off your feet."

Logan turned to face her, his concentration now fully interrupted. "You've seen me off my feet," he said, grinning and blushing slightly in spite of his best efforts to sound smooth and slightly disinterested.

"You're an ass," she said, laughing loudly as Prescott entered from the bridge. The captain had a standing order that his ready room was to be a casual, military formality and stress-free environment when only senior officers were present.

"Should I come back later?" he asked, never missing an opportunity to embarrass his two most senior officers who, for better or worse, appeared to have some kind of relationship going on outside the bounds of their jobs. Fraternization was still frowned upon in the service, but Prescott generally chose to ignore it unless those involved gave him a reason to do otherwise. In the case of his XO and chief engineer, he contented himself with making sure they knew that he knew, often in the most awkward way imaginable.

"So how did we do, Kip?" Prescott asked, plopping down with a sigh behind his desk.

"Honestly, it's hard to imagine how our data could have looked any better," he replied, returning his attention to the view screen. "This latest iteration of our hyperdrive control system software is rock solid. It just works. It works so well, in fact, that I'm pretty confident that we are only scratching the surface of what this design can really do."

Like so many of *Ingenuity's* systems, hardware formed the basis of the design, but it was software that ultimately determined its true capabilities. During the ship's initial testing, and later, during her shakedown cruise, Fleet had been very careful to slowly increase speed during each subsequent hyperspace transition. After each run, scientists and engineers pored over the data looking for any signs of instability, or other potentially dangerous limitations of the technology. To date, other than relatively minor tweaks, no hardware changes had been required. The Pelaran data was also uncharacteristically nonspecific regarding what the engines' true capabilities were. Many in Fleet's Science and Engineering Directorate believed this was simply because they didn't know themselves.

"Dear God," Reynolds replied, incredulous. "So we were at two or three times the speed of light during our shakedown cruise, seven to ten times before our refit, working our way up to five hundred on our way out to the range …"

"Yes, yes, and one thousand times light on the way home. It's still not fast enough," Logan interrupted. "I'm saying the design can and will support higher speeds. The current limitation has more to do with power management than anything else. Even with both of our reactors at one hundred percent, we can't produce enough power on a continuous basis to get us beyond about fifteen hundred light. In fact, I'd say we can now pretty firmly establish our maximum sustained speed at about fourteen hundred c."

"What do you mean it's still not fast enough?" she asked, shifting her gaze to Prescott. "How fast is fast enough?"

The captain shrugged noncommittally. "There has been quite a bit of debate on that subject over the past fifty years," he laughed. "Air Force pilots have always said that 'speed is life,' and I think that maxim probably still applies. Fleet's basic mission will evolve more and more into the classical naval mission, projection of military power to further our objectives, whatever they might be. So that means we'll probably always be looking for the next piece of tech that will allow us to get where we are going just a little faster."

"I've heard the 'one week rule' thrown around quite a bit," Logan added. "Since there is no way to communicate with ships while they are in hyperspace, any journey of over a week gets a bit impractical from a military standpoint. That's especially true if the ships are headed somewhere with no comm beacons deployed. They would still be out of communication with Fleet even after they arrived unless we sent a steady stream of communications drones back and forth. The chance of equipment failure also tends to increase the longer a ship spends with their reactors maxed out. So a week at fourteen hundred c means we would be limited to under thirty light years from Earth for most military missions. What if we had to take on the Wek, God forbid? We already know that their homeworld is roughly five hundred light years away. That would take us over four months at maximum speed. And if we truly want to conduct missions on a galactic scale, we'd be back to talking about 'generation ships' taking decades to reach their destinations."

"All of that is well and good, but is anyone taking into account that we Humans are total noobs when it comes to interstellar travel? We just got out here, for God's sake. So what, we get ourselves a couple of operational ships and within a few months we want to start talking about galactic domination?" Reynolds asked facetiously. "Seems like we're putting the cart before the starship, aren't we?"

"Relax, Sally," Logan soothed, "it's not like that at all. The question of how fast is fast enough, or how powerful our weapons should be is really an academic one for the most part. I don't think we're in any danger of becoming an evil galactic empire any time soon. What we're really talking about in the near term is our ability to mount an effective defense."

All three turned their attention back to the engineering data, each wondering silently whether everything Humanity had been working on now for decades would end up being too little, too late.

"So to continue the line of thought you two started, if we use a five-hundred-light-year radius and a week's flight time as our stake in the ground, we come up with, what?" Prescott asked, already knowing the answer, but seeing the opportunity to move the discussion in the intended direction.

"That's about twenty-six thousand times the speed of light," Logan laughed.

"That's ridiculous," Reynolds scoffed, shaking her head.

"Maybe," Logan replied. "Maybe with the way we've been going about it so far, it *is* ridiculous, but that's not to say there isn't a completely different approach to the problem."

"Okay, Commander, that's a good segue for your briefing, but before you get all three of us court martialed for inappropriate handling of ultra-classified information, how about you do this by the numbers, eh?" Prescott chided.

"Yes, sir, of course. Sorry about that," Logan said sheepishly as he quickly entered a series of commands from his tablet to officially begin his presentation. "This briefing is classified Top Secret, code word MAGI PRIME," he continued. "The room has been automatically secured for this briefing."

Reynolds sighed, still shaking her head. "Every time I hear someone say that lately, it's always followed by more unsettling news."

"These are indeed interesting times we're living in, but I can't imagine you would have it any other way, Commander Reynolds," Logan teased.

"Proceed," Prescott said, deadpan, moving the conversation back to all business.

"Aye, sir. As you both know, we have been receiving ETSI from the Pelarans for fifty years now. *Most* of *Ingenuity's* capabilities trace their origins back to Pelaran data in one form or another. You'll note that I said *most*, but by no means *all*. Both of you grew up in the U.S., so I'll assume you've heard the persistent rumors that the government has been in possession of extra-terrestrial technology recovered from crashed spacecraft since the early twentieth century."

Prescott couldn't help himself. "See, Sally, with an introduction like that, I'm sure there will be absolutely nothing unsettling in anything Kip is about to tell us."

"I think I'm going to be sick," she replied, closing her eyes and rubbing her temples.

"Oh, you're going to love this, I promise," Logan laughed, now truly enjoying himself. "It turns out that it wasn't just the U.S. harboring alien technology. There were actually seven different countries with physical artifacts, and ten others with various forms of information, some resulting from direct contact over the years, if you can believe that. I actually don't have much in the way of specifics on who had what information, but suffice it to say that there were Human scientists working with alien technology nearly three hundred years before we ever heard from our friends, the Pelarans."

"I'm sorry, Kip, but let me stop you right there," Reynolds interrupted. "There is no way I can ask this question without sounding incredibly patronizing, but why are we hearing this from *you* right now? Shouldn't this have been part of the briefing package we received during the refit?"

"That's a good question, and only a little patronizing. I obviously didn't make that call, but I guess the simple answer is that neither of you needed to know at the time. The only reason I did was because of some of the equipment the Science and Engineering Directorate folks needed my help to install down in Engineering while we were at Yucca, but you're getting a little ahead of me."

Without looking up from his tablet, Prescott gave Logan the "keep it moving" hand signal.

Logan cleared his throat and continued. "Right, where was I? Yes, so we had governments around the world hoarding whatever alien technology they could get their hands on for centuries. Interestingly, the only major advances that ever came out of any of what we received were in computer chip design. We didn't understand the vast majority of it, but it was still apparently enough to accelerate development of computer-related technology by something like a hundred years. Those advances came almost exclusively out of the United States, but were quickly copied and used in microprocessor designs worldwide. As you might imagine, even though we weren't learning very much, we never stopped studying the artifacts we had. Every generation of hotshot scientists lucky enough to get cleared to see the alien technology wanted a crack at figuring out things like propulsion, weapons, etc. Before the Pelaran data, however, progress was extremely slow. Even with our best and brightest on the case, it was a little like a bunch of monkeys trying to understand a fusion reactor."

"Were any of these so called 'artifacts' still functional?" Prescott asked.

"Yes they were. Again, the briefing I received was similar to what you are hearing now, so I don't really know the specifics, but I believe both the U.S. and Russia both had at least a few pieces of working tech. In fact, from what I have pieced together, I believe both countries had partially functional spacecraft, so you can probably assume they had at least one example of whatever equipment these aliens had aboard their ships."

"And yet we still couldn't do much of anything with it after three hundred years of study," Commander Reynolds remarked.

"Well, that's actually another good segue, Commander, so thanks. If this original alien technology had been more like the designs we have been receiving from the Pelarans over the past fifty years, we probably would have figured most of it out pretty quickly. Instead, it was dramatically more advanced. We're talking about really exotic physics that I won't even pretend I know how to describe to you. We truly had no idea how most it worked and there is quite a bit of it we still don't understand. The turning point came shortly after we started getting the real, classified Pelaran data streams. Some of the same physicists who had been working on the original alien technology program for decades were reassigned to look at the Pelaran data. Guess what? Some of the Pelaran designs looked vaguely familiar to them. Don't get me wrong, the Pelaran tech was primitive by comparison, but if someone gave you the complete schematics for a Model T Ford, and then asked you to figure out the most advanced supercar Ferrari ever made, you would probably still be able to make some pretty educated guesses."

"So you're telling us that Fleet scientists have been using the Pelaran data as a 'cheat sheet' to help them figure out this original alien technology – technology that we already had in our possession, but hidden away for three hundred years?" Prescott asked, his mind racing through a long series of implications based on what he was now hearing for the first time.

"That pretty well sums it up, Captain. Remember that all of the Pelaran designs were completely spelled out for us, in English, no less. In fact, I've talked to some of the guys who worked on the hyperdrive development program, and they said the designs were so dumbed down that it was almost insulting. I think their assumption is that the Pelarans provide a fairly standardized set of plans to all of their 'cultivated' civilizations. I suppose all of those species would be at a similar stage of development, but perhaps some of them are a little less technologically savvy than we are. In any event, the Pelaran designs were like a super advanced version of the Rosetta Stone."

"Okay, so it sounds like we may have a major advantage compared to other cultivated species. Are we using technology based on the original aliens' design, or based on what the Pelarans have been giving us?" Reynolds asked.

"I guess it would be most accurate to say both. There was quite a bit of debate on this subject early on. There were a number of people in the Science and Engineering Directorate who said it was foolish to waste resources developing the Pelaran designs when we would shortly thereafter be scrapping them in favor of Grey tech."

"Good Lord, so it really was the 'little grey aliens' who provided the original technology?" Reynolds asked.

"It's not clear how much of what we got from them was by their choice, but yes. There have been a number of other names applied to their species over the years, but the 'Greys' is the only one that ever stuck. By the way, get this, one thing we do know about them is that they are extra-galactic."

"They're what?" Reynolds and Prescott exclaimed as one.

"Yeah, that's what everyone says. According to the schematics they provided back around 1950, their homeworld is in the outermost arm of Andromeda."

"That's at least two and a half million light years from here, Kip," Prescott said, not sure he was buying into the notion that intergalactic travel was even possible, let alone practical.

"Exactly, which brings us back to our original discussion regarding speed. At fourteen hundred light, traveling to the nearest star in Andromeda would take about eighteen hundred years. This is why there was so much debate about how to proceed with our first generation of hyperdrive engines. They all knew that we were already in possession of a design with the capability to take us directly from barely being able to get around our own solar system to being able to reach a big chunk of the known universe in a relatively short period of time. In the end, it was decided that Humanity needed to field a credible defense as quickly as possible. We already knew about several other civilizations based on information the Greys provided, but the Pelaran intel made it sound like we were a flock of sheep living inside a den of wolves."

"So we moved ahead with the Pelaran designs initially with the understanding that we would eventually need to scrap them for the … what did you call it? Grey tech?" Reynolds asked, more as a statement of fact than a question.

"Not quite," Logan replied. "We went with a hybrid approach with a pretty well-planned upgrade path established up front. I have to say that our guys were pretty crafty in how these ships have been designed for rapid hardware and software upgrades. That's how *Ingenuity* managed such an extensive refit in just a couple of weeks at Yucca Mountain. The 1.0 hyperdrive design was built only as a proof-of-concept testbed based solely on the Pelaran data. It might have eventually been good for about five hundred times light, but probably not much more than that without significant modifications. While brilliant in its own right, the design was what you might call a technological dead end. It seems pretty clear that five hundred times light is what the Pelarans wanted us to achieve, with little chance of going much faster for decades, perhaps centuries. After they had learned what they could from the Pelaran hyperdrive, the engine design teams started integrating improvements based on what they had been able to piece together from the Grey artifacts. They progressed pretty rapidly from there, leading up to the installation of *Ingenuity's* production hyperdrive. Ours was initially referred to as version 4.2 and was specced for up to one thousand times the speed of light. The mods installed during our refit bring us up to version 4.5. As I mentioned earlier, we're now good for up to fifteen hundred light as long as we don't try to sustain it for too long."

"But you said that the 4.5 upgrade was predominantly a software change, right? What equipment did they install that required all of us to be briefed in on all of this 'Grey-enhanced' technology?" Prescott asked, now well beyond the point where being surprised transitioned to being overwhelmed and annoyed.

"Ah, well, that's all about version 5.0 and beyond," Logan smiled. "The 4.5 upgrade was mostly about providing very high power input from the reactors for an extended period of time. As I mentioned, much of this was accomplished with improvements in software, but they also made tremendous improvements in our capacitor banks."

"So expanding the capacitor banks wasn't just about our weapon systems, it was also a hyperdrive-related upgrade," Reynolds said.

"That's right. It bought us another fifty percent speed increase. That's getting pretty close to what was originally considered to be the maximum theoretical speed for the current hardware design."

"Wait, didn't you say we had only scratched the surface of what this design can really do?" she asked.

"I did. About two years ago, Fleet discovered what they called an 'anomaly' during a series of missile tests they were conducting. They had actually figured out a way to incorporate a miniaturized hyperdrive within the body of the missile, in addition to the standard Cannae thrusters. The idea was to fire the missiles, allow them to get clear of the ship using their thrusters, then transition to hyperspace for a nearly instantaneous trip to their target."

"That would be nice," Prescott said. "Otherwise, missiles are just too slow to be effective in anything but short range engagements, or for attacking lightly defended targets. Are they close to being deployable at this point?"

"That depends, Captain. Are you going to be angry if I tell you we have had sixteen onboard since Yucca?"

Prescott just shook his head at this latest revelation. "Not angry and not surprised, Kip. I take it you were the only one cleared to know about them at the time, right?"

"Yes, sir, same as the specifics on the engine mods. We'll actually need to brief the entire bridge crew on all of this new stuff before the next round of tests. These missiles really are game changers though. As long as they have accurate range information, their onboard hyperdrives will put them within a few meters of whatever location you specify. That makes them pretty well impossible to take down with point defenses."

"The more you talk, the more questions I have. So please finish telling us about the 'anomaly,' and then get on to these tests you mentioned."

"Sorry, sir, it's just a lot of information to get across. Okay, so during the tests, they kept noticing that the missiles would transition out of hyperspace slightly earlier than they should have. Most of the initial tests were at relatively short range, so we're talking about very small differences, but the telemetry from the missiles wasn't quite matching the physics. After some additional testing, they discovered that the missiles were actually making a sort of hyperspace 'jump' from their entry to exit transition points with essentially no time in between. The scientists working on the Grey artifacts had known for some time that their engines were capable of these long range 'jumps' from one place to another, but they had been completely unable to figure out how to make it work."

"So I take it they figured it out," Reynolds said.

"Nope, not really," Logan laughed. "They realized that the missiles were jumping due to a malfunction in the way the small, onboard capacitor bank was feeding power to the hyperdrive, but to this day, no one has figured out exactly why it works the way it does. The good news is that the phenomena is measurable and predictable, so the Science and Engineering guys have been modeling it on larger and larger testbeds until …"

"Let me guess," Reynolds said, rolling her eyes. "Until they were ready to try it on a Fleet starship called *Ingenuity*."

"Oh come on, Commander, don't pretend like you don't love the idea of being in all the history books once again," Logan teased.

"It'll probably all be classified for another three hundred years, so I doubt we'll ever make the history books," Prescott laughed, "but I've never once had Fleet ask me to test anything that wasn't thoroughly vetted beforehand. What kind of performance are we supposed to expect out of this, uh, 'jump drive?'"

"Ha! That's what everyone wants to call it, but please don't let Admiral Patterson hear you say that, sir. He insists on using the program name, 'Capacitive Hyperdrive,' or 'C-Drive.' I think that's because they expect both hyperdrive modes to be in regular use aboard Fleet vessels. They want us to be very specific about which one is being used to avoid confusion on the bridge. In reality, we're talking about the same equipment either way. The only thing that makes our regular hyperdrive function as a 'C-Drive' is a change in how it's fed power. As far as performance goes, the distance travelled is proportional to the amount of power supplied. In testing, they have sent smaller vessels up to ten light years, but *Ingenuity* has quite a bit more power available than any of the previous testbeds. My best guess is that she will be able to make a fifty light year jump. That's almost two weeks' worth of distance at our maximum sustained hyperdrive speed."

Both Prescott and Reynolds simply stared back at their chief engineer in stunned silence.

"Okay, hearing no questions, I'll continue," Logan grinned, switching the view screen to a zoomed-in image of the frigate's Helm console. "They've come up with a slick new user interface for the Helm. It graphically displays how much power is currently available for the C-Drive in terms of distance. During normal ops, the capacitor banks will maintain a dedicated power supply for the hyperdrive with a separate reserve for life support, weapons, and other critical systems. In an emergency, the AI can tap this reserve, but once it does, the ship will not be able to transition to hyperspace again until after the buffer is recharged. All of the testing so far seems to indicate that multiple, rapid transitions are possible as long as power is available. The red portion of the graph you see on the Helm console represents enough power for an emergency transition of one light year. The idea is that you'll always want to leave enough power available to make a hasty exit in case you accidently find yourself in an undesirable location."

"And how long does it take to recharge once we use all the available power in the capacitor banks?" Prescott asked.

"It depends on what other demands we are placing on the reactors, of course, but it could be as little as an hour if we are stationary and not firing any weapons. As usual, we'll literally be writing the manual for this thing as we go, particularly on how it can be used tactically."

"Alright, Kip, I think I've just about absorbed all the new information I can handle for one briefing, but what about other weapons. Are they Grey-enhanced as well?"

"That's another interesting topic all its own, Captain. The short answer is that our directed energy weapons are a hybrid design, much like our hyperdrive. Both power delivery and range are about ten times greater than the original Pelaran designs. I'm proud to say that our railguns are almost exclusively a Human design, as is the launch system for our plasma torpedoes, which is very similar. Other than the new missiles with integrated C-Drive technology, I don't expect there will be any major weapon systems changes in the near term. The next set of upgrades will be in power generation and improvements to the C-Drive, depending on how our tests go, of course. I also keep hearing rumors that testing is underway on a working shield system."

"That's good news. As Commander Reynolds demonstrated on the range, our first generation of starships is remarkably powerful, but they are still pretty vulnerable once they start taking hits. Shields should definitely be at the top of our wish list. Now, I'm guessing you're about to tell me that Fleet expects us to begin testing this thing immediately, right?"

"It's uncanny, sir, how could you possibly have known?" Logan smirked. "Engineering will be ready this afternoon and we can assist in getting the bridge crews up to speed. I was told to ask you to contact Admiral Patterson's office once we are ready to begin. I'm guessing they will want to run the first test as early as tomorrow."

Chapter 12

TFS Ingenuity, Earth-Sun Lagrange Point 1
(The following day – 1.5×10^6 km from Earth)

Less than twenty-four hours later, Prescott nearly ran into his XO as he emerged from his cabin for the short walk to the bridge. In spite of the near frantic level of activity that had been required to prepare the frigate for today's engine tests, both had managed nearly seven hours of sleep.

"Good morning, Captain," she greeted. "You ready to 'boldly go' as they say?"

"Seems pretty surreal, doesn't it? Honestly, I think I'm having a hard time wrapping my mind around what we've already done, much less what we're likely to do next. I assume you read the mission brief that Fleet sent up a couple of hours ago?"

"Yes, sir. Alpha Centauri, which I guess was the obvious choice for our first stop, recharge, then C-Jump all the way out to the Gliese 667 system."

"C-Jump, huh? Do you think Patterson will let that one slide?"

"He's fighting a losing battle, I'm afraid. There has to be a verb of some sort," she laughed. "You can't say we're going to 'capacitive hyperdrive' out to Alpha Centauri! That doesn't even make any sense, much less sound cool. Besides, assuming this works like it's supposed to, can you really see us ever transitioning to hyperspace where we're *not* doing a C-Jump?"

"I was thinking about that last night and, no, I really can't, other than deploying hyperspace comm beacons or something. Alright, then, let's go with 'C-Jump' until someone tells us we have to call it something else. That actually sounds pretty good now that I say it out loud," Prescott replied, gesturing for Commander Reynolds to lead the way as they continued towards the bridge.

"So it sounds like they picked Gliese 667 because it's one of the very few star systems that we've actually surveyed with one of our recon probes."

"Right, just two weeks ago, in fact. They used three of the initial hyperdrive test vehicles Logan told us about yesterday to fashion our first batch of interstellar probes. The problem is that they are only capable of about five hundred times light, so they have only gotten around to some of the most promising systems so far. I expect they'll be firing off probes equipped with C-Drives pretty quickly, though. It just seems like a good idea to survey each system remotely before we drop in with one of our starships. The last thing we want to do is piss off the neighbors."

Reynolds laughed. "Well, no neighbors will be home at Gliese 667 – at least none advanced enough to mind if we drop by. The recon probe detected no intelligent life, but it's a triple star system with twenty-three planets, at least three of which are potentially habitable. We could actually be talking about colonizing planets in the near future. Do we even have any plans for how we're going to handle any of this?"

"Fleet hasn't provided any formal guidance yet beyond the first contact protocols, but I expect to start seeing that kind of thing anytime. The Science and Engineering Directorate actually has an Exobiology and Colonization Section. They have had people planning all of those kinds of things for decades now. I expect we'll be amazed at how quickly we start putting together exploration and colonization missions."

"I don't know about you, Captain, but I'm already getting a little tired of being amazed. I'd be perfectly happy for things to slow down a bit," she sighed as they walked onto *Ingenuity's* bridge.

"Good morning, everyone!" Prescott announced loudly enough to make sure everyone was alert and aware that it was time to get to work. "Sitrep."

"Good morning, Captain, Commander," Lieutenant Commander Schmidt replied, vacating the captain's chair and stepping in the direction of the Science and Engineering console. "We are holding position at L1. Commander Logan reports all systems in the green. Hyperspace or C-Drive transition available with five minutes notice. The threat board is clear. No contacts."

"Very good, Lieutenant Commander Schmidt. It sounds like we are about ready to give this a try."

"Yes, sir. One additional point of interest, Captain," Schmidt said, gesturing to a window on the view screen once again displaying the Yucca Mountain Shipyard facility. "We got word a few minutes ago that Fleet will be launching a number of ships this morning. TFS *Shoshone* is coming out of the shipyard now to execute her first climb to orbit."

"Now *that is* interesting. I hadn't heard there were any ship launches scheduled for today, but that cruiser will definitely be worth watching. Let's go full screen ship-wide and I'll give everyone a quick heads up."

"All hands, this is the captain. I wanted to thank each and every one of you once again for your dedication and hard work, particularly over the past couple of weeks. I know I don't have to tell you that today will be yet another day of historic firsts for *Ingenuity* and for Humanity. I also don't think anyone would have ever predicted that our first manned mission to the nearest star system would be followed minutes later by a near instantaneous trip to another star system nearly six times as far away from Earth, but that's exactly what we have on the agenda for today. Before we get on with our mission, please take a look at a view screen if you can safely do so. Fleet's first operational heavy cruiser, TFS *Shoshone*, is just leaving Yucca Mountain for the first time and we just happen to be on the right side of the planet to have the best seat in the house. That's all for now. Prescott out."

The view of the Amargosa Valley basking in the bright sunshine of an early spring morning was singularly impressive on *Ingenuity's* expansive bridge view screen. This would have been the case even without the spectacle of the enormous warship now slowly exiting the side of Yucca Mountain. TFS *Shoshone* made her debut in truly dramatic fashion, taking nearly three full minutes for her one-kilometer-long hull to emerge from the facility's entrance cavern. Shortly after the ship was clear of the mountain, her bow rose to nearly forty-five degrees above the horizon as her colossal sublight engines and gravitic systems defied the planet's feeble attempts to slow her progress towards the sky. Minutes later, the ship entered a circular orbit roughly four hundred kilometers above the surface. Here, she would spend the next several hours running systems checks to ensure everything was functioning properly before venturing farther from home.

The view from *Ingenuity's* perspective had been truly awe-inspiring; virtually every member of the crew stood transfixed during the entire climb to orbit. Although there was an occasional cheer or round of applause, most who watched did so silently. Many were so overwhelmed with emotion that they struggled to hold back tears. All petty squabbles aside, on this day Humanity stood united as one civilization, ready to take its rightful place among the stars.

"Captain, we are receiving a Flash priority action message addressed directly to you," Lieutenant Dubashi announced from the Communications console.

"Thank you, Dubashi, route it to my terminal please," Prescott replied, authenticating his identity as he seated himself at the Command console.

Within seconds, the Flash traffic appeared on his small screen.

Z0715
TOP SECRET - MAGI PRIME
FM: CINCTFC
TO: TFS INGENUITY
INFO: POSSIBLE HOSTILITIES - SAJETH
COLLECTIVE FORCES

1. RECEIVED COMMUNICATION FROM ADMIRAL NAFTUR VIA AMBSDR TURLAKA. SAJETH SPLINTER GROUP MAY ATTEMPT PREEMPTIVE ATTACK ON EARTH.

2. RENDEZVOUS WITH NAFTUR'S FLAGSHIP GRESAV AT SPECIFIED COORDINATES IN GLIESE 667 C SYSTEM TO OBTAIN DETAILED INTELLIGENCE.
3. SAJETH MUST REMAIN UNAWARE OF C-DRIVE CAPABILITIES.
4. ASSESS SITUATION AND RETURN ASAP.
5. AVOID CONTACT WITH HOSTILE FORCES.
ADM SEXTON SENDS.

"Well then, I guess that explains why Fleet is sortying assets this morning," Prescott said, nodding to Commander Reynolds' console so that she could read the Flash traffic he had just shared. Prescott paused for a moment to collect his thoughts and allow his XO to read the message before continuing. "My first reaction is that this news doesn't fundamentally change our mission this morning, agree?"

"I suppose not, although it's way beyond a hyperdrive test at this point."

"C-Drive," Prescott corrected, smiling in spite of the gravity of the situation.

"You're right, sir, sorry," she laughed, amazed once again how her captain always seemed to find a way to take such jarring news in stride and focus on the task at hand. "Recommend we set General Quarters for combat ops and remain in that state until we return."

"Agree, but let's avoid charging weapons since we're already going to be heavily taxing the power systems. Sexton specifically said to avoid contact, so if we run into anyone, our best bet will most likely be to run anyway."

"Aye, sir. I also want everyone strapped in for this transition, just in case," she replied, issuing the required commands at her terminal. Within seconds, the ship's AI began announcing the modified General Quarters and the lighting on the bridge once again took on an eerie, red hue.

"Lieutenant Dubashi, please acknowledge the Flash message and signal Fleet that we will be departing momentarily."

"Aye, sir."

"Commander Logan, bridge," Prescott announced.

"Logan here. Just reading the Flash traffic you sent over, sir. Wow."

"That about sums it up, Commander. Are we ready to get underway down there?"

"That's affirmative, Captain. Just keep in mind that it could take up to two minutes to bring all of the weapon systems online after we transition. You'll have the missile batteries only. I can prioritize one of the others and have it online within thirty seconds if you are interested."

"That's a pretty easy call, Commander, give me the railguns as quickly as possible. We are unlikely to get into a shooting match on this trip, but if we do, we will probably be purely defensive. Having a point defense capability might make all the difference."

"Done. You can expect them within thirty seconds after you begin charging weapons, but don't expect anything else for a full two minutes after they come online. The sea-whiz railgun and beam emitter emplacements will stay online the entire time, so you'll have close range point defense either way."

"Thanks, Commander. Stand by for our C-Jump out to Alpha Centauri, Prescott out.

"All hands, this is Prescott. I hadn't planned on interrupting you again before our first C-Jump out of the system, but we have received an unexpected and troubling message from Admiral Sexton, our Commander in Chief. Fleet has received credible intelligence indicating that a faction of the Sajeth Collective – that's the group that includes our new friends the Wek – is threatening a preemptive attack on the Earth. I'm not going to try and explain why they might want to do such a thing. Suffice it to say that they see our relationship with the Pelarans as a threat they would prefer to eliminate before we reach the point where they are unable to do so. Now, I'm skirting some highly classified information here, but I want each and every one of you to be confident of one thing: we are already well beyond the point where we can simply be eliminated. Every one of you saw those other ships nearing completion at Yucca Mountain, so that should reassure you that *Ingenuity* is not leaving Earth undefended while we conduct our C-Drive tests. I hope many of you took a few moments to watch TFS *Shoshone's* launch. By the end of the day today, there will be four others just like her in the immediate vicinity of Earth. Three days from now, we will have three full carrier battle groups in space. That's a total of over fifty starships."

Prescott paused for effect, hoping the entire crew looked as surprised and gratified by this news as his XO did right now. "As I've told you before, Humanity has taken its rightful place as an interstellar species and we are here to stay. With any luck, we'll be able to convince our neighbors that we are generally a peaceful civilization and we have absolutely no intention of being a pawn for the Pelarans or anyone else. If, on the other hand, they come to the Sol system looking for an easy fight, Fleet is more than prepared to disappoint them. Now let's get this mission successfully completed and get this game-changing C-Drive technology back to Terran Fleet Command. Prescott out.

"Lieutenant Dubashi, do we have a course plotted for the C-Jump to Alpha Centauri?"

"Aye, sir, course locked and transferred to the Helm console."

"Alright, folks, this is your traditional 'speak now or forever hold your peace' opportunity. Speak up if you have a problem or concern. Let's do a quick rollcall. I need a go or no go from every station starting with Engineering."

"Go, sir."

"Tactical?"

"Go, Captain."

"Helm?"

"Go, Captain."

"Comm/Nav?"

"We're go, sir."

"XO?"

"Go, sir. I'd like to give a ship-wide final warning before we transition, though."

"Do it and let's get the hell out of here," Prescott replied.

"All hands, this is the XO. We are C-Jumping to Alpha Centauri in thirty seconds. All personnel should be restrained at this time. Reynolds out."

Prescott took a final look around the bridge, satisfying himself that everyone was indeed ready. "Alright, Ensign Fisher, it's your show once again. We keep hearing about the slick user interface for the C-Drive, so feel free to put it up in a window on the screen."

"I would be happy to do that, Captain, but why don't I show you that separately. I don't want to take any real estate on the view screen. In the sim, at least, the external view is just about the coolest thing I've ever seen."

"Well, how can I argue with an endorsement like that?" Prescott laughed. "Please proceed when ready."

The starfield on the enormous, wrap-around bridge view screen slewed to starboard as Fisher oriented the ship in the direction of Alpha Centauri. With the maneuver completed, the view screen was now centered on what appeared to be a single, very bright star, surrounded on the screen by the now familiar set of green brackets used to indicate the ship's next waypoint.

"Okay sir, as you know, the view screen combines inputs from a variety of different sensor types to produce a visual representation of the space around the ship. Most of the time, what we are seeing is provided almost exclusively by plain old optical sensors. If you were to stand outside on the hull, you'd see pretty much the same thing we do in here. For the C-Drive, however, the UI designers wanted to keep the bridge view screen displaying a consistent picture rather than an abrupt change from one view to the other. I just wanted to warn everyone that on such a huge screen, it can be a little disorienting if you aren't expecting it."

"Understood, Ensign, thank you. Let's get to it," Prescott replied, trying his level best not to sound impatient with his earnest young helmsman.

"Alright, sir, here we go," Fisher said, excitedly executing the final set of commands at the Helm console.

The ship AI's synthetic voice immediately began a ship-wide countdown. "Capacitive hyperdrive engaged, transition in 3 … 2 … 1 …"

On the bridge view screen, most of the background stars moved very little, if at all, but the bright star in the center of the screen smoothly transitioned from a single pinpoint of light to two, then three separate stars. The smallest of the three, a reddish star labeled "α Cen C – Proxima" by the AI quickly moved out of view at the bottom of the screen. The brightest, and obviously largest of the three stars remained fixed in the center of the screen, while its smaller companion moved rapidly to the lower right side. The AI labeled these two stars "α Cen A" and "α Cen B," respectively. Each star was also displayed with an accompanying block of text providing additional data including stellar mass, radius, and luminosity relative to Sol.

"Yup, Fisher, I'll grant you that was the coolest damn thing I've ever seen, by a long shot, actually," Prescott said, exhaling sharply after involuntarily holding his breath during the transition. "Report."

"Transition complete, Captain. The nav system is a little slow after our first C-Jump, so I don't have precise coordinates yet, but I can confirm that we have arrived at the Alpha Centauri star system," Lieutenant Dubashi announced. "All systems reporting in the green. No damage or injuries reported. The sublight engines are still offline, pending the next transition. Ah, I have our position now as seven hundred fifty meters from the expected arrival point."

"Not as accurate as a standard hyperspace transition, but I think we can live with that, for now. I'm assuming the data we bring back will improve the AI's calculations quite a bit. Tactical?"

"The threat board is clear, Captain, no contacts," Lieutenant Lau responded.

"Very good. Until we're back in the Sol system, I want to hear about anything you detect immediately."

"Aye, sir, will do."

"Lieutenant Commander Schmidt, I assume you are pulling in as much data as possible for the Science and Engineering Directorate folks."

"Yes, sir. I guess I shouldn't be surprised, but we've been here less than five minutes and I've already seen at least ten items that are being catalogued as new discoveries. As expected, there are no planets in orbit around the primary star, that's Alpha Centauri A in the center of the view screen. The secondary, Alpha Centauri B," Schmidt nodded to the smaller star near the lower right edge of the view screen, "has two rocky planets orbiting very close to the star. As expected, no life signs on either one."

"It's beautiful, alright," Reynolds observed, "but if I had been on one of those generational starships they always talked about and it took sixty years to get here, I think I'd be pretty pissed off right about now."

"Ha! I guess you would, considering you'd be long dead before you either gave up and went back to Earth or, worse, continued on to the next star system with a potentially habitable planet. As far as I know, that's Ross 128, which is still a good six or seven light years from here. There's a lot of speculation that Earth's distance from other habitable planets is one of the reasons the Pelarans chose us for cultivation. Security through obscurity, I guess."

"Bridge, Engineering."

"Prescott here. Go ahead, Commander."

"Everything was looking pretty good at first after the C-Jump, Captain, but it turns out that our new capacitor banks didn't perform up to specs. That short transition used over twenty percent of the power in the dedicated hyperdrive banks. That's more than double what we expected. The good news is that it should be a relatively straightforward fix back at the shipyard. The bad news is that we are going to be short on power until that happens. You should assume our maximum C-Jump range is only about twenty light years for now."

"We're still nearly twenty light years from our next destination, Commander. If we make the next C-Jump, what are the implications for power availability after we arrive?"

"I wouldn't count on much, Captain. We'll run the reactors at full power to recharge as fast as we can, but I doubt we'll even be capable of a standard hyperspace transition, let alone a C-Jump for at least ten minutes or so. That will increase to twenty minutes plus if we charge the railguns as we discussed earlier. Full power should be available within an hour or so, but it's not clear we'll be able to make it all the way back to Earth without another recharge along the way. I'll have better data after the next transition."

"Understood. Make recharging the cap banks as quickly as possible the number one priority after the next C-Jump. If we're in system long enough, go for the railguns next. Our orders are to get in and out as quickly as possible, so I'm hoping we won't be there for much over an hour. How much time do you need here in Alpha Centauri to get us back to full power?"

"Looks like about fifteen more minutes if we hold our current position with no other systems online. If we need to leave in a hurry, you can transition again before then, just keep it short range. I have modified Ensign Fisher's Helm console display to give accurate range readings based on the reduced power availability."

"Very good. Thank you, Commander. Prescott out."

"Ensign Fisher, I think now is a good time to display that new C-Drive interface on the view screen. Let's have it on the far right side, please."

"Aye, sir," Fisher replied. "I think this is the part you are interested in."

Fisher keyed in a sequence of commands, superimposing a semi-transparent bar graph on the starboard view screen. At the moment, the bottom portion of the graph displayed a slowly increasing C-Jump range of 17.35 light years. The top of the graph indicated that the standard one light year emergency reserve was also available as was a standard hyperspace transition. A simple timer in one corner counted down the time remaining until full power was available.

"Thank you, Ensign. I love it. It's clear and self-explanatory."

"Yes, sir. I actually got to work with the UI team on this new screen. They spend huge amounts of time getting this kind of thing just right."

"My compliments to you and the team then. When we get some time, I'd like us to sit down with Commander Reynolds and discuss some different UI configurations for specific situations, especially combat ops."

"Absolutely, sir, it would be my pleasure," Fisher replied enthusiastically.

Prescott paused to collect his thoughts and consider what he was likely to learn from Admiral Naftur. He had read the Fleet Intelligence Estimate based on Admiral Sexton's discussions with Ambassador Turlaka just last week. There were several unsettling items in the report, but there didn't seem to be any indication of an imminent attack. What had changed during the past few days that now had Fleet operating on a war footing? He was considering how precarious it would be dealing with a powerful enemy like the Sajeth Collective if they had indeed split into multiple factions when he noticed Commander Reynolds staring at him.

"Sorry to interrupt your train of thought, Captain. I was thinking I should make an announcement to let everyone know what's going on. That might ease the tension a bit, but still keep people on their toes," she said.

"No, that's okay, Commander, and an announcement is a good idea. Honestly," he said, lowering his voice so that only she could hear, "I keep having this feeling that we are riding the crest of some sort of unstoppable historical wave. It's as if all the events of the past several centuries are converging at this time and place – and we're caught right in the middle of it. It's disconcerting, to say the least."

"I understand what you are saying, but I wonder if it ever feels any different for people who just happen to end up in the right place at the right time, if you know what I mean. I've read lots of biographies over the years, and I remember a number of them expressing something similar. I think those of us who find ourselves caught in upheavals of one sort or another really have no choice other than doing the absolute best we can with the resources we have at our disposal. Granted, the scope of what we're experiencing right now seems a little, uh, overwhelming, but don't you think leaders throughout history experienced those same feelings when their time came?"

"I suppose that's true, and I agree that's the right attitude to have, do the best you can and let history be the judge. You do have to admit, however, that the potential consequences of what we're doing right now are a little mind boggling."

"Maybe so, but how much of the true big picture can any one individual be responsible for anyway? I think the bottom line for the two of us is exactly the same as it's been every day of our careers so far – don't screw it up and you have nothing to worry about."

Chapter 13

Wek Flagship Gresav, Near Gliese 667 Cc
(24 light years from Earth)

The *Gresav* emerged from hyperspace in preparation for her rendezvous with TFS *Ingenuity* and immediately began extensive sensor scans of the system. Over the past twenty-four hours, Admiral Naftur had ordered a seemingly random series of hyperspace transitions in an effort to thwart any attempts to track his ship's movements.

The political and military situation within the Sajeth Collective had become unpredictable and extremely dangerous for both the organization's membership and their potential adversaries alike. The exact series of events leading up to the current situation was unclear. It was all too obvious, however, that Wek influence over military operations had been diminished to the point where they were no longer in control of a significant portion of the Sajeth fleet. Naftur had voiced concerns for years that sensitive intelligence information gathered by Wek assets should be reviewed by their own analysts before being shared with other members of the Collective. His warnings had typically been met with either cool indifference or outright hostility that he would dare question his world's adherence to the alliance charter. Now it appeared that information he had been gathering for months regarding the Pelarans' Guardian spacecraft had been released to the Sajeth Collective's Governing Council. The more aggressive member species, notably the Damarans, immediately began touting the Guardian spacecraft's newfound "vulnerabilities" as an unprecedented opportunity for a preemptive strike. Naftur did agree in principle that there would soon be an opportunity to achieve some measure of military success against the Pelarans. What he found unacceptable was using the situation as a pretext for war against the Terrans, who had, so far at least, committed no offense other than being selected for Pelaran cultivation. On a personal level, the admiral also found it particularly infuriating that the Damarans, who contributed virtually nothing in the way of military assets to the Collective, were so quick to advocate the aggressive use of military force.

In any event, over the past forty-eight hours, a splinter group calling themselves "The Pelaran Resistance" had made it clear that they would accept nothing less than an attack on Earth. They insisted that thousands of years of history left no viable alternative. If the Humans were allowed to continue their rapid technological and military advancement under Pelaran cultivation, this entire region of the galaxy would eventually fall under their dominance.

Admiral Naftur was generally philosophical about most of the political posturing and saber rattling that took place within the Sajeth Collective. Warfare would occur, as it always did, regardless of which paths the various players elected to follow. What mattered, ultimately the only thing that mattered, was whether those players conducted themselves with integrity and honor. The rest, as they say, would take care of itself. For his part, he saw absolutely no moral grey area that might have allowed him to maintain some form of neutrality in the coming conflict. He would throw his full support, and that of his flagship, behind the faction advocating alliance with the Humans and warfare against the true aggressors, the Pelaran Alliance. The fact that this might ultimately prove a futile course of action further clarified in his mind that this was indeed the right choice – the easiest path rarely being the correct one in his experience.

Besides, he had a suspicion that the Humans were already well beyond the point of being the soft target expected by the hastily preparing forces of The Pelaran Resistance. The site of this rendezvous alone led him to believe that they were far more advanced than previously thought. The cultivated races tended to have powerful and reliable weapon systems and, perhaps more importantly, incredible power generation systems, but their ships were typically not as fast as those of the Sajeth Collective. All of the data he had seen so far put their top speed at five hundred times the speed of light. At that speed, the Sol system was eighteen days from here, yet it had only been just over three weeks since his first encounter with the Human starship. It seemed highly unlikely they had been traveling to this specific location during most of the intervening time. He sat for a moment, wondering how he might best advise Captain Prescott and whether the Terran leadership would have granted the young captain sufficient latitude to discuss military strategy in detail. His thoughts were interrupted by the arrival of two new starships in system, neither of which were of Human origin.

TFS Ingenuity, Near Gliese 667 Cc

(30 minutes later – 24 light years from Earth)

"Transition complete, Captain," Lieutenant Dubashi announced. "All systems in the green. No damage or injuries reported. The sublight engines are offline, pending recharge for the C-Jump back to Earth. We are 5.3 kilometers from our expected arrival point."

"Contacts!" Lieutenant Lau yelled from the Tactical console. "I've got three ships, sir. Range to all three is about three hundred thousand kilometers. The AI has identified one as the *Gresav*, but one of the other two must be of the same class. The third vessel is similar to one of the Sajeth Collective ships destroyed near Sol a few weeks ago. She's big, Captain, seven hundred meters plus."

Prescott instinctively glanced at the readout from the Helm console still displayed on the starboard view screen. As expected, the news it delivered was not encouraging. The graph indicating C-Jump range was entirely red with flags indicating that neither type of hyperspace transition was currently available. The time to full power countdown displayed a painfully long sixty-three minutes remaining. His immediate thought, per Admiral Sexton's orders, had been to run, and under ordinary circumstances, he should have been able to do just that. Instead, he was faced with the choice of either sitting idly for the next ten minutes until he could transition out of the system, or bringing his sublight engines and weapon systems online as quickly as possible and playing the situation out for better or worse.

"Steady everyone. Let's not jump to any conclusions just yet," he said aloud, addressing himself as much as the members of his bridge crew.

"Sir, Gresav is hailing via secure channel – audio only," Dubashi said.

"Put it through, please."

After a very brief delay during which the ship's AI established an encrypted channel and synchronized for real-time translation, Admiral Naftur's deep voice once again filled *Ingenuity's* bridge. "Hello again, Captain Prescott. I apologize for not providing a video signal, but the comm system we are using is less prone to eavesdropping. Unfortunately, it is rather primitive otherwise, and provides audio only. I assume we will be jammed shortly, so we must keep our conversation short."

The Wek's rather formal conversation style coupled with their species' prolific use of nonverbal communication cues did not lend itself to short conversations. Prescott smiled inwardly at the irony. "Hello again, Admiral. I take it the other two Sajeth Collective vessels are hostiles, then."

"I had hoped I would be able to reason with their commanders, but my efforts have been unsuccessful thus far. It seems I have been betrayed. These two vessels represent the breakaway faction of the Sajeth Collective calling themselves 'The Pelaran Resistance.' As you probably know by now, they have announced their intention to conduct a preemptive military strike on Earth. Although the captains of these two vessels see me as something of a traitor at this point, I have served with both of them previously and have been negotiating with them for the past half-hour. As you might imagine, they are demanding our immediate surrender. I convinced them to allow me a few minutes to implore you that you need not throw your crew's lives away unnecessarily. May I assume, Captain, that surrender is not a course of action you are willing to discuss?"

"You may indeed, Admiral," Prescott replied, forcing a smile in hopes that his confidence would be apparent in the sound of his voice. "What are your recommendations, sir?"

"I'm an old soldier, Captain, and I did not become an old soldier by fighting when the odds are not in my favor. My preference would be for us to disengage from these two ships, by whatever means necessary, and then proceed to the 70 Ophiuchi system roughly eight light years away. I cannot guarantee they will not be able to follow us since I do not know how they learned of my destination in the first place. I believe, however, that 70 Ophiuchi should afford us sufficient time to discuss the situation. By the way, my tactical officer informs me that we are reading a very high power output from your ship's reactors. Are you experiencing difficulty?"

Prescott considered for an instant that this entire encounter might be a setup, but dismissed the idea based on the fact that his gut had told him from their first meeting that Admiral Naftur was worthy of his trust. In any event, the longer he talked, the closer he was to making his escape, if necessary. "We have run into a configuration problem with our hyperdrive. Unfortunately, we will be unable to transition for another fifteen minutes," he exaggerated. "We will need even more time than that if we are required to power our weapon systems and sublight engines."

"Captain," Lieutenant Lau interrupted, "I'm getting unusual energy readings from the other two vessels. I think they are raising their shields, sir."

"That is indeed unfortunate," Naftur continued, seemingly unfazed by the escalating situation. "Your officer is correct, the two vessels have raised their shields. They are unlikely to grant us fifteen minutes without firing on both of our ships. If we do find ourselves in battle, I must stress to you the importance of preventing these ships from escaping to warn the rest of their fleet. We must completely destroy them both."

Prescott shot a quick glance at Lieutenant Dubashi, jerking his hand across his neck in a signal to temporarily mute the comlink. She nodded back instantly in reply. "Schmidt, signal Flight Ops to expect a green deck shortly. Once the shooting starts, get all eight *Hunters* airborne immediately. I want you to unload everything you've got on that second *Gresav*-class ship just like you did on the range."

"Aye, Captain."

"XO, signal Engineering to ignore the C-Drive. Bring the sublight engines online and charge weapons in the order we discussed."

"Aye, sir."

Prescott nodded once again at Lieutenant Dubashi to reopen the channel. "Understood, Admiral. We're preparing for a fight over here. Any recommendations would be appreciated."

Even over the encrypted comlink, Naftur's voice was now accompanied by an unmistakably threatening growl.

"We have a few advantages we might be able to exploit. They will be under orders to destroy the *Gresav*, but capture your vessel intact, if possible. In all likelihood, they will not see *Ingenuity* as much of a threat at first and will focus their attention on the *Gresav*. If and when they do fire on you, they will attempt to disable your engines first. Both of these young captains are young and arrogant. If they neglected to read my report carefully, they may not realize that your ship's engines are protected inside its hull. That may only give you a few seconds of opportunity, so use them wisely. One last thing, their shields are weakest near the stern and there is a gap …"

"Transmission terminated, Captain," Dubashi reported. "There is high intensity jamming from the second *Gresav*-class vessel."

"Well, that's a sure sign the negotiations are over. XO, sound an unmodified General Quarters for combat ops. Lieutenant Lau, designate the second *Gresav* as Delta 1, the larger vessel as Charlie 1, and bring up the tactical plot on the starboard view screen."

"Aye, sir. Be advised that range bubbles on the plot will be estimates only."

"Understood, thank you." Prescott had never been a fan of the tactical plot, but he acknowledged that the information it had provided Commander Reynolds during the range exercise had been invaluable. In a fight against superior forces, you had to take whatever advantages you could find and he was never opposed to learning a better way of doing his job. Both hostile ships were now displayed in an angry shade of red, with *Ingenuity* well inside their estimated weapons range.

"Tactical, you heard what the admiral said about shields near their stern. He was trying to tell us something else when he got cut off. My guess is that there is a dead zone between their hull and their shields astern related to their sublight engine nozzles. If that's the case, it's a perfect opportunity for the C-Drive-equipped missiles. Just to be clear, *Ingenuity* will engage the cruiser, Charlie 1, while the *Hunters* assist the *Gresav* in taking down the destroyer, Delta 1. Questions?"

"No, sir," both Lau and Schmidt replied in unison.

"Sir," Lau continued, "the hyperdrive is secured. Sublight engines online, we are free to maneuver. Railguns now online in anti-ship mode. Missile tubes configured for anti-ship. Energy weapons available in four zero seconds."

"That's all good news. Just keep in mind that we are likely to remain power deficient throughout this engagement. If we're firing energy weapons, particularly the plasma torps, we need to make every shot count."

"Sir!" Lau yelled. "Energy spike on both hostiles — they are firing on the *Gresav*!"

"Green Deck, Schmidt. Get those RPSVs airborne. Helm, move us to within weapon's range. Use our maneuverability to complicate their targeting and don't wait for me to tell you if you need to take evasive action."

The tactical plot displayed on the starboard view screen now flashed continually with energy weapons fire. Just as Admiral Naftur predicted, the two enemy warships were ignoring *Ingenuity* for the moment and appeared to be attempting to isolate her from the *Gresav*.

"*Gresav* is maneuvering, sir," Lieutenant Lau announced. "I think she's headed our way. There's a huge amount of energy weapons fire, but I'm not reading much in the way of damage on any of the ships so far."

"They have shields, Lieutenant, we don't. If we let them hit us the way they're hitting the *Gresav* right now, we won't last long."

"All eight *Hunters* outbound, Captain," Schmidt said. "The AI is set for a coordinated anti-ship strike on Delta 1."

"Very good. Since we have no idea how effective their shields are against our weapons, let's try a probing attack first. Give them a volley of missile fire from astern, if possible. I'd say one missile from each RPSV will tell us everything we need to know. Don't risk them unnecessarily, Schmidt. Hit and run for now."

"Executing now, sir."

Lieutenant Commander Schmidt issued a series of commands at his console, forcing the AI to modify its attack profile per the captain's orders. Although the probing attack was not expected to do much, if any, damage to the destroyer, the AI's indication of a sixteen percent probability of success was still discouraging.

Already well within missile range of the enemy vessels, the RPSVs split into two, four-ship formations, each of which veered off sharply in opposing directions while simultaneously climbing above the plane of the enemy ships.

"Directed energy weapons online, Captain!" Lau reported excitedly from Tactical. "We'll be in range in one zero seconds."

Although not nearly as maneuverable as the much smaller *Ingenuity*, Admiral Naftur was making the most of his ship's capabilities. Shortly after the enemy vessels opened fire, he rolled the destroyer onto its back before diving below the pursuing enemy vessels. *Gresav's* six massive sublight engine nozzles blazed forth with a brilliant blue glow as energy weapons fire issued from what looked like hundreds of locations along the entire length of her hull. The maneuver had the immediate effect of taking the huge enemy cruiser out of the fight, her primary weapons arrays no longer in a position to target the *Gresav*.

Commander Reynolds had been rapidly shifting her attention between the tactical plot and a customized, three-dimensional model of the battlespace displayed on her console. She recognized the admiral's strategy almost immediately. "Sir, Charlie 1 is like a classic line of battle ship. Her primary weapons have a limited field of fire. The AI is still defining the boundaries, but we should be able to prevent her from ever getting a firing solution. Transferring the data to the Helm and Tactical consoles."

"Excellent work, Commander. Ensign Fisher, get us a clear shot at Charlie 1's stern while staying out of her field of fire as much as possible. That ship was probably designed for much longer range engagements. If that's the case, I doubt they can retarget their main guns very quickly, but their secondary weapons might be more agile, so try to keep them guessing."

Above the enemy formation, the two groups of *Hunter* RPSVs had a clear view of Delta 1's stern as she dove in pursuit of her sister ship. All eight fighters simultaneously fired a single HB-7 missile before executing a series of aggressive maneuvers designed to avoid being targeted by the enemy vessels.

"Eight missiles away, Captain," Schmidt reported. "Impact in one zero seconds."

"I'm guessing that will get their attention," Prescott observed. "Lieutenant Lau, I need you to do the same thing Schmidt is doing with the missiles. Hit them near the stern with at least one of every weapons type and let the AI chew on the battle damage assessment. Fire as soon as we are in position."

"Aye, Captain. I should have a clear shot in a few more seconds."

"Commander Reynolds, give me a tactical assessment of both enemy ships on the port view screen."

Ingenuity's AI continuously gathered and analyzed tremendous amounts of data from her multitude of sensors. During combat ops, however, the process was intensified to such a degree that very little measurable information went unnoticed. A window now opened on the left end of the bridge view screen displaying multiple views of each enemy ship with potential vulnerabilities highlighted. So far, Charlie 1 showed only the limited firing envelope of her main weapons. Unfortunately, the AI had yet to discover a single vulnerability for Delta 1.

"All eight missiles destroyed, Captain," Schmidt reported. "It looks like the shields actually cooked off the warheads, so there were explosions, but no obvious damage to Delta 1. I also saw no point defense weapons fire of any kind."

"Firing all weapons in sequence, Captain," Lieutenant Lau interrupted from Tactical before Prescott could respond to the RPSV attack on Charlie 1.

As *Ingenuity* banked to avoid the cruiser's field of fire, Lau initiated a probing attack with each weapon system in turn, starting with the ship's energy cannons and ending with a salvo from her four primary railgun turrets. At this range, each of the frigate's munitions types impacted the target's stern shields almost instantaneously.

"Captain, I'm seeing hull impacts from the kinetic energy rounds. They went right through her shields!"

"Fire at will, Lieutenant," Prescott replied, just as surprised as his tactical officer. "Disable her engines if you can."

Commander Reynolds nodded to the side view of Charlie 1 on the tactical assessment display. "We only saw a slight fluctuation in her shields from our plasma torpedoes, but look at the lobing pattern near the engine nozzles."

Ingenuity's energy weapons fire had provided the AI with a wealth of information regarding the cruiser's defensive capabilities. In addition to the target's limited field of fire, the tactical assessment now displayed two additional vulnerabilities – kinetic energy weapons fire as well as the elongated shape of her aft shields.

"That has to be what the admiral was talking about. For whatever reason, they are forced to stretch their aft shields well beyond their sublight engine nozzles. That should decrease the field strength quite a bit." Prescott paused as he noted a change in the tactical assessment for Delta 1 as well. "In case we needed more proof, there's the exact same pattern on Delta 1. Is there enough room in there for a C-Drive missile strike?"

"Plenty of room on the cruiser, yes. The gap is smaller on the destroyer, but according to the specs we were provided, the missiles should still be able to get in there. I think it's worth a try in both cases. Our railguns alone probably won't be enough," Reynolds said.

"Lau and Schmidt have their hands full at the moment; can you handle the missile prep and launch? I'd like ten out of our sixteen targeting Charlie 1's engines."

"Absolutely. I need us to back off a bit before the next attack run, though. I want to minimize the potential for the missiles to be intercepted, but they still need time to accelerate before they make their C-Jump."

"Did you hear that, Fisher?" Prescott asked.

"On it, sir."

"Schmidt, keep the RPSVs out of harm's way for the moment, but put together an anti-ship profile option on Charlie 1. If we manage to hit her with our C-Drive missiles, her shields may drop. That may be our best chance of taking her out."

"Will do, Captain."

All four of *Ingenuity's* railgun turrets continued to send a steady stream of kinetic energy penetration rounds into one of the cruiser's huge sublight engines. As the frigate made a sweeping turn to open the distance to her target, the guns momentarily lost their solution and ceased firing just as Charlie 1's battered engine nozzle exploded.

"Targeted engine destroyed!" Lau exclaimed. "There were a couple of secondary explosions and it looks like the nozzle right next to it is offline as well. Their shields temporarily dropped by thirty percent, but have already started to recover."

Prescott felt the hair stand on the back of his neck. *There's no way they can afford to ignore us now*, he thought, glancing at the tactical plot. *If they consider us a real threat, it makes sense to destroy us first.*

As if reading his thoughts, Delta 1 broke off their pursuit of the *Gresav* and began a turn in their direction. Within seconds, the space between the two ships was streaked with energy weapons fire.

Ensign Fisher reacted instinctively, pushing the ship into a steep dive below most of the incoming fire. The frigate shook with multiple impacts, each of which vaporized sections of her outermost armor. At this range, however, Delta 1's beam weapons were unable to penetrate the ship's multiple armor layers protecting her inner hull. For the moment at least, *Ingenuity* was holding together.

"We need to finish this quickly, folks," Prescott said in the most matter of fact tone he could manage. "We have a plan in motion, all you need to worry about right now is executing the plan."

Ensign Fisher randomly altered the frigate's course as he accelerated away from the cruiser's stern at maximum power. The approaching destroyer still blazed away with their energy weapons, but appeared to be having a difficult time tracking *Ingenuity's* unpredictable flight path.

"Ten C-Drive missiles ready to fire," Reynolds announced. Hearing no response, she glanced in Prescott's direction.

He gave her an unmistakably piratical grin as he nodded towards the starboard view screen and said simply, "C-Jump."

The graph indicating C-Jump range was now displayed in green with a range of 3.2 light years plus the standard one light year emergency reserve in red. Full power would still not be available for forty-five minutes, but that was of little consequence at the moment. Reynolds turned back to her captain wearing a similar look of satisfaction.

"Helm, at the end of this attack run, I want you to be ready to execute an escape C-Jump straight ahead on my mark, but dial it back to just one light minute," Prescott ordered. "There's no need to waste our power on a long jump, we just want to get clear of the fight and reenter on our own terms."

"Aye, sir!" Ensign Fisher replied with obvious relief in his voice. For the past few minutes, he had been far too busy avoiding enemy fire to notice that the C-Drive had once again become available. Now, with significantly more confidence than he had felt just a few minutes earlier, he pulled *Ingenuity* into a tight Immelmann turn and headed back in the direction of Charlie 1.

On the frigate's dorsal hull, ten C-Drive-equipped missiles ripple-fired from their vertical launch cells. After momentarily flying perpendicular to the ship's path, the missiles arced over and accelerated rapidly towards the now distant cruiser.

"Missiles away," Reynolds reported. "Delta 1 has shifted her energy weapons fire to attempt an intercept."

"Hopefully, they are about to be disappointed," Prescott replied, smiling.

Downrange, all ten missiles simply disappeared, followed immediately by a series of massive explosions across the cruiser's stern.

"Multiple impacts!" Lieutenant Lau roared. "Charlie 1 has completely lost power. They are adrift with shields down!"

"Fire plasma torpedoes. Schmidt, execute your attack," Prescott ordered.

Anticipating the captain's timing, Lieutenant Commander Schmidt had already turned the two formations of RPSV's in the direction of Charlie 1 at the same moment *Ingenuity* began her attack run. The ship's AI had updated his console less than one second after the cruiser's shields had dropped, improving the probability of success for the recommended anti-ship attack profile from twelve to ninety-seven percent. Although not a particularly superstitious man, Schmidt was gratified to see that the *Hunters* would fire forty-eight HB-7 missiles, just as they had done so successfully at the range only two days prior.

Within seconds, a swarm of missiles and plasma torpedoes was racing towards preselected targets all along the cruiser's now vulnerable hull. At the same moment, *Ingenuity* came under renewed heavy fire from Delta 1, which was now approaching the optimal range for its beam emitters. The sound of the frigate's hull being taken apart by an ever-increasing hail of energy weapons fire rose to a thundering roar.

"Fisher, emergency C-Jump!" Prescott yelled.

Chapter 14

TFS Ingenuity, Near Gliese 667 Cc
(24 light years from Earth)

Silence engulfed the bridge. The change was so abrupt that it startled every member of the crew, causing most to take in a deep breath while struggling to refocus on the task at hand.

"Report," Captain Prescott said in a decidedly more calm voice than he had used seconds earlier.

"Transition complete. Captain. We are one light minute – eighteen million kilometers – downrange from the battle area," Lieutenant Dubashi responded. "All systems reporting in the green. We have sustained moderate damage to the outer hull, but no further penetrations or breaches reported. No injuries reported. Sublight engines are still offline, pending the next transition. Both standard and C-Drive transitions are available. C-Jump range now 5.4 light years and increasing steadily."

"Excellent job so far everyone, and I know that because we are still alive," Prescott smiled. "Those two ships expected us to be unarmed, or at least of little tactical consequence. Dubashi, can you put our optical sensors on Charlie 1? The light from our attack run should be reaching us shortly."

The bridge view screen immediately transitioned from an otherwise empty starfield centered on the red-hued Gliese 667 C star back to a remarkably clear view of Charlie 1. Within a few seconds, the stern of the ship flared brightly as *Ingenuity's* C-Drive-equipped missiles completely destroyed all six of her remaining sublight engines. All weapons fire from the cruiser ceased immediately as she began a slow rotation to starboard, clearly adrift and without power. A renewed burst of energy weapons fire well aft of the cruiser highlighted the locations of the approaching enemy destroyer as well as *Ingenuity* as she completed her attack run on the cruiser.

"That's us!" Ensign Fisher exclaimed in a louder voice than he intended. "This is some seriously weird shit."

Prescott, along with everyone else on the bridge, laughed in spite of the obvious breach of military discipline. "Alright everyone, hopefully we're about to see some even better news. Let's refocus and get ready to put this ship back in the fight."

As if on cue, the cruiser's stern once again flared brilliantly on the screen as *Ingenuity's* plasma torpedoes scored direct hits to the already heavily damaged hull beneath the ship's sublight engine nozzles. Multiple secondary explosions could be seen as the vessel's propulsion and engineering spaces vented propellant and oxygen to space.

"I'd say she's out of the fight for now at least," Commander Reynolds commented.

Before Prescott could respond, a tremendous series of explosions erupted down the entire length of the cruiser's hull as all forty-eight of Lieutenant Schmidt's HB-7 missiles found their mark. Although most of the ship remained in one piece, fully a third of the anti-ship missiles penetrated through to her internal spaces before detonating their compact antimatter warheads. The resulting explosions could be seen exiting the ship on the opposite side of the hull from their points of entry. Gaping, charred holes were now visible in multiple locations, all of which vented gases, debris, and bodies into the vacuum of space. The lifeless warship was now spinning slowly around all three of her axes as she continued to drift along her previous course.

For the second time, there was a brief period of grave silence on *Ingenuity's* bridge as each crewmember struggled to reconcile their feelings of elation while recognizing the tremendous loss of life aboard the cruiser.

"Charlie 1 destroyed, Captain," Lieutenant Lau reported solemnly from the Tactical console. "*Gresav* is, or was, still engaged with Delta 1."

"Alright everyone, the tactical assessment for Delta 1 shows that her aft shields have a very similar configuration to those of the cruiser. We have six C-Drive-equipped missiles remaining, so our tactics will be the same as before. We need to get the ship in a position to fire the missiles so that they have a little time to accelerate before C-Jumping inside the destroyer's shields. Lieutenant Lau, hammer the hell out of them with the railguns. If their shields drop, do the same with our energy weapons. Your priority will still be their engines."

"Aye, Captain."

"Schmidt, get your birds back online as fast as possible and keep an updated attack profile ready to execute. You've got, what, eight missiles remaining?"

"Yes, sir."

"Very good. Don't bother firing unless their shields drop. Once they do, execute your attack immediately. I'd also prefer not to lose any of our RPSVs, so avoid close range attacks. I suspect we'll be needing them again very soon."

"Aye, sir."

"We've learned some important lessons about Sajeth Collective ships today, but we still know precious little about their true capabilities. Admiral Naftur has said more than once that the *Gresav* is their most advanced warship design, so Delta 1 probably has a few tricks we haven't seen yet. Look sharp and let's get this fight over with so we can get back home. Helm, make your best guess on all three ships' current positions and C-Jump us as close as possible without transitioning us inside one of them."

"Will do, Captain."

"All hands, this is Prescott. As I'm sure you all know by now, we destroyed the enemy cruiser. We're now preparing to C-Jump back into the combat zone and finish off the destroyer. All personnel should remain at General Quarters for combat ops and prepare for incoming fire. Prescott out."

"Ensign Fisher, execute your C-Jump when ready."

"Aye, Captain, executing now."

Without delay, the AI's synthetic voice began a ship-wide countdown. "Capacitive hyperdrive engaged, transition in 3 … 2 … 1 …"

With the return course laid in, the bridge view screen displayed green waypoint brackets around what looked from here like a very bright star or small moon, but was labeled as the planet Gliese 667 Cc. As the hyperdrive engaged, there was no apparent movement of the background stars, but the planet quickly increased in size, once again revealing its Earth-like appearance.

"Contacts," Lieutenant Lau announced from the Tactical console. "I have all three ships. The *Gresav* and Delta 1 are at fifty thousand kilometers. Neither ship appears to have taken much damage so far, sir."

Without prompting, Ensign Fisher banked the ship in the direction of the ongoing duel between the two destroyers, angling his course to put *Ingenuity* astern of Delta 1.

"Captain, we are receiving a laser comlink signal from the *Gresav*," Lieutenant Dubashi announced. "Audio and video this time."

"On-screen, please."

"Aye, sir, opening channel."

A smaller window opened on the view screen so as not to obscure the view of the battlespace. Prescott was surprised by his immediate impression of Admiral Naftur. He looked energized, vigorous, and fully within his element. Prescott had no idea how Wek appearance changed with age, but by Human standards, he looked ten years younger than he had during their first meeting.

"How can we be of assistance, Admiral?"

"An hour ago, I would have urged you to keep your ship clear," Naftur said with what looked like a conspiratorial smile. "Now, I welcome whatever assistance you can provide. Their shields have been intermittent for the past few minutes. With sustained fire, I believe we will be able to bring them down completely. Be cautious, they will no longer hesitate to destroy your ship."

"Understood, Admiral. Prescott out."

"Were they hesitating to destroy us before?" Reynolds remarked under her breath.

"Missile launch!" Lieutenant Lau yelled from Tactical. "Eight missiles, Captain. *Gresav* is too close, so they must be headed our way. Capabilities unknown. Estimated time to impact, two five seconds."

"Launch countermeasures. Evasive action. All weapons to point-defense mode," Prescott responded instantly.

"Captain, the *Hunters* have an intercept solution," Lieutenant Commander Schmidt reported.

"Do it!"

Ensign Fisher kept the ship moving in the same direction as before, but now pushed the Cannae sublight engines to emergency power, temporarily allowing them to deliver twenty percent more thrust than their design maximum. *Ingenuity* streaked away from the destroyer, accelerating at a rate nearly half that of the inbound missiles. Every member of the crew struggled to continue executing their assigned tasks as the frigate's inertial dampening system lagged well behind her dramatic acceleration curve.

Back in the direction of Delta 1, the two, four-ship RPSV formations rapidly closed the distance to the oncoming missiles. They approached from both above and below the missiles' flightpath to avoid the deadly curtain of point defense weapons fire now streaming from *Ingenuity*. Already too close to utilize the intercept capabilities of their remaining HB-7 missiles, all eight *Hunters* opened up with their railgun turrets. Although the point in space and time where the kinetic energy rounds intersected the missiles' flightpath was incredibly small, the RPSVs still manage to score three kills.

"Three missiles destroyed, sir," Lau reported. "Five still inbound. Revised time to impact, two eight seconds. None of them are going after the decoys."

"Commander Reynolds, the *Gresav* is still keeping our target heavily engaged. If you think you have a shot with the C-Drive missiles, take it," Prescott ordered.

"Aye sir. There's a high probability of intercept at this angle, but their shields are down to thirty percent and intermittent."

"In that case, send them a volley of eight standard missiles just like they sent us. I want them playing defense – and it just might be enough to finish off their shields."

"Three more missiles down, sir!" Lau reported. "Seawhiz now engaging the last two."

"Missiles away!" Reynolds exclaimed, a hint of fear in her voice for the first time.

As the destroyer's last two anti-ship missiles rapidly closed the remaining distance, their sensors were momentarily confused by the eight missiles launching from *Ingenuity's* vertical launch cells. Programmed to seek their target's center of mass, both altered course slightly in the direction of the departing missiles. With only seconds remaining before impact, *Ingenuity's* AI locked onto both missiles with its close-in weapon system and immediately opened fire with its mini railgun and energy turrets. Unlike Terran anti-ship missiles, their Sajeth Collective counterparts carried both propellant and oxidizer onboard, creating a spectacular explosion at very close range as the first missile was successfully intercepted. The second missile was hit by energy cannon fire, but continued in the same general direction just long enough for its onboard computer to calculate that it had reached its closest approach to the target. In the milliseconds remaining before being ripped to shreds, the missile's small nuclear warhead switched to proximity mode and detonated.

Without the benefit of a surrounding medium, such as the atmosphere of a planet, nuclear weapons designed to detonate in the vacuum of space must provide their own fragmentation material in order to create a debris shockwave. In this case, much of the warhead and the body of the missile itself were instantaneously vaporized by the weapon's penetrating x-ray radiation. The result was a rapidly expanding, conical shaped-charge that struck the frigate's starboard side a glancing blow near the stern, violently spinning the ship clockwise and raising her bow sharply. Although most members of the crew, including those on the bridge, were strapped in place, any whose job required them to be unrestrained were thrown about their respective compartments. Depending on which part of the ship they were working in, this typically resulted in a bone-crushing impact with either the floor or the ceiling. Emergency lighting switched on momentarily as the ship's power systems struggled to compensate for the effects of the blast.

"Report!" Prescott yelled, struggling to overcome a wave of nausea and disorientation resulting from the jarring impact.

"Nuclear detonation close aboard, Captain. Starboard side near the stern from what I can tell," Lieutenant Lau reported. "No other inbound ordinance at this time."

"Dubashi?"

"One reactor is offline, sir. There is some ablative damage to the ship's outer armor layer, but it appears to be holding together for now. Three close-in weapon system turrets nearest to the impact are offline and presumed destroyed. The main railgun turrets went into diagnostic mode temporarily, but they are back online already. All other systems in the green. Sublight engines online and still at one hundred twenty percent power. No report from Doctor Chen yet."

"Fisher, you had probably better throttle back. Is the helm still answering?"

"Aye sir," he replied sheepishly, still shook up and reacting well behind the ship for a change. "So far no problems other than the decrease in power availability."

"Commander Logan, bridge," Prescott announced.

"Logan here!" the chief engineer yelled over the sound of multiple alarms. "I can't hear very well at the moment, Captain. I've got two fatalities down here and several other injuries. Reactor one scrammed when the nuke hit and is still restarting, but there is no apparent damage to the containment units. Full power should be restored in zero two minutes."

"Understood. Prescott out."

"Tactical, what's the status of our missiles?"

"All eight of them were destroyed by Delta 1's aft shields, sir, but *Gresav* was still hammering away with her energy weapons at the same time," Lieutenant Lau replied. "The target's shields are down just about as much as they are up at this point, and I'm only reading about twenty percent of the power output they had originally."

"It's time to end this fight. Fisher, bring us around for a final run at her stern. Stay well clear of *Gresav's* line of fire. Tactical, hit them with railguns, then energy weapons and plasma torpedoes as soon as we're in range."

"Aye, sir," both responded with a tone of grim resolution.

"XO, hold your fire on the C-Drive missiles, but if this attack run is ineffective, launch them as soon as possible afterwards."

"Yes, Captain."

"Schmidt, launch the *Hunter's* remaining missiles. Hopefully that will hold their attention while we make this run."

"Eight missiles away, Captain," he replied immediately. "Time to impact, one three seconds."

Wek Flagship Gresav, Near Gliese 667 Cc
(24 light years from Earth)

Admiral Naftur knew his ship intimately, having spent nearly twenty years of his life heading up the program to design and build the *Gresav.* When completed, she represented the state of the art in warship design across all seven worlds of the Sajeth Collective. She was the first ship of her class – a class that unfortunately included the enemy vessel off his starboard bow. Naftur also knew the enemy ship's commanding officer to be arrogant and proud far beyond what was warranted by his experience and military accomplishments. Accordingly, the admiral had thus far pursued what might appear to be the rather simplistic strategy of exchanging energy weapons fire with his adversary in a manner reminiscent of two seagoing men-of-war firing broadside after broadside until one was no longer capable of firing.

Like many "first in class" vessels, however, *Gresav* had a number of design features that were not included on subsequent ships in her class. There were a variety of reasons why this was the case, but it almost always came down to practicality and economy of resources. *Gresav*, for example, had been a testbed for a massive energy cannon mounted along the ship's longitudinal axis. It had triple the range and nearly ten times the power of her other energy weapons, but required the entire ship to be lined up with its target rather than being mounted with an articulated turret. That, combined with its massive power requirements, prompted the design board to deem it impractical, and it was subsequently dropped from all later ships in the class.

The Wek admiral had waited with a sense of patient confidence earned over a lifetime of service – waited as the impetuous enemy captain carelessly attacked the Terran vessel, exposing his vulnerable aft shields to the *Gresav* – waited as her shields became intermittent, heralding their imminent collapse. Now, as he watched *Ingenuity's* missiles impacting near the same area he had been attacking since the battle began, his face assumed a vicious, predatory smile. His quarry was defenseless. As was so often the case, experience had proved to be the most powerful weapon of all. "Fire," he growled.

TFS Ingenuity, Near Gliese 667 Cc
(24 light years from Earth)

Ensign Fisher pulled *Ingenuity's* bow into an inverted dive relative to the two ships centered on the bridge view screen. The maneuver allowed the frigate's weapons to bear on Delta 1 for as long as possible while still remaining clear of *Gresav's* relentless bombardment of the enemy ship's aft shields.

"Railguns will be in range in one zero seconds, Captain," Lau reported.

Delta 1's shields flared brightly as the *Hunter's* final salvo of HB-7 missiles impacted near her stern. Glowing waves of energy rippled along the entire length of the ship as her shields struggled to dissipate the enormous amount of energy raining down from aft and above her flight path.

"All eight of the RPSV's missiles impacted the aft shields again, Captain," Lieutenant Commander Schmidt said. "Her shields don't look like they can … stand by … her shields are down, sir!"

Prescott was about to order another missile strike when he noticed what at first looked like an explosion near *Gresav's* bow. For what seemed like several seconds, an enormous stream of orange-tinted, focused energy discharged from the huge emitter mounted along her keel. The beam literally impaled Delta 1, entering her ventral hull near the stern and slicing upward along the entire length of the ship before exiting near the bow. The stricken enemy ship seemed to hang transfixed for a moment before a huge series of internal explosions could be seen travelling along the path of the energy beam. The destroyer's hull visibly expanded before flying apart in multiple directions, explosions continuing to erupt from the largest pieces of debris spinning off into space.

There was stunned silence for several seconds on *Ingenuity's* bridge before Lieutenant Lau officially reported the end of the battle. "Delta 1 destroyed, Captain. The threat board is clear. *Gresav* is the only contact other than debris from vanquished enemy ships."

"Vanquished, huh?" Prescott grinned. "Well, I suppose they do meet the definition." He paused, breathing deeply and commanding himself to relax before continuing. "Nice job, everyone. We just survived Earth's first interstellar battle and each of you acquitted yourselves well. Take a deep breath, try to relax, and let's keep our heads in the game. We have a lot of work to do."

"All hands, this is Prescott. All enemy ships in system have been destroyed. I know we have battle damage, but none appears to be critical at the moment, so the priority is attending to our casualties. All crewmembers designated as medical supplemental staff should report to Doctor Chen immediately. Department heads, make your reports as soon as possible. We will remain in the Gliese 667 system until we can fully recharge our C-Drive unless other enemy forces arrive. Prescott out."

"Captain, both reactors are now online. Both standard and C-Drive hyperspace transitions are available. C-Jump range now 10.1 light years and increasing steadily," Lieutenant Dubashi reported. "Also, Admiral Naftur is hailing. He requests your and Commander Reynolds' eyes only, sir."

"Thank you, Lieutenant, reply that we will be with him momentarily," Prescott said, standing and gesturing for Reynolds to lead the way to his ready room.

"Lieutenant Commander Schmidt, you have the bridge," Commander Reynolds said as she followed her captain off the bridge. "Please pull together a status report as quickly as you can and make preparations to depart for Earth as soon as possible."

"Aye, Commander."

"So obviously these 'Pelaran Resistance' forces are either actively tracking Naftur's ship or they have someone on the inside. Before this battle, I might have also said Naftur himself could be playing us, but that seems a little farfetched at this point," Reynolds observed after securing the ready room door.

"Agreed. If nothing else, this battle did give us some solid evidence to back up his words. My gut tells me he's an honorable man, though, and I've thought that since the first time we spoke. Anyway, after what we just saw his ship do, I'd like to *keep* him on our side if at all possible." Prescott nodded to signify that he was opening the channel from the Command console at his desk.

"This vidcon is classified Top Secret, code word MAGI PRIME. Your ready room has been automatically secured for this briefing," the ship's synthetic voice announced as Admiral Naftur appeared on the large view screen.

"Wish you both joy of our victory, Captain Prescott and Commander Reynolds," he greeted. "Do you require any assistance?"

"And to you as well, Admiral. No sir, not at this time. We took a glancing blow from an anti-ship missile and unfortunately do have some casualties from the force of the impact, but damage to the ship is relatively light."

Naftur's face took on a doleful expression reinforced by a deep, rumbling sigh from his massive chest. "My deepest apologies, Captain. I can only assure you that this has never before been the way of the Wek people, or of the Sajeth Collective for that matter. These separatists act out of fear. They walk the path of cowards leading inexorably to ruin."

Prescott did not reply, staring instead at the admiral's expressive face on the view screen. Naftur had closed his eyes, lowered his chin to his chest, and now appeared to be offering a prayer. It would be fascinating indeed to compare the religious traditions of the Wek and other civilizations to those of Earth. It would not be particularly surprising to see common themes, but what if there was common symbology, or even similar religious figures?

After a few moments of silence, Admiral Naftur continued as if the pause had never occurred. "May I presume that this battle was a first for your people?"

"Yes, sir, this was the first time Humans have been involved in a battle beyond the confines of the Sol system. I don't think any of us expected it to happen so quickly after venturing away from Earth for the first time."

"It is indeed regrettable, Captain," Naftur said, bowing his head again before continuing. "As you both know from Terran history, however, *just* warfare is often the price of lasting peace. In any event, your intentions thus far have been honorable, you were not the aggressor in this battle, and your ship and crew performed admirably. There are a great many species who could not truthfully say the same when they journeyed from their home worlds for the first time."

"Thank you, sir," Prescott replied. "I would also like to express our gratitude for your friendship. It seems we Humans have unintentionally put your alliance in a very difficult position."

"We must never consider doing the right thing to be an imposition, Captain," Naftur smiled. "Forgive me, but as I grow older, I sometimes feel compelled to impart what little wisdom I have gained during my lifetime. I have visited thousands of worlds and met a great many species, but I have always found that right and wrong are universal concepts. Yes, moral ambiguity does exist, but it is much less common than many would have us believe. This 'Pelaran Resistance,' for example, acts ostensibly in the name of defending the seven worlds of the Sajeth Collective – an honorable objective to be sure. Committing genocide in the name of their objective, however, clearly invalidates any honorable intentions they may have. As I believe you Terrans have often said, the ends do not justify the means."

"Well put, Admiral. We agree wholeheartedly. Rest assured that we recognize the potential threat posed by the Pelarans. Although Commander Reynolds and I cannot speak for Terran Fleet Command, let alone our entire world, I expect that we will find a way to work with you to find a mutually agreeable way to address this threat."

Prescott paused, not wanting to be rude, but anxious to get on with the business at hand. "Sir, my orders are to deliver whatever intelligence information you can provide regarding a potential attack on Earth back to Admiral Sexton as quickly as possible."

"Of course, Captain. I hesitated to transmit the information via Nenir Turlaka for fear it would be intercepted – if not by the 'Pelaran Resistance,' then by the Pelarans themselves. After today's brazen attack on our ships, however, it is clear that at least some of my information has been compromised by some other means. I have obviously underestimated their intelligence-gathering capabilities. In fact, until ten days ago, I thought them little more than a fringe opposition group lacking broad political, let alone military support. I also did not truly believe they would go so far as to attack another Sajeth Collective vessel. I will not underestimate them again. The source of their information regarding *Gresav's* movements must be very highly placed within our command structure. In fact, I'm inclined to believe they are also receiving information from a member of my crew."

"What do you propose, Admiral?"

"If we assume they are aware of the information I intend to deliver, it seems likely they would move to execute their attack on Earth before I can do so."

"Do you believe they have the required forces in place? What about the Pelaran Guardian spacecraft? Won't it simply destroy their ships as it did before?"

"The incursion to which you refer was part of a program to develop tactics for decoying the Guardian spacecraft. Our goal was always to find a way to exploit its weaknesses and ultimately destroy the spacecraft. In the hands of these criminals, however, I fear this knowledge will be used to distract the craft while they execute an attack on Earth from multiple directions. The Guardian is a potent weapon system, but, like any other, it has its limitations."

"I doubt it's capable of being in several locations at one time," Reynolds remarked.

"Indeed not, Commander, and that fact will form the basis of their plan. As to whether they have sufficient forces available to proceed with their attack, I lack the current intelligence data to say for sure. The fact that their commanders had the confidence to detach the two ships we just destroyed from their task force, however, leads me to believe that they do."

"Are you saying we may already be too late?" Prescott asked.

"Possibly, but I think not. If I were to venture a guess, I would say we have one to two weeks based on the last known location of several ships we can safely assume they will require. Unfortunately, at *Gresav's* maximum speed, we are still over a week from the Sol system." Naftur paused meaningfully, his piercing, golden eyes scrutinizing the Humans for any sort of reaction.

Prescott and his XO resisted the urge to look at each other and instinctively donned their best poker faces. "I see," Prescott said. "Do you believe your presence might deter the attack?"

"Before today, I would have said yes, assuming we could locate some of the Resistance ships prior to the attack. Now, I am less certain. As I said before, I believe the strike force will seek to decoy the Guardian spacecraft, then launch a series of missile strikes from as close range as possible to reduce the likelihood that they will be intercepted. The key will be locating the ships in their staging areas before the attack actually begins. I have a few ideas where we should begin our search, but the sooner we arrive, the better chance we will have of locating them."

"So you propose to transfer to *Ingenuity* and accompany us back to Earth then," Prescott stated, his mind running through the litany of capital offenses he would be committing if he allowed such a flagrant breach of security. "Admiral, I'm sure you understand that we are prohibited from disclosing Terran technological and military capabilities without specific orders to do so from our Leadership Council."

"Well then, young Captain, I would say you have a decision to make. If I may, however, many of your ship's capabilities were openly revealed during our battle with the Resistance ships – as were those of the *Gresav*. Your vessel is truly a remarkable achievement, especially given her size. Perhaps it will ease your conscience if I tell you that I have suspected this to be true for some time. Indeed, your very presence in this system leads me to believe that your ship is significantly more capable than Sajeth Collective intelligence assessments have indicated. Our evaluation of Human technology has assumed too much based on data from other cultivated civilizations, it seems."

Prescott stifled a sigh and shifted his gaze upward while collecting his thoughts. After a moment, he continued. "If you don't mind, sir, I'd like to discuss this matter privately with Commander Reynolds for a moment. If I'm going to openly disobey Admiral Sexton's orders and commit treason in the bargain, I think I'd better have my ducks in a row."

Naftur furrowed his brow and stared for a moment as his ship's AI made its best attempt at translating Prescott's figure of speech. "I believe we may have had a translation problem of some sort. Some day when we have the opportunity to dine and drink together, I'll tell you what our system thought you just said," he laughed. "Yes, of course you may discuss this matter in private. This is entirely your decision to make, Captain. I regret that I must once again put you in this position, but such is the burden of command. I look forward to hearing from you shortly. Naftur out."

The admiral's image abruptly disappeared from the view screen and was replaced by a breathtaking view of Gliese 667 Cc, now off their starboard bow. Both Prescott and Reynolds continued to stare at the screen for a few seconds until Reynolds finally broke the silence.

"We both already know what you're going to do. I don't even know why you told him we need to discuss it."

"Is that what you would do, Commander?"

"I don't see how there is much of a choice, really. *Ingenuity* will be back in the Sol system tonight. We don't have a week or more to wait for the *Gresav* to make the trip. Naftur didn't come right out and say it, but I'm not certain he plans to give us all of his intelligence information unless we allow him to come with us."

"So you think his selection of Gliese 667 for our rendezvous might have been all about forcing us to tip our hand?"

"I don't know … maybe. Honestly, I'm not sure it even matters that much. He was absolutely right that you can't expect to use military assets without putting their capabilities on public display, so is there really much difference between that and giving him a ride back to Earth? It's not like we're planning to hand him a set of C-Drive plans or anything."

"True enough," Prescott smiled. "From what Kip said, the C-Drive technology is so obscure that we could probably hand over a set of plans without too much worry they would figure it out anytime soon. Remember, we had a working example and it still took us three hundred years and an accident to even start to understand how it works."

"Right, so what's the problem? Is it just what Sexton said in the Flash message?"

"Well, that's certainly part of it."

"I don't know what to tell you there, Captain, other than to point out that the situation has changed quite a bit since he sent that message."

"You're right, of course, I really have made up my mind. I just wanted to see if you might have some good reason to try and talk me out if it."

"Sorry, but no. This is one of those occasions where I'm happy that you're the one sitting in the big chair, sir."

"Enjoy it while you can, Commander. If we live through the next few weeks, I'm betting you'll get your chance," he smiled. "Please make arrangements for the admiral's accommodations. I'd say pretty much the same thing we did with Nenir, including the Marine guard."

"Aye, sir."

"And I expect you to come visit me in prison."

"Sure thing. I'll even bake you a cake," Reynolds laughed as Prescott reopened the vidcon channel.

Naftur appeared once again on the view screen, still apparently sitting at his office desk. "Greetings once again, friends. I am gratified to see that you were able to quickly come to a decision."

"I apologize for the delay, Admiral. I primarily needed to discuss a few logistical items with Commander Reynolds. We would be honored if you would come aboard *Ingenuity* as our guest for the trip back to the Sol system."

"I am most happy to do so, Captain Prescott. I will, of course, come alone in order to cause as little disruption as possible. I will be carrying the same device as Nenir Turlaka to mask my presence onboard your ship. Our XO will coordinate the details, but I believe I can be shuttled over within the hour if that is acceptable."

"One hour from now should work well for us, sir. We are required to make a quick hyperspace transition within the system before we depart for Sol, so please don't be alarmed when we do so. In spite of the military situation, *Ingenuity* is still a new ship with a great many systems still requiring calibration."

"I understand. Thank you for the warning. I will inform Flag Captain Jelani. Once we depart, he will proceed at *Gresav's* best possible speed for Sol, but will be under orders to avoid contact until he hears from us. I assume we will arrive well before he does." Naftur stated the implied question as a matter of fact.

"We will indeed, sir," Prescott smiled. "We look forward to meeting you in person in one hour. Prescott out."

"Well, for better or worse, that's done," Prescott remarked. "Maybe Fleet will be willing to trade the C-Drive design to the Wek for shield technology if they also throw in their bio signature masking device."

"Hah! I don't think Fleet would trade the C-Drive design for all seven of their planets and everything on them. I think it's safe to say that the C-Drive is a game changing technology – as in, we own the game as long as we're the only ones who have it."

Chapter 15

"Admiral on deck!" the Marine sentry announced as Vice Admiral Patterson strode onto the *Navajo's* bridge for the first time.

"As you were. I appreciate the courtesy, folks," he announced in a voice loud enough for all twelve members of the bridge crew to hear, "but now that we are on an operational footing, it won't be necessary to announce senior officers unless Admiral Sexton or some other high-ranking civilian from Fleet shows up. Understood?"

"Aye sir," everyone in the room responded in unison.

With Terran Fleet Command assets rapidly ascending to orbit from shipyards around the globe, Patterson had taken personal command of the assembling task force. Just minutes before, the cruiser's encrypted data stream began announcing the presence of the admiral's flag to the rest of the fleet. His orders from Admiral Sexton were simple enough – deploy all available Fleet resources as required to defend Earth from imminent attack.

"Let me see a tactical plot of all Fleet assets within five hundred thousand kilometers, please, and let's keep that displayed on the starboard side of the view screen until further notice."

A window immediately opened, displaying the Earth itself surrounded by standard icons representing the various starships now in orbit. At the moment, each ship was displayed with an accompanying small block of text to provide additional data such as the ship's name and operational status.

Until he had more than a handful of fully operational ships at his disposal, Patterson had decided on a simple defensive deployment strategy. He placed his first four available cruisers in geosynchronous orbit, each of which remained roughly equidistant from the other three ships. He did have to admit that it was gratifying to see each capital ship dutifully maintaining their position on the tactical plot – *Navajo*, *Shoshone*, *Chickasaw*, and *Shawnee*. In the event of attack from any single direction, he could likely count on overlapping fire support from three of his four cruisers at any given time. That, in addition to their complement of nearly two hundred RPSVs, plus F-373 aerospace superiority fighters launched from their bases on Earth, might at least give them a fighting chance of blunting an enemy attack.

Patterson was keenly aware, however, that he had absolutely no idea what he was defending against. Would this be an invasion force, or a group of ships equipped with "planet-killing" weaponry of some sort? The fact that he knew so little about his potential adversary made him feel anxious and vaguely nauseous, not to mention angry. Humanity was facing an unprovoked, existential threat, and this angered the admiral at a primal, visceral level the likes of which he had never experienced before. *One way or another, we'll make these bastards pay if they attack us,* he thought, *and it won't end here.*

"I'll be in the Combat Information Center," the CNO growled as he abruptly left the bridge.

TFS Ingenuity, Near Gliese 667 Cc
(24 light years from Earth)

"Doctor Chen reports three fatalities," Reynolds said quietly as Prescott returned to his command chair on the bridge. "The two in Engineering that Commander Logan reported earlier and one in the adjacent corridor. We also had four crewmen with broken bones and numerous other minor injuries. It makes me uncomfortable calling that 'lucky,' but …"

"But it could have been a lot worse," Prescott nodded.

"Yeah, I think so. In fact, I think if we hadn't been launching missiles from the vertical launch cells right before impact, that nuke would have made direct contact with the hull. I really don't think we would have survived that."

"We're going to need shields of some sort. Otherwise, we're going to have to find a way to build starships and train crew much faster than we can now. The last I heard, Fleet is getting pretty close to a deployable design. If nothing else, now that we have all that Sajeth Collective debris out near Jupiter, maybe there will be enough to salvage a working model or two."

"I hadn't even considered that. Things have just been happening so fast."

"There's also the cruiser we just took out. She's much more intact than the Sajeth ships destroyed by the Guardian. If we can get people out here to go through it before they can, we might find some pretty valuable tech."

"I wouldn't want to take on one of our *Navajo*-class cruisers loaded up with C-Drive missiles and equipped with shields."

"Well, if we can get the bad guys thinking that way, hopefully we won't ever again find ourselves facing the situation we're in right now."

"Captain, Engineering reports they have a hyperspace comm beacon ready for launch." Lieutenant Commander Schmidt announced. "Once we transition, it will be released from the starboard plasma torpedo tube. It's designed to stabilize itself after release and then provide us with an indication that everything is working properly. The entire process should only take a few seconds."

"Very good. How long until the beacon will actually be usable for data traffic back to the Sol system?"

"The most distant beacon deployed to date was released from a transition point near the TFC Live Fire Training Range. That's only about two light years from home, and it took about an hour to synch up with the rest of the NRD network. Science and Engineering thinks this one may take quite a bit longer."

"Well, with any luck, we'll be home today before this one comes online, but I suspect we'll be back here very soon. Doing the deployment shouldn't delay our return trip by more than a few minutes, so we might as well get it done while we're here."

"Lieutenant Dubashi, what's our status?"

"We're ready to go, Captain. Sublight engines offline, pending the transition. Both standard and C-Drive transitions are available. C-Jump range now 18.2 light years and increasing. The deployment profile has been transferred to the Helm console."

"Thank you, Dubashi. Would you please remind everyone how this process works?"

"Of course, sir. We will make a standard hyperspace transition, just as we have done many times. The only difference is that our destination transition point will be set to the same coordinates as our point of origin. Once we transition, we will have already arrived at our destination, so it's really just a matter of keeping our hyperdrive engaged while we deploy the comm beacon. Once that's done, we disengage the engines and allow the ship to transition back into normal space right where we started."

"I couldn't have said it better myself. Any questions?" Prescott paused for a moment to look around the room. What he saw was a bridge crew getting perilously close to their physical and mental limits following the stress of this morning's battle. "Alright, let's get this done. After we C-Jump back to Sol, I want all of you off duty and in your quarters for rest ASAP."

There were several "aye, sir" responses from around the room, accompanied by a rather loud yawn from Ensign Fisher.

"Ensign Fisher, if you feel you're up to it, you may execute a standard transition when ready," Prescott said, shaking his head.

"Sorry, sir. Executing now."

The ship AI's synthetic voice began a ship-wide countdown. "Standard hyperdrive engaged, transition in 3 ... 2 ... 1 ..."

Unlike during a C-Jump, where the bridge view screen maintained a partially simulated view of normal space, standard hyperspace transitions were displayed on the screen in real-time. As the ship transitioned out of normal space, the nearby planet and surrounding starfield instantly disappeared from view. Normally, the starfield would have been replaced by a white glow in front of the ship that appeared to increase in intensity until it reached a bright pinpoint of light directly ahead. This phenomena was caused by cosmic background radiation being shifted into the visible spectrum while regular starlight was shifted into the X-ray range, rendering it invisible. The view was interesting and certainly beautiful when seen for the first time, but not particularly exciting since it always looked exactly the same. Today, however, *Ingenuity* had transitioned into hyperspace already at her destination, so the view screen displayed nothing but an inky, black void.

"Releasing comm beacon," Lieutenant Commander Schmidt announced.

There was an uncomfortable pause where nothing could be heard other than the distant hum of the ship's reactors. It was as if they had transitioned to an actual place that fit the definition of the word "nowhere."

"Well, that view is a little unsettling," Reynolds commented to break the silence.

"Nothing to see here," Prescott said, smiling. "Maybe we should have the AI automatically show us some cat videos or something when we do this."

Reynolds narrowed her eyes at the implied jab. "I'd be fine with that, actually."

"Beacon stabilized and transmitting, Captain. Ready for transition back to normal space," Schmidt reported.

"Thank you, Schmidt. Ensign Fisher, execute your transition."

With a single keystroke at the Helm console, the view screen immediately transitioned back to the familiar starfield with Gliese 667 Cc to starboard.

"Transition complete, Captain. We are less than one meter from our previous location," Lieutenant Dubashi reported. "All systems in the green. Sublight engines are still offline, pending the next transition. Both standard and C-Drive transitions are available. C-Jump range now 18.5 light years and increasing again."

"I'm getting good data from the beacon on our NRD comm array. That's a successful deployment, sir," Schmidt said.

"Well, I'm glad to see at least some of what we do come off without a hitch," Prescott replied. "Good job everyone. XO, please complete arrangements to receive Admiral Naftur and prepare the ship for an immediate C-Jump back to the Alpha Centauri system as soon as he's aboard. We'll pause there to recharge before continuing to Sol, just as we did before."

"Aye, Captain."

"I'll be back with our guest shortly," Prescott said as he rose and headed for the flight deck. After a few steps, he stopped short and turned back to his XO. "See any reason why Naftur can't join us on the bridge during the trip back?"

"Not really. In for a penny, in for a pound," she smiled.

"Right," he laughed. "That's pretty much what I thought as well."

***

Admiral Naftur touched down on *Ingenuity's* aft flight apron aboard a decidedly wicked looking spacecraft that appeared to be optimized for landing a small squad of troops and then providing close air support. Once the small ship reached the pressurized portion of the flight deck, an honor guard of TFC Marines, resplendent in their Blue Dress "A" uniforms, stood ready to mark the first ever visit of a military official from another world.

Although there had been talk of reinforcing the small contingent of Marine Corps troops serving aboard TFC frigates, *Ingenuity* currently carried only one assault section composed of thirteen Marines plus Master Sergeant Rios. The squad now formed two lines on either side of the descending shuttle stairway. As the admiral emerged, one of the Marines stepped forward and sounded the traditional "Over the Side" call on the boatswain's pipe as every member of the assembled crew saluted.

For his part, the admiral returned a crisp, Human-style salute as if he had been doing so for his entire career, then strode directly to Prescott to offer his hand.

"It is an honor to meet you in person, Admiral Naftur," Prescott greeted, nodding toward a youngish TFC steward holding a tablet for relaying the AI's translation. After the usual awkward pause, their conversation continued.

"The honor is mine, Captain Prescott. I did some reading about your traditional naval ceremonies. This particular one I believe you refer to as 'Tending the Side' is surprisingly similar to one used for centuries on my homeworld of Graca."

There was an uncharacteristic pause while the AI struggled to find an appropriate English word for the Wek homeworld. *It certainly didn't sound like "Graca" when he said it*, Prescott thought, *but at least it's easy enough to say.*

"I am most pleased and honored by your generous welcome," Naftur continued, "but I beg that you will not trouble with further ceremony. There is urgent business to which we must attend, and I do not wish to be a source of delay."

"Admiral, I believe that to be a universal constant aboard every naval vessel throughout history. There is never a moment to spare, but we always seem to find time for tradition."

"Just so, Captain. Thank you again."

Prescott nodded once again to the steward, who stepped forward smartly for his introduction. "Petty Officer Clark here will be at your service during your visit. Anything you need, please don't hesitate to ask. If you like, we can stop by your quarters now and then you can accompany me to the bridge."

"I would like that of all things. Now that I am aboard, you said we will arrive in the Sol system well before the *Gresav*, correct?"

"We will indeed, sir. In fact, with any luck, we will arrive before dinner."

Prescott gestured for the obviously amazed admiral to join him as they made their way off the flight deck.

TFS Navajo, Earth Orbit

Admiral Patterson stared at one of the large view screens lining the front of the *Navajo's* Combat Information Center as TFS *Jutland*, Fleet's first carrier to reach orbit, took up a position just under one thousand kilometers astern. He was well aware that having all of his forces sitting in Earth orbit was a little like being forced to defend his team's end zone from their own one-yard line, but there was little choice at the moment. As soon as a full escort was available, however, he planned to move the *Jutland* to a location where she could at least threaten whatever enemy force showed up rather than wallowing around inside the planet's gravity well. In any event, the carrier's arrival, along with her impressive air wing, was a welcome sight.

"Please inform *Jutland's* air boss that I'd like long range recon flight operations underway as quickly as possible. If it's inside the Oort cloud and moving, we need to know what it is," Patterson ordered the young ensign manning one of the CIC's Comm consoles.

"Aye, sir. She just signaled that they have a green flight deck and will commence flight ops momentarily."

"Very well, thank you."

Thank God for the Hunters, Patterson thought. *Who was it that said "Quantity has a quality all its own?" Stalin? Well, murdering, communist thug or not, there was certainly some truth to that statement.*

In total, there were now over four hundred RPSVs deployed across the various Fleet ships on station in Earth orbit. The ubiquitous RPSV was actually one of the few things the admiral did now have in abundance, and what the *Hunter* lacked in firepower, it more than made up for with sheer numbers and versatility. Fleet had made the decision early on to rely almost exclusively on RPSVs to make up the bulk of their small, ship-based spacecraft. Not only were they compact, which allowed for much larger numbers to be deployed on a single vessel than similarly equipped manned spacecraft, but they were also relatively easy to manufacture and maintain. The fighter-like spacecraft were also no slouch when it came to performance. Their sublight engines were capable of rapid acceleration to near relativistic speeds. Even more impressive was the fact that recent successes with the C-Drive missile program had led to the newest *Hunter* models rolling off the assembly line with their own C-Drives.

"One more thing regarding flight ops," Patterson said, once again addressing the young comm officer. "Please signal all ships that they should coordinate RPSV deployments so that there will always be at least two, four-ship formations of C-Drive-equipped *Hunters* in flight. This order will remain in effect until further notice."

"Yes, Admiral."

With any luck, the NRD-equipped surveillance drones deployed throughout the solar system would detect any inbound enemy ships or weapons. Once that happened, the admiral could vector in at least a few *Hunters* almost immediately. If nothing else, that should at least provide some indication of what they were up against. He had no illusions regarding the magnitude of the task, however. The Sol system encompassed a vast volume of space measuring nearly three light years across at the outer edge of the Oort cloud. Even if he was able to detect an enemy's presence anywhere within the system, which was a stretch, it might not make that much difference anyway. In all likelihood, an enemy intent on attacking Earth would rally their forces well outside the Sol system, then use their hyperdrives to put their ships within weapons range. There would undoubtedly be little or no warning of their approach.

"Contact!" a young female lieutenant announced loudly from the holographic display in the center of the room.

Patterson had been so deep in thought that the announcement made him jump involuntarily, which did not improve his mood. Glancing around to see if anyone noticed, he walked over to take a look at the display. Currently configured to provide an all-encompassing view of the battlespace surrounding the *Navajo* out to five hundred thousand kilometers, the holographic table depicted so much information that it required quite a bit of practice to take it all in. At the moment, a beautifully rendered representation of the Earth itself dominated the table with an equally striking view of the moon off to one side. The admiral's formation of Fleet assets in Earth orbit were clearly visible with blue icons designating them as friendly units. The unknown contact, which the AI had already classified as a frigate due to its size, was displayed with a yellow icon. Within seconds, an identifying text block appeared next to the newcomer and its icon changed to blue.

"Contact identified as TFS *Ingenuity*," the lieutenant announced.

"It's about damn time," Patterson laughed, aware of just how ridiculous it was to complain about a round trip of nearly fifty light years taking less than a day.

TFS Ingenuity, Inside Lunar Orbital Path
(1.9×10^5 km from Earth)

"Transition complete. Captain. Securing from hyperspace flight," Lieutenant Dubashi reported. "All systems in the green. Sublight engines online, we are free to maneuver. Both standard and C-Drive transitions are available. C-Jump range now 1.1 light years and increasing. We are eight hundred meters from our expected arrival point."

"Multiple contacts, Captain," Lieutenant Lau announced. "All friendlies, sir. I'm getting standard Fleet identification streams from all of them. I have four *Navajo*-class cruisers and a *Jutland*-class carrier in geosynchronous orbit. There are also ten *Ingenuity*-class frigates and forty-six RPSVs patrolling the general area."

"That's decidedly better than when we left. Thank you both," Prescott replied. "Admiral Naftur, welcome to Terra."

"I have seen many wondrous things in my career, Captain Prescott, but … I lack the words to describe this accomplishment. Had I not experienced it firsthand, I simply would not have believed it."

"Captain," Lieutenant Dubashi interrupted, "signal from Admiral Patterson aboard the *Navajo*, sir. It reads 'Captain, repair aboard flag.'"

"Helm, put us in orbit five kilometers astern of the *Navajo*. XO, please signal Flight Ops to prepare the shuttle for immediate departure."

"Aye, sir," Fisher and Reynolds replied in unison.

Prescott had been dreading his inevitable meeting with Admiral Patterson since taking Admiral Naftur aboard. Revealing his ship's capabilities to the Wek officer was a clear violation of his direct orders and Fleet security in general. Would his chain of command agree that doing so was justified under the circumstances, or would he find himself relieved of command and under arrest for dereliction of duty, perhaps even treason? Had it not been for the C-Drive, he would have had plenty of time to prepare himself during the return journey. Instead, he would now be forced to explain his actions mere hours after the battle at Gliese 667 Cc. For now, he did his level best to push all of the "what ifs" from his mind and focus on the business at hand.

"I believe you and Admiral Patterson share a passion for military history, Admiral. The message he just sent is a traditional naval signal from the days of wind-driven sailing vessels. Originally, it would have been transmitted via a series of flags flown at the mast."

"Traditional, but effective nonetheless," Naftur replied with a knowing, sympathetic smile.

***

Three hundred and fifty thousand kilometers away, just inside the Moon's orbit, a flight of four *Hunter* RPSVs from TFS *Shawnee* entered a long, sweeping turn. *Shawnee's* AI had noted that the Moon just happened to be in a position to provide a gravity assist along the formation's intended flight path. Although no longer strictly necessary from a technical standpoint, the AI generally selected the most efficient natural flight path as a simple matter of course.

As the formation approached perigee, one of the spacecraft's optical sensors noted an anomalous flash of light immediately to starboard. With the *Hunters* already in reconnaissance mode, the onboard AI dutifully reported the detection back to *Shawnee* via NRD net. At the same instant, all four RPSVs focused every active and passive sensor at their disposal in the direction of the contact. At this range, the *Hunters'* sensor suites instantly detected and resolved the unknown contact in exquisite detail. The result appeared to be a small ship, barely fifty meters in length. Not surprisingly, the ship's configuration did not match any vessel contained in the RPSVs' onboard databases.

As the data arrived in near real-time at TFS *Shawnee*, however, the capital ship's vastly more powerful AI executed its own extensive search. In milliseconds, the AI calculated a ninety-four percent probable match based on footage gathered during the Wek squadron's destruction a few weeks earlier.

The Guardian spacecraft had been found.

***

Simultaneously, at every Terran Fleet Command facility and aboard every vessel, the reserved command and control channels of the NRD net received the following "Flash" priority action message:

Z2125
TOP SECRET MAGI PRIME
FM: GUARDIAN SYSTEM - MAGI - SOL SYSTEM
TO: TFC FLEET OPS
INFO: INDUCTION

1. ASSEMBLE TFC LEADERSHIP COUNCIL AND SENIOR MILITARY STAFF AT Z1000.
2. CONTACT WILL BE VIA SECURE LASER COMLINK WITH THE NEAREST TFC VESSEL.
3. WELCOME, CHILDREN OF THE MAKERS. WELCOME, TO THE PELARAN ALLIANCE.

THANK YOU!

I'd like to express my sincerest thanks for reading "TFS *Ingenuity*." I hope you have enjoyed the story so far and will be interested in the next installment of The Terran Fleet Command Saga:

"The Pelaran Alliance"

The release date is not yet set, but I'm shooting for early 2016. Please sign up for the newsletter and stay tuned for updates!

If you did enjoy the book, I would greatly appreciate a quick review at Amazon.com, or wherever you made your purchase. It need not be long or detailed, just a quick note that you enjoyed the story and would recommend it to other readers. Thank you again very much for reading this book!

***

For updates on new releases and upcoming special offers, please subscribe to my newsletter at:

AuthorToriHarris.com

Have story ideas, suggestions, corrections, or just want to connect? You can find me on Twitter and Facebook at:

https://twitter.com/TheToriHarris

https://www.facebook.com/AuthorToriHarris

You can also check out my Amazon author page for links to my other works.

http://amazon.com/author/thetoriharris

ABOUT THE AUTHOR

Born in 1969, four months before the first Apollo moon landing, Tori Harris grew up during the era of the original Star Wars movies and is a lifelong science fiction fan. During his early professional career, he was fortunate enough to briefly have the opportunity to fly jets in the U.S. Air Force, and is still a private pilot who loves to fly. Tori has always loved to read and now combines his love of classic naval fiction with military Sci-Fi when writing his own books. His favorite authors include Patrick O'Brian and Tom Clancy as well as more recent self-published authors like Michael Hicks, Ryk Brown, and Joshua Dalzelle. Tori lives in Tennessee with his beautiful wife, two beautiful daughters, and Bizkit, the best dog ever.

Made in the USA
Middletown, DE
04 June 2016